When famous Berkeley writer India Wor woman writer in the Bay Area attends, eve: college graduate in creative writing, who never dared hope to meet her idol in her own home, among so many famous friends. After midnight, when the party has thinned to family and close friends, Jessamyn is awed to find herself among them. Yet, within moments her awe turns to horror as India Wonder collapses and dies, poisoned.

To assuage her own grief and shock, Jessamyn works with the handsome young homicide inspector to find the killer. Was it prolific but underrated Jane, who envied India's fame? Was it Yolanda or Margot, both of whom believed India used her influence to injure their careers? Was it her husband or daughter, both portrayed falsely in her writing, which they had sacrificed so much to foster? Was it India's disciple Sylvia, whose imitation of India's writing had brought her to a dead end? Or Antonia, who had neither forgiven India for betraying their youthful radical ideals, nor stopped coveting India's husband? Or Carla, whose sexual advances had been spurned? Or Pamela, who claimed India destroyed her father? Or Celeste, self-proclaimed witch?

As Jessamyn uncovers contradictory facets of her idol's life, and discovers unsuspected motives among the other writers, she also confronts her own conflicting feelings about the place of writing in her own life. Suspense mounts as she realizes that she may also be in danger.

KILLING WONDER is not a *roman a clef.* It is a "novel of ideas" which uses the traditional mystery format as a vehicle to make an entertaining commentary on the current (perhaps perennial) writing and publishing scene, and on the joy and pain of writing.

KILLING WONDER

KILLING WONDER

a mystery novel by
Dorothy Bryant

Ata Books
Berkeley, California

Ata Books
1928 Stuart Street
Berkeley, California 94703

Cover Photos	Jane Scherr
	Felicia Liu
Cover Design	Robert Bryant
Production	Kathy Vergeer
Assistance	Anne Fox
Typesetting	Ann Flanagan
	Typography

*My thanks to my friends in the Bay Area literary community
who joined in the spirit of fun in which this book was written
by allowing themselves to be photographed for the cover.
They helped set the scene for the book, but they are not in it.
It is fiction.*

1.

I was the only one there who was nobody, and everybody was there. Women crowded around Jessica Mitford, then broke up, shifted, and regrouped around Tillie Olsen. Charlotte Painter and Mary Jane Moffat swooped in together announcing their completion of a "final, final draft" of something. Susan Griffin and Kim Chernin proposed toast after toast to Sandy Boucher, who had just won a big grant. Celeste West and Nancy Schimmel compared printers while Jennifer Stone sat glaring at them, waving a red rose slowly back and forth. Karen Jacobs jogged in, her hair wet from swimming.

India Wonder introduced each woman as she came in, kissing her, singing out her name. I knew most of them by sight from the pictures on their jackets of their books, or from interviews in newspapers. J. J. Wilson looked younger than her pictures, Diana O'Hehir thinner, Mary Mackey smaller.

The only man was mixing drinks and bringing out chips, but mostly staying back in the kitchen, sitting quietly, giving a tired old smile to anyone who came in for ice or water. Someone told me he was Reuben Wonder, India's husband. I thought she had left her husband.

I didn't pinch myself because I knew I wasn't dreaming. My dream had come true. Ever since I started to write I had imagined a community of writers, a network, a sisterhood. My dream was that they came together to talk about what inspired them, that they argued about great issues, that they shared each other's creative plans. I knew it would be years before I was published and accepted into this creative sisterhood. Yet, here I was already, with practically every important woman writer in Northern California, at a party in the home of the greatest of them all, India Wonder.

All because I had written a letter I almost didn't mail because it was so stupid.

Dear India Wonder,

When I was sixteen, your classic *Emma Pride's Journal* inspired me to begin writing. I have just earned a BA in Creative Writing from San Francisco State. And now what? I feel so confused, so lonely, so inadequate to meet the demands of life as an artist.

I thought of you, of your journal telling how you overcame. I felt you would understand.

Forgive me for bothering you. I know you are too busy to answer.

Sincerely,
Jessamyn Rebecca Posey

Her answer came two weeks later. It wasn't just a card or a polite note. It was a real letter, longer than mine, full of comfort and encouragement and advice to keep trying but to "be gentle with yourself." It ended asking whether anything of mine had been printed where she could read it. I sent her a copy of the college literary magazine. I didn't hear from her again, but I didn't expect to. Then the note came.

My mother India Wonder is having a get-together of women writers at her home on Friday 5 September. She hopes you can come.

Georgie Williams

So there I was, too excited to say a word or swallow a drink, terrified that someone like Jessamyn West would speak to me and expect an intelligent answer. Luckily they all left me alone except for the weak but kind smile Reuben Wonder gave me when I brought some dirty glasses into the kitchen.

Every once in a while—four times in three hours, to be exact—India gave me a hug, squeezed my hand, then said to anyone who happened to be near, "Jessie Posey. A truly serious young writer. She's going to amaze us all!" Then whoever she said it to would smile politely, except for Sylvia March, who turned away as if she didn't hear, and Carla Neeland, who stared at me hard, like a black Amazon taking aim to throw her spear.

Except for Carla and Celeste Wildpower, the other women disappointed me. They didn't look like writers. They looked dumpy or had blotchy skin or jowls or wore glasses with out-of-style frames. Only India Wonder looked like a writer, the way I imagined a writer should look. Tall and thin and artistic. She wore blue, of course. She always wore blue, not as bright as royal blue or as dark as navy blue, but somewhere in between. I had seen her speak at least a dozen times, and only once was there a little white scarf at her throat. Blue made her skin, which was unusually white, look even whiter. She had wrinkles, like any woman over sixty, but no jowls. But it was her hair that finished off the picture of genius. Bright white, not yellowish or dirtied with leftover gray, but white-white and thick and long. It waved gently back from her face, twined into a thick braid, thick as my wrist, that hung down the middle of her back. She wore no makeup, no jewelry. She didn't need them, for she had the eyes of an artist, a strange, piercing light gray, intense and pure, looking deeply into me each time she turned toward me smiling, as if she and I shared a sweet secret.

As the women came and left, I moved around watching them and looking at the house. It was a very old wood-frame house in west Berkeley, the part known as Ocean View, where there's no view of the ocean or even of the bay that comes in between, because the few houses left there are surrounded by warehouses and factories. Years ago houses had been torn down to make an "industrial park." But the few people living there organized a tremendous campaign for an initiative to save the few blocks of homes, and, "admiring their spunk," as my father put it, the Berkeley voters supported them. India had been one of the leaders, and one of her speeches had made me cry as much as I had when I read her journal.

The house was a two-storey narrow box with wiggly ornaments on peaked windows. Women bunched up in the small, high-ceilinged living room, dining room, front hallway. Some stood or sat on the stairway. I convinced myself that I had to go to the bathroom, so that I could zigzag among them, climbing the stairway to see the rest of the house.

Someone was already in the bathroom, so I stood in the narrow hallway and looked around. The ceiling peaked up high, then sloped sharply; the old attic had been made into three bedrooms. Two of the doors were open. I saw one small room with an unmade double bed, with books and medicine bottles on a table, like an invalid's room. The other room was like an office, with a typewriter, files, a narrow cot, no books. Neither could be India's room.

The closed door swung open, and Jane Lee came out carrying a thick envelope. When she saw me, she blinked a little scared look behind her round glasses, then gave me a tiny smile, ducked her head, brushed past me, and hurried down the stairs. Her face was as familiar to me as my own. I had seen it under short straight bangs on jackets of twenty books, the bangs starting out dark and getting grayer and grayer on later books.

She had forgotten to close the door. I stood on the threshold as if I were in a museum where a velvet cord stops you from going into an antique furnished room. I wouldn't cross the threshold and violate this room. I was content just to stand there and look at the room where *Emma Pride's Journal* had been written, where India had written that wonderful letter to me, where she now was working on her new book. I stood there just breathing, as if I could inhale the magic of her genius.

An old, huge roll-top desk sat open, a mess of papers spread all over it. The desk stood under the only window, dark, so I couldn't tell what view India looked out on when she worked here during the day. The drawers of the desk were all open, two inches, six inches, one pulled way out and hanging near one of three cardboard boxes on the floor. Between the boxes stood a modern office chair, plastic on wheels, half-turned toward me.

Against the wall to my left was a narrow bed covered by a Mexican blanket and topped with four or five big pillows, piled up, then crushed and dented from her head and shoulders. Paralleling the bed, one long shelf hung on the wall holding about twenty books. The opposite wall was hidden by a row of six tall filing cabinets with boxes and folders piled on top of them almost to the ceiling.

I resisted. I didn't let myself pass the imaginary velvet ribbon. I just imagined the contents of those file cabinets and the boxes stacked on them: the lifetime of journals, notes, articles, lectures. Somewhere in this room, probably on the desk, lay the current draft of her new novel.

I heard the toilet flush. Whoever was in the bathroom would come out and see me, exposed, as if I were making love or stealing something. I reached in, grabbed the doorknob, and pulled the door shut. I could feel myself blushing as I stood there in the hall waiting for the bathroom door to open.

2.

Women came and left, came and left. Left. First the stairs cleared, then the front hall, then the kitchen. By midnight only ten of us were left sitting in the living room with India's husband Reuben standing in the doorway to the kitchen with a towel over his arm. He reminded me of the boys' gym teacher in my junior high school. I was sitting on the floor next to India's daughter Georgie. The other women were old friends of India. I didn't belong. But when I got up, mumbling, "I guess it's time to..." Georgie shook her head at me, a short, impatient shake that sat me down again. I knew Georgie's father had been a black man, but it still felt strange to watch that dark tan face with India's pale eyes staring out of it, staring at India.

"Dear friends." India stood in front of the fireplace. The flickering flames made changing tones of blue on the folds of her gown. "Dear friends, old and...new." She nodded at me, and I blushed, and everyone quieted down to hear her. "Friends to have near, friends to celebrate...." She paused as if she didn't want to finish.

"Celebrate what?" Jane Lee asked in a small but clear voice. "The book?"

"Oh, when will it be out?" I forgot to be shy. I think it was the first time I had said anything. India just tilted her head at me and smiled. I turned away from her to look at the others, expecting someone to raise a glass and toast her new book. Everyone looked suddenly cold, as if a chill wind had blown away their smiles. All their faces had closed up over something. Even India's husband had stopped smiling.

But that chill was only a flicker, like the slow tick of an old clock before the pendulum swings back the other way. All the faces were smiling again, and some started talking until India silenced them with a graceful wave of her half-filled glass. "Celebrate friendship. Celebrate all the talent gathered here, all the wonderful women's creativity." She turned to her right. "Georgie, my dear firstborn, into whom I poured all my early longings, naming her after my heroine, Aurore, after George Sand."

Georgie sat stiffly on the edge of the green armchair by the fireplace and made a thin-lipped smile. She and India looked more like sisters than like mother and daughter. In a way Georgie looked more like the mother, with her tight-jawed, thin-lipped smile, very maternal and middle-aged, next to India's bright, intense face, full of childlike wonder. Her name—Reuben's name—suited her perfectly.

"And my newest little friend, I mean young friend, but she's little too, Jessamyn Posey." She reached behind her to the mantelpiece and picked up the literary magazine from San Francisco State. I sank into myself while she read that awful prose poem of mine. Before I could say that it had been printed two years ago and I'd really improved since then, she had gone on to the next person, and I realized she was going to make a speech about each of us. Well, at least she was done with me. I could relax, listen, enjoy what she said about the others. She stammered over a word and laughed. She was just a little bit drunk, drunk with style, with elegance, waving her glass without spilling a drop.

"From my newest friend to our oldest." She raised her glass to the woman next to me, who looked much older than India, but maybe that was because her hair was bleached yellow and she wore bright red lipstick and was fat and chain-smoked the way older women do. "Antonia Moran, dear Antonia, who shared our young, idealistic passions." India nodded toward Reuben, then at Antonia, but neither of them looked pleased, and I noticed that some of the other women smiled with sucked-in cheeks. "Once we thought we were going to change the world. We failed. But Antonia goes on. And on. She has what I lack—consistency!"

Antonia Moran blew out a mouthful of smoke as if she were spitting at India. Now I recognized her. She had been in front of the co-op every Saturday for my whole life, passing out leaflets or selling *Peoples World*. I hadn't seen her there for a long time, not since her book on radical heroines was published.

"Jane, our wonderful Jane Lee, the most underrated writer in America!" Not by me. I'd read all sixteen of her novels, her collected poems and her three biographies. All night I had wanted to tell her so, but I was too shy, and now I couldn't interrupt India. I could only look at her, and all I could see was her head, the straight silver hair cut Dutch-boy style. Her head was down and her hands folded in her lap. She raised her head slightly, but the light shone on her little round glasses, blanking out her expression.

"Yolanda Dolores! Listen to that name, my lovely friend with a name like music. Yolanda Dolores. I refuse to use that awful name you married, McVittey! Ah, Yolanda, Yolanda," she sang, and we all laughed. "How could we have realized the Mission *barrio* would give us a new muckraker, our own Latina Jessica Mitford?" One of Yolanda's articles had saved me a lot of money by warning about crooked agencies. Her style was so formal and serious—not like Mitford at all—that I was surprised she looked so soft, so Latin, so plump and golden, soft as the couch she shared with Jane. Except for her steady black eyes, watching India.

"Margot Stackpole, our success, our super success, our regular little tapdancer!" It had been in the papers, the huge advance for Margot's first novel. The title of it *Reserved for Love* was printed across her purple T-shirt, which was so tight you had to study her big pointed breasts to read it, as I'd noticed Reuben doing while she hung around the kitchen earlier. Margot sat on the end of the couch. She wiggled her crossed legs, letting her skirt hitch up a little more, then swished her long blonde hair back and smiled. She had an amazing row of big, even, white teeth. Anyway, it was good to see someone smile.

"Carla Neeland. Carla." India was holding up a copy of *Herland Newsletter*. I had subscribed to it last year and read about the conference Carla organized. "Our very own Delilah." Of course, everyone had seen Carla's play *Delilah*, with the famous hair-shearing scene. But this was the first time I had seen her up close, and now I took a good look because she'd finally let go of the woman she had come with. They'd been hugging and kissing and stroking the way lovers do when they're mad at everyone or at each other, making everyone look all around them pretending not to be embarrassed. Now they sat apart, and Carla was sprawled on the floor, her long, black legs spread as she leaned back on her elbows, watching India. She was a lot darker than India's daughter, with a face like an old Egyptian statue, hair wound up in a shimmering white satin scarf. Margot tried to look beautiful, but Carla really was beautiful.

"And Pamela, our visitor from New York, a real scholar in our midst, Doctor Pamela Righbottom." Now that Carla was off her, I recognized her from San Francisco State. She had been a visiting lecturer last term, and my advisor talked me into sitting in on some of her classes, where she mostly read from her father's books and told us how boring and illiterate we were compared to her students at Eastward U. "Brilliant Pamela. Of course, it runs in the family."

She meant Pamela being the daughter of the great critic Murray Righbottom. She looked a little like her father, with his wide face, fat cheeks and heavy black eyebrows. Her hair was light and slicked back to a roll at the back of her neck, so she even looked a little bald like her father.

"And my dear Sylvia March." India's voice dropped to a low, soothing whisper. "The disciple, the survivor, the exposed one." I recognized all these words as titles of journal fragments Sylvia had read in open workshops around town. India took a few sheets of paper from the mantelpiece (she must have prepared it before the party) and started reading aloud from "The Survivor." Sylvia looked as embarrassed as I had felt. She had one of those white, broad, Scandinavian faces that looks mongol, narrow-eyed and puffy, as if she has been crying or is about to cry. And she had that lank, fine blonde hair that looks fantastic until about the age of thirty, when it begins to thin and dull out, which was what had happened to Sylvia. She was on the floor on her knees, sitting back on her heels, but rocking forward as if to beg India to stop. India went on and on, swaying slightly, waving her glass as if conducting an orchestra while she sang Sylvia's sad phrases.

Suddenly she stopped in mid-sentence and put the papers back on the mantel. "And last but very certainly not least, the witch herself, who writes by alchemy, by enchantment!" Another round of sucked-in smiles? What did they mean? India was looking at Celeste Wildpower, who stood in the corner farthest from her, near the door to the hallway. She almost blended into the shadows because she was dressed all in black, in something like an old-fashioned nun's habit. Her long, pale face stood out because of her hair, which probably was as thin as Sylvia's but had been dyed orangy-red and frizzed so that it stood out as if electrified.

"Dream, Witch!" said India. That was the title of the only book by Celeste Wildpower, a fantasy about an island ruled by people's dreams. It was a much better book than the title would make you expect. It had inspired me to try writing a fantasy, which died on about page sixty. "Celeste tells us of hidden powers to awaken. Celeste promises everything." India giggled, but Celeste didn't even smile. "Come, Celeste, cast your spell, show us your wild power!" India raised her glass toward Celeste, then drained it. Everyone was turning toward Celeste's corner, smiling at her still, black-shrouded body. I could see that Celeste didn't like it, and I thought India would stop, but she kept saying, "Show us your wild power!"

Suddenly Celeste Wildpower's arm shot upward through arm slits in the folds of her black habit. Her long, bare arm stopped level with her shoulder with her hand making a fist, her thumb extended, pointing at India.

India screamed. She fell. I couldn't believe what I was seeing, India screaming, falling, now lying on the floor, her blue-draped body shaking.

"Someone call an ambulance."

"India!"

"Grab her head."

"India!"

"Dial 911."

"India!" Reuben was on the floor, holding her and rocking her and calling her name. Her daughter Georgie had pulled an afghan from the couch and was wrapping it around her. Yolanda, whose plump body had moved faster than any of ours, was already hanging up the hall phone after calling for help. Everyone else was standing up as if we had somewhere to go but had forgotten where. All except Celeste Wildpower, who had come out of the corner and had fallen on her knees beside India. She was passing her flat-palmed hands through the air a few inches above India's body. Suddenly she stopped doing that, pushed Reuben away, felt India's wrist, lifted an eyelid, probed her mouth. "More blankets." She sucked in a gasp of air and put her mouth to India's, her orange-red hair quivering over India's face, hiding it.

I don't know how long this went on. It seemed like forever, it seemed like what they must mean by eternity in hell, but I guess it lasted for about five minutes before we heard the siren and horn of the fire department emergency truck.

The firemen were running up the front stairs, but inside everything had stopped. India lay still. Celeste leaned back, looked at Reuben. "I think...." He shook his head at her. His face was fierce, furious, forbidding her to finish. But then his face crumpled into misery and he pulled India's body close to his chest, looking around as if he was sheltering her against all of us. "You did it. You." I thought he was accusing Celeste, but then I saw he was looking across the room to where Yolanda stood in the doorway to the hall. Everyone turned to look at Yolanda except for Sylvia

March, who was mumbling something to herself as her narrow eyes squeezed out tears. I read her lips. "Free at last, free at last," she was saying. I thought I saw satisfaction on Antonia Moran's face and solemn, cool interest on Jane's. I thought the others just looked stunned. I thought...but I couldn't think at all anymore because I was trying to understand that India Wonder was dead.

3.

I never got to bed that night. The firemen said that because India was dead the police had to come. A cop came and asked Reuben questions. I heard him give India's age, sixty-four. Health problems? Reuben recited in a dull monotone. "High blood pressure. Fibrillations. Asthma." An ambulance came to take the body away for an autopsy. "Routine," said the cop, apologetically. Nobody mentioned the way Celeste Wildpower had pointed at India, and nobody looked at Celeste. She looked scared, or was it only the way her orange hair frizzed out? She kept watching Reuben, but he never once looked at her.

Reuben collapsed as soon as they took the body away. He sank into the green armchair near the dying, smoldering fire and began rocking back and forth mumbling in a singsong way. I recognized that motion from my Jewish grandfather's funeral last year in New York, where I watched old men rock and mumble that way. It was as if Reuben wasn't himself anymore, he was millions of old men who had rocked and groaned that way.

Georgie stood behind his chair, her hands gripping the chairback as if to hold him without touching him. The look on her face was something terrible. Rigid. Blank. I had never seen such control. Jaw, lips, nostrils—even her eyelids seemed tight and taut. Her whole face looked ready to explode. But it never did. She just stood there, her bloodless face turning to a muddy gray color, like a statue standing guard over her stepfather.

No one wanted to leave as soon as the body was gone, but no one would go near Reuben. It seemed cruel to go near him, yet cruel to leave him. So we all started cleaning up the room, putting food and liquor away, washing the dishes. I swept up the bits of India's glass which had broken when she fell, and threw them into the garbage.

No one said a word. What we needed to tell, we managed by signs. It was a weird scene, all of us doing these ordinary women's chores in total silence except for Reuben's singsong moans. No one cried. I thought we were all too shocked to cry. Later I wasn't sure.

We left one by one, nodding to Georgie, still saying nothing. Down in the street, women got into cars: Jane with Yolanda and Antonia; Margot and Sylvia in Celeste's car. Carla Neeland motioned to me, a silent offer of a ride with her and Pam, but I had my bike.

I pedaled up University Avenue, which was brightly lit and quiet. It was almost three a.m. and even the hookers had quit for the night. I saw only one car. Within five minutes I was at the restaurant named after my mother, Okita, and I saw that the working light was still on in the kitchen. That meant Mom and Dad were still up cleaning, waiting for me, probably worrying. I was so glad they were still awake that tears filled my eyes. I ran the bike up the alley and in through the kitchen entrance. Then I fell off of it into my dad's arms, let him put me in a chair, and with him and Mom on either side of me, each holding one of my hands, I told them everything.

My mother and father are very special people. My father's parents came from Poland, from the part I.B. Singer writes about, and our name, Posey, was shortened from something like Posznzihwki. Dad left New York when he was my age to get a PhD at UC. He never went back to New York. For a while he was married to a black woman, so I have two black half brothers. My mother is half Japanese and half Mexican, an orphan adopted by a Quaker couple. She was first married to a Japanese man, so I have two mostly Japanese half brothers. I'm the only girl and the only child my parents had together because I was my mother's third Caesarean and, besides, they were near forty by the time they got together. My Quaker grandparents, pure WASP from an Indiana farm, both in their eighties, still do Thanksgiving for the whole family, full of pride as they look at the mix sitting around the table. But my dad laughs and says we're nothing special, just a typical Berkeley family. It was my dad who got interested in Japanese food and got my mom to start the restaurant with him. They work hard and make a bare living, and all of us kids have worked off and on in the place for more money than we are worth.

I love my parents. I admit it as if it were something to be ashamed of, like some kinky sex practice. I love them. I think they're the most interesting people I know, and when I read a book or have an important experience, they're the first ones I want to tell about it. That's why I still live with them above the restaurant, grateful that they'll have me and let me work in the restaurant.

While I was telling them about India, I was looking at their gray hairs, realizing they were sixty now, they were old, they could suddenly die, just like India. The thought of it was like a knife in my heart. I guess a writer, a would-be writer, shouldn't use a phrase so corny, but that's the trouble, cliches are true. That's what it felt like, a knife in my heart.

After a while, I ran out of words, ran out of tears. It was nearly five o'clock. My mother looked really tired. So my dad did what he has done so many times, stood up, long and lank and skinny, put an arm around each of us—we come up about to his armpits—and walked us three abreast up the stairway to the apartment. Then my mother made me a cup of camomile tea to take to bed with me and sat on the edge of my bed until I made her go, because I knew that even if I slept all day, she would be up in a few hours doing the flower arrangements for the restaurant tables. I looked at her dark broad, smooth face and thought again how glad I am that I look like her, except for a kink in my hair from Dad. It was the last thought I had before I fell asleep.

4.

I slept past lunch but woke in time to start getting ready for the dinner crowd. By three-thirty I was down in the restaurant sitting at the big round table in front of a mound of snowpeas. Stringing snowpeas was my favorite job, and Mom had saved it for me. I like holding the flat, cool, smooth pods, snapping off the top and pulling away the hair-like string, all in one smooth motion. Usually I make up stories while I do it, but that day my mind was numb, and I hoped it would stay that way. Mom and Dad were working in the kitchen, and whenever there was a lull in the roar of traffic on University Avenue, I heard their low voices.

It was one of those hot, still days we get in September. We had left the front door open, hoping for some air along with the noise and fumes. I sat with my back to the door, but I knew someone had come in because the light changed, was cut off by someone standing in the doorway. I turned around. "We start serving dinner at five." I couldn't see who it was because the light was behind him, and then a bus roared by so I couldn't hear if he answered me. He stood there for a minute, then came in, making his way around the tables toward me. "We're closed!" I wanted to be left alone with those quiet, cool snowpeas.

"Are you Jessamyn Posey?" He moved around close to the table where I could see him. He was short and broad, compact. He had curly brown sideburns and thin, brown straight hair on his head. He wore a light tan suit with a white shirt and tie, and he looked vaguely familiar. He reached for his wallet and pulled out a business card. A salesman? I started to wave him toward the kitchen to see my mother, but then I remembered that he had asked for me. I took the card and read it: JAMES MERINO. Then, in delicate letters on the side: Inspector, Berkeley Police Department.

My mind woke up, producing an instant list of charges. The people next door had a backyard plot of marijuana, from which a few cuttings were drying in my room. I hadn't renewed my bike license for two years, nor returned that copy of Charlotte Gilman's autobiography to the library. And a girl I hardly knew had asked me to store some boxes of stuff for her while she was in Mexico. They were in the basement, and I'd never looked at them. Explosives? Obscene books?

"You look familiar to me," he said, squinting at me. He let his mouth soften into a little smile, and I saw that he was younger than I thought at first. It must have been the suit.

"So do you," I said, and waited. I'd gotten past my first flash of paranoia and felt pretty sure I wasn't going to be arrested for overdue books. I guess I was ready to let myself face the real reason why he had come.

"You were one of the guests last night at the home of... India Wonder?" He hesitated as if he couldn't believe the name, and I wondered if there really could be someone who had never heard it. I nodded, then nodded again at a chair. He sat down and said, "Don't let me interrupt." I started picking up the snowpeas again, something for my hands to work on while I tried to keep back the sting and the tears from my eyes. "You were there when she... collapsed?" I nodded. "What is your relationship to... Ms. Wonder?" His voice was very gentle, and each sentence stopped midway while he chose the right word, like a football team waiting for a substitution.

I shook my head. "No relationship. She was a great writer. I'm nobody to her. I wrote her a letter. She invited me...." I was pulling at a stubborn pod; it wouldn't give. I stopped and looked at him. I guess my mind was finally really waking up. "Why are you asking questions about her?"

He smiled again, but this time the smile was phony. "Routine. In a case of sudden death, we have to file a report." He pulled out a sheet of yellow paper. "Is this a complete list of the people at the party?" Names were scrawled in a round, foreign-looking script. "Mr. Wonder made this list for us."

I shook my head at it. "People were in and out all night. Dozens of people. She was a very great lady and..." I stopped because I was close to crying again.

"Some stayed late. Could you check and see if all of them are on the list?"

I went over it, pointing to each name, trying to think. "Sylvia March. He left her off."

"Could you give me her address?" he asked as he added the name to the list.

"I don't know it. I didn't really know anyone there. I can't help you." I told him how I came to be at the party. The phony smile was gone. He was listening and nodding, even when I explained why I had written to India, though I hadn't really intended to tell him that.

"San Francisco State." His smile had become a wide grin.

"What?"

"That's where I know you from. Didn't you go to State?"

"Yes."

"We had an English class together, three—four years ago. Your paper was read in front of the class. It was great. I dropped out when my shift changed."

Now I remembered him. He had more hair then, but he was still a little older than most of the freshmen. Everyone knew he was a cop and wouldn't have anything to do with him. "I just graduated," I told him.

"I still have another year, at least. Late starter, working, you know. I just made inspector." His grin was as fresh and proud as his little business cards. Good for him. I gave him a smile that said it.

He stopped smiling, squinted at me again as if he'd made up his mind about something. "Look, that wasn't true, about this being routine. The toxicology reports won't be back for a few days, but the pathologist is sure, spotted the signs even before cutting her. It was cyanide."

My hands went on moving. I watched them slipping green, smooth, flat pods from one finger to another.

"I said..."

"I heard what you said!" So he waited and gave me a chance to take it in. Even if he was new at this, he must know that a person needs time to take it in. He was quiet for a long time before he started again.

"Death is either natural or unnatural. If it's unnatural, it's either an accident, suicide or homicide. Now, if it's an accident, how could it happen? How could one person be poisoned, and not any others?"

I started shaking my head.

"Okay, not absolutely ruled out, but unlikely. What about suicide? Need a reason. The pathologist found no sign of cancer or anything. She had a heart condition, high blood pressure, but her family doctor said she could have gone on another twenty or thirty years. Can you think of any other reason?"

I kept shaking my head.

"She was famous, admired?"

I nodded. "At the height of her career...new book coming out ...millions of readers...loved her." I was clamping my jaws, holding back those damned tears again.

"Okay, some personal problem? But you don't know her well enough. I'll have to get what I can from the family. Now. That leaves homicide. Do you know of anyone there—let's just say among the people who stayed late—anyone with a motive?"

"I told you I don't even know those people."

He nodded. "Now. Cyanide can be inhaled or swallowed or even absorbed through the skin." I was beginning to be interested in the methodical way he was moving. "I think we can rule out skin absorption because death was so sudden. Also, inhalation—as a gas it would have affected others in the room. So she swallowed it, in food, in a drink."

I nodded. "She drained her glass just before she fell."

"Then someone cleaned up the place, washed all the glasses."

"We all did."

"Who suggested that you clean up?"

"I...we all just...I can't remember that any one person suggested it. Wait. I remember. India's glass broke when she fell. I swept it up myself and put it in the garbage. It must be there, in a green plastic pail under the sink."

He was nodding. "I know. Mr. Wonder told me."

"You were testing me, weren't you? If I hadn't remembered about the glass, you'd have thought..."

"That you forgot, maybe." He shrugged. "But you did tell me. And it's not in the green pail. Somebody emptied the garbage into the can outside, and it was collected this morning. Can you remember..."

"Let me think." My head felt tight, knotted like a fist. "No, I can't. I think I saw Yolanda...no, I can't be sure. Does that matter a lot?"

"Probably not, since we know anyway it was cyanide, but it could be handy to know how administered. Who poured that drink for her?"

"Let me think...her husband made the drinks at first. But later on everyone was doing it." I shrugged and sighed. He imitated me almost exactly, then stood up. "What are you going to do?"

"Go around with this list, work my way through it. Look into the usual things—who would benefit financially if she died, that sort of thing."

"...is usual? You mean her family? What awful things to have to dig up about people."

He sighed again. "Well, thanks, Jessie. Are you still writing?" I nodded. "Good. I mean, you're really good. I'd better get going. If you think of anything else, or if anyone tells you something, anything at all, just call me. The number's on the card."

After he left, I went back to the snowpeas. I could tell Mom and Dad were still in the kitchen, moving around but not talking the way they usually did. They must have heard everything. I was glad they didn't come out and ask questions. I wanted to be quiet, to keep my hands busy, to think.

I finished the pile just at five, when the first dinner customer came through the doorway. By that time I knew I wasn't going to just wait for Jim Merino to work his way through his list. My grief and anger were too strong for that, intolerable unless I did something. Just as I always turn pain into writing, I could turn this pain into action, into trying to find out who killed the woman who stood for everything I ever wanted to be.

5.

Reuben Wonder was sitting in the same green armchair as if he hadn't moved since India died. The only difference was that now the fireplace was cold and black, and the windows were light. He was very pale, but he made an effort to look at me, even to smile. "They won't release. . .the body until all the reports come back. Three—four days." He seemed to be talking to himself while resting his eyes on me. The phone rang, but he didn't move.

"Should I get that?"

He shook his head. The morning sun came through the front room windows, shining on his round, bald head. He had few wrinkles; the skin of his face just seemed to have slipped to hang loose around his jaw and neck. His eyes were red, maybe from crying, but maybe it was just the usual red of old eyes under drooping lids. His nose spread with a pushed-in look, and his mouth was wide. He had that sad look I recognized from the description in India's journal. I glanced at his arm, but the tattooed concentration camp number was covered up by his shirt sleeve.

"I appreciate your seeing me so soon after. . . ." It was as hard as I thought it would be to get started. He just shrugged. I had rehearsed, but it was still an effort to go on. "I want to find out who killed her."

"Well...the police...." He sounded so vague, indifferent. He wasn't even looking at me anymore.

"I know I sound stupid to you. Just a kid with..."

"Not at all, no, not at all." At least he was looking at me again.

"My being young is an advantage. People are off guard. You'd be surprised at the things people say to me, just because I look about sixteen. I wouldn't tell anyone I was trying to find out who killed her. I would say—that I was writing an article about her."

"Why should..." He could shrug so hopelessly.

"Mr. Wonder, I'll go crazy if I don't do something. She was surrounded by her friends, the people she loved best, and one of them killed her."

His tired old eyes filled with tears. "Friends? Were they? Who knows? India had her ideals...bonding. Bringing women together. She thought she could be the person that all these women could gather around, come together, using her as the center. Using her. Friends?"

"Do you have any idea who might have done it?"

"I accuse..." He shrugged that awful shrug again. "I...no one."

"You *do* have some idea. Did you tell the police?"

He shook his head.

"Why not?"

He wrung his hands. I don't think I had ever seen anyone wring his hands before, but I knew what wringing was when I saw it. "If I only knew what she would want me to...."

"You think she wouldn't want her killer punished? Maybe not. Maybe she was that good. But I'm not. Are you that good, Mr. Wonder? Do you want to protect the person who killed her?" His tears were falling now and I felt like a monster for yelling at him. "What did you mean when you said 'you did it'? Who? You were looking at Yolanda. What did you mean?"

"Nothing, nothing."

"But you knew someone had reason to kill her, didn't you? Who had something against her? Or don't you care?"

He sat still for a long time. I couldn't see his face. His head hung over his hands. He didn't have any intention of answering me. He was just waiting for me to give up and go away. I decided that I could sit there as long as he could, longer. I kept staring at the top of his bald head as if I could bore two holes into it, until finally I saw it begin, slowly, so slowly, to move as he raised his head to look at me. He had stopped crying and was looking at me, but when I looked back at him, into his eyes, he blinked as if he had seen something ugly. The phone was ringing again. Neither of us moved. "Don't I care? Don't I care." He shook his head at me, a slow motion that didn't mean no; it meant he didn't think he could make me understand. "She was my life. I owe her my life. When I came here from Europe, alone, my whole family dead, my friends, everyone. Nothing but death, I came from. In the camps. After the camps, I was death, I killed, when I escaped and joined the British commandos. More killing and death until I was dead inside, ready to kill myself when I came to America. And then I met India. Then. . ."

I kept nodding as I listened. It was all like an echo of *Emma Pride's Journal*. At least the man knew it, I would give him credit for that. At least he knew how he had sucked her dry, how she had carried him. At least he admitted it. I knew all this, so I interrupted him with my question again. "Who had something against her?"

He hesitated, then turned his eyes away from me and sighed. "All of them, I guess. They were all in it."

"In what?"

"The book."

"India's new book?"

He nodded. "She worked on it for a long time. Once or twice she read a page to me. She talked about it. Maybe she talked too much about it. A *roman a clef*. They were all in it."

"May I see the manuscript?"

He nodded but did not move. I was getting impatient. "You want me to get it? Where is it, upstairs in her room?"

He shook his head. "Georgie takes care of all that, all India's work, correspondence. Talk to Georgie about it."

"Georgie lives here with you?" I remembered that office room upstairs. Cold and plain like Georgie.

He was nodding. "But she's out now. She's. . .making the arrangements."

"When can I talk to her? I could come back."

Now he was drawing back, shaking his head. "She's very upset, very busy. The phone keeps ringing." It started ringing again as if to prove him right.

"Well, you could give me what you gave the police. A list. Phone numbers, addresses of the. . .friends who stayed late at the party."

He didn't move right away. Finally he got up and walked slowly through the doorway to the kitchen. He was gone for a long time. I looked around the living room as if I might find some clue, but I didn't even know what a clue was. Everything was bland and ordinary: armchairs, couch, shelves of books, everything faded and dull in daylight. Ashes spilling out of the dead fireplace. Stains on the rug. Water streaks on the thin window curtains. Why was he taking so long? Was he still hoping I'd give up and go away?

Finally he came back, moving slowly, dragging one foot slightly. Suddenly I remembered a story of his concentration camp torture from India's journal, and I felt a stab of guilt for pushing at him this way. "This is India's." He handed me a thick address book. "She kept it by the phone. She had so many...people who called on her. Maybe...maybe you shouldn't tell Georgie what you're doing. She feels...." He shrugged again.

I shook my head. "I'll tell Georgie I'm writing an article about India. I'll tell the others that I'm writing an article about women writers for...for *Ms. Magazine.* Then they'll all want to see me and talk to me. Off guard."

"Clever girl." He took my hand and tried so hard to smile that I didn't mind being called a girl. I even forgot to ask why I shouldn't tell Georgie I was investigating her mother's murder. "May I keep this for a few days? I'll just copy the addresses and phone numbers and then bring it back to you."

He nodded.

I remembered another question. "Who emptied the garbage?"

His faint smile was gone, his face blank, unreadable.

"The police think the cyanide might have been in India's drink. The glass broke when she fell, and I swept up the pieces and put them in the pail under the sink, but someone else took the garbage out. I can't remember who...can you?"

He didn't move for a while, as if he hadn't heard me. Then his eyes shifted away. After a while he shook his head. I couldn't figure him out. Was he hiding something? Or was he still in shock? I opened my mouth because I had more questions, but his head went on shaking, and he raised his hand as if he could stop my words with it, as if to say he couldn't take any more. I knew he wouldn't listen to me. I watched him sink back into the green armchair as the phone started ringing again.

6.

I went straight home and started going through the address book. The names were all printed in India's slanty, crisscross hand, like the letter she had sent to me. Hers was the only printing I'd ever seen that was less legible than script. The book was thick and worn, all pages covered with names and addresses on every line, with more running along the edge of each page. My name was there in fresh green ink, squeezed between Marge Piercy and V.S. Pritchett.

I turned pages, wondering why I had taken the book, except that returning it would give me an excuse to see Reuben Wonder again. I couldn't contact the hundreds of people in this book or even the dozens who had been at the party, any one of whom could have slipped something into her drink and then left. I could be wasting my time.

I copied the names, addresses and phone numbers of the people who had stayed late. There were eight of them, plus Reuben Wonder and India's daughter Aurore—Georgie. Neither name suited her, one too romantic, the other too playful. If this were a movie, I thought, she would be the prime suspect, with her grim jaw and her hard eyes, like Judith Anderson in *Rebecca*.

Now what? I decided to start with Jane Lee, just because I admired her so much, and this time I would have reason and courage to speak to her. I dialed her number.

No answer. It wasn't noon yet. Where had I read that she worked in the morning and never answered the phone while writing? What discipline, to be able to ignore a ringing phone. When the phone rings, I always think it's just the call I've always waited for—though I can't think what that call could be.

I dialed India's number. If Georgie was home by now, I could ask her about the new manuscript. The phone rang and rang. I could almost see Reuben sitting there alone, head in his hands, deaf to the phone. I was about to hang up when I heard the click and the soft, "Yes."

"Miss Williams? Georgie?"

"Yes."

"This is Jessamyn Posey. I...I wanted to say again how sorry I am about...and to...and if there's anything I can...."

"Yes. Thank you." Now she would hang up. How could I keep her on the line? It was so hard to talk to her.

"I wonder if you could tell me when the funeral will be."

"The coroner expects to release the body by Wednesday. Probably the funeral will be Friday. At St. Joan's. We prefer to keep it quiet, small."

Did she mean I shouldn't come? I wouldn't ask, so she couldn't tell me so. "St. Joan's? Isn't that Catholic?" I remembered that part in the journal, how India had wanted to run away from her big, suffocating Catholic family to be a nun, and how she actually had run away from all of it, family, church and all.

"Supposedly." How sarcastic that sounded. What did she mean? "About a year ago she began attending mass there."

"I'd like to see you before..."

"Impossible."

I could see that telling her I was doing an article was hopeless. But I had another idea. "Surely, you're planning a larger ceremony, a public memorial service later?"

"I'm planning nothing."

"No, I mean others should. I would. I could help."

No answer.

"And at the memorial service, someone should read from your mother's new book. I understand you have the manuscript and if I could come to look at it and...."

She hung up on me. I couldn't have done any worse if I'd just come straight out and told her that I wanted to catch her mother's murderer and that the new book was an important clue. Why didn't I? I didn't trust her. I even suspected her. She was so cold, so different from anything I had expected after reading *Emma Pride's Journal*.

I remembered the part about her so clearly, as I usually remember the beginnings of books. The young "Emma," only seventeen, already deserted by the black man she ran away with, desperately trying to survive with her tiny baby girl, the sweet, golden child she held and loved and called her "miracle." That part had been anthologized so often, such a perfect expression of mother love, that I must have read it many times. I'd seen it pantomimed and heard parts of it sung by folksingers. There was a famous drawing inspired by it, and one year I'd received it on a Christmas card.

I looked at my list. I had to do better than I had so far! If I really had been working on an article for *Ms.*, I probably would have started with Margot Stackpole. She was the logical one, with a first novel about to be published, a big advance, lots of talk about movie options and promotion campaigns. Margot, with her novel spread all over her chest, wasn't the type who'd refuse to talk to me. She'd be expecting to hear from *Ms.* If she hadn't already. I'd better make sure about that. I splurged on a call to New York and asked some editor at *Ms.* if they planned a story on Margot Stackpole. She hesitated, then said no, in a funny, cool way, almost like Georgie. Why did everyone I talked to seem weird today? Maybe it was me.

I called Margot and got a recording saying that her phone had been disconnected. It couldn't be because she hadn't paid her bill! For a minute I had a crazy vision of her being packed and ready to fly away after poisoning India. That's what comes to you when your experience with homicide is only in movies and television.

I looked at her address again and saw that it was just down on Ashby. So I got out my bike and went to find her.

7.

Margot's address was a small, dirty, backyard cottage on the western part of Ashby Avenue, where the traffic and fumes and dust were so bad that I started wishing for some kind of space helmet with a supply of air. Or any kind of helmet, to keep my head from getting broken if one of those cars knocked me flying.

Margot wasn't there. The new tenant, a student at Cal, told me she had moved. "She's up the other end of Ashby. Here, you can take some mail up to her." He handed me some envelopes with the new address scribbled on them, and I got back onto my bike.

I hoped I would live to make it up to her new place. Traffic moved fast along the narrow, two-lane street. During rush hours no parking was allowed, but now, in the middle of the day, it was legal, and a parked car ahead could mean disaster if some impatient driver decided to smash me into it.

Ashby widened out at Grove, then narrowed again, and the worst stretch of all was the business-lined block before College Avenue. But as soon as I crossed College I was in winding residential streets, where I turned off to the address on the envelopes: a huge lawn, wide marble steps, a massive front door, like City Hall. I chained my bike to a tree in a concrete urn on the front porch, then banged the big brass knocker on the polished wood, listened to the echo, and waited until the huge door swung open.

Margot was still wearing the RESERVED FOR LOVE T-shirt, with shorts so short they must be digging into her crotch. Her thighs were a little flabby, but her legs were long and smooth and tan. She uncovered a row of deep wrinkles in her forehead when she tossed her long blonde hair back from her face and started finger-brushing it back like a veil, the way we used to when styles were more hairy. I wondered how it felt to have a big advance on a first novel and be written up in all the papers. I thought she should have looked happier. But when she recognized me she made a wide smile and her eyes brightened, even though the wrinkles above them stayed deep. "Hey, uh. . . ."

"Jessie."

"Right, Jessie, hi. Come on in." The foyer alone was bigger than the place she had lived in on lower Ashby. She led me into a front room filled with satiny, spindly antiques. "Isn't this something?"

"You collect. . . ."

"Oh, no, none of this is mine. I'm renting the whole thing. Until I can get my own place, what I really want, you know. Maybe I'll build something. I always wanted to design my own house. I studied architecture for a while. When I was painting. No time since. . . ." The phone rang. "Sit down." She wiggled all over as she left the room. It was the high heels. I never saw such high heels. My mom told me when she was young you just had to wear them or you were a frump. I tried once but couldn't stand them.

I could hear Margot talking from the other room. It was someone who wanted to interview her. I hoped it wasn't *Ms.* suddenly pushed by my call to do something. No, it sounded like some Marin County paper with an early deadline. "*Reserved for Love,* that's right, it's a sort of modern Berkeley Gothic romance, but comic, you know."

A manuscript was spread out on the carved, leather-top table near my chair. I stood up to look at it. The first few pages were covered with blue pencil marks, corrections of spelling mostly. The margins were full of questions in blue pencil. In the middle of page eleven, the blue-penciling suddenly ended, as if someone had given up. Margot's interview went on and on, so I read a few pages.

I couldn't believe how awful it was. Could it be parody? Mysterious sexy strangers leaping out of dark corners to pounce on a blonde, bosomy heroine with a wide smile, who told jokes about demonstrations and dope. Was that Berkeley Gothic? The jokes reminded me of my junior high school toilet walls. And it wasn't parody. Something about it was very earnest, dead serious.

When I heard her conversation stop, I jumped back and found a chair far away from the manuscript. I didn't want her to catch me reading it and ask me what I thought of it.

"Sorry about that. They needed a few details for this big spread —local girl makes good and all."

"You must really be enjoying it."

She spread her lips out over her teeth again, but the lines in her forehead showed even through the hair. Then her lips closed again as if smiling made her tired.

"Actually that's why I'm here. I'm doing an article for *Ms.* on local women writers, and I thought I'd start with you."

"Well, for a minute or two, but I have to get back to work on this mess." She pointed to the manuscript.

"Have you been writing for a long time?" I pulled out a 3 × 5 card and pretended to concentrate on writing down her answers.

She shrugged. "I only write when I'm inspired. I can't sit there day after day the way Jane does. *Reserved for Love* took six weeks, then those editors tackled it with their blue pencils. Clean-up. I won't write again till something hits me. That's not the only thing I do. I believe in the renaissance woman." I waited for her to laugh, but she didn't. So I didn't.

"You paint too?"

She shook her head. "Film, I'm a film-maker. That's the only form that expresses the consciousness of our time."

"Oh. Did you...would I have seen any of your films?"

She shook her head. "I could never get any backing. Takes money, you know. I went to UCLA, hung around down there for a while, but it's hard for a woman to get anywhere."

"But now, with your own book, that's all changed," I said. "Maybe you'll get to film it."

She nodded absentmindedly.

"Maybe you could play the lead," I said.

She just gave me another absent-minded nod. Then she remembered her hair, her T-shirt, her smile, and she turned them all on

again. "It's true, I'm an actress. I had a couple of roles on TV."
She named some serial shows I had never watched. She shrugged.
"Bits. I decided if I was ever going to get a good role, I'd have to
write it myself, film it myself. I see it like this." She started describing the opening scene of the film she would make. She used movie
jargon I didn't understand. I was wondering why the conversation
hadn't turned to India's death and how I would get it there. And,
when I did, what questions would I ask? I had thought that pretending I believed India's death was natural gave me an advantage.
But it only seemed to limit the questions I might ask. I watched
Margot as she talked and gestured. She didn't look sad that India
had died. She didn't look guilty either.

Then she suddenly turned her talk in the direction I wanted.
"...that's how I met India. I was going to make a film of *Emma
Pride's Journal*. But it never worked out. Money, you know. It's
always money."

I nodded. "I'm still in shock over her death, and I hardly knew
her. You must feel terrible."

"Yeah." I waited, but that was all she said. She was looking
around the room as if taking inventory of all the antiques, the lines
deepening across her forehead.

I tried again. "Now all we have is her new book. Have you seen it?"

Margot shook her head, fingering her hair. "But I'm in it, of
course. I know how she did me, stupid, illiterate broad from L.A."
She surprised me. Was she smart enough to know how dumb she
looked? "India was rough on her friends. You noticed how furious
Jane was at the party?"

"Jane? Why should..."

"And Sylvia! All of them. All except me because I'm going to
be three times as famous as India ever was."

"You mean they were jealous of her fame. But Sylvia loved her,
and Jane is famous in her own way. She..."

"You know, Jessie, I've got a terrible headache, and all this
work to finish." The phone started ringing as she stood up. She
went to answer it, and this time I could hear her voice more clearly.
"No, no, that is not correct, no, I have no comment on that. No."
I heard her hang up, but I waited a long time for her to come back
into the living room. She wobbled into the room holding her head.
"They wanted to interview me about India's death. I think that's
ghoulish. I told them where to go." I didn't believe her, but I couldn't
think why she would lie.

"I didn't even know she was sick. Did you notice anything about her recently that would make you expect...."

"You mean how scared she was," Margot murmured absently as if she wasn't talking to me at all. She was going to the front door, and I was rushing after her.

"Scared?"

"You'll have to come back to finish this. My head just..." She held the door open and gave me a little shove out onto the front porch.

"Scared of what?" I was asking, as she shut the door. There was nothing to do but unhook my bike and head for home, where I called Sylvia March and, dangling my bait of a write-up in *Ms.,* got an appointment to see her the following morning.

8.

The next morning *The Chronicle* had the story: India Wonder had died of cyanide poisoning. The paper ran a lovely picture of India, taken when she was younger. Her hair hung loose, but it was already white and her eyes shone with the same pale intensity. There was a picture of Jim Merino too, with his statement that police were investigating but had "no clues."

Sylvia March might be on her guard. What would she say when I told her I had heard her say, "Free at last"? Or had I imagined that? No one else had noticed, and I hadn't actually heard the words, only watched her mouthing them.

I headed my bike north toward Albany, and soon I was coasting past the rows of tiny stucco houses that always made me laugh. Most of them were little boxes no bigger than an apartment, but some had turrets like Spanish castles or columns like southern plantation mansions. They looked like play houses, doll houses.

Sylvia's house was one of the tiniest, with a row of little columns across the front porch, like a two-bit Parthenon. It needed paint and the little patch of lawn was scraggly and gouged out in places. A tricycle blocked the tiled stairway. I climbed over it, rang the doorbell, and waited. I tried to remember what India had said when she introduced Sylvia: the disciple. I guess she had meant that, like

India, Sylvia wrote journals. I had heard her read from her journal three or four times, explaining the value of "the uniquely feminine quality of spontaneous and experimental writing." Her style was like India's, intense and maybe even more exposed. She had been keeping a journal daily for ten years. The first time I heard her read, I was shaken. Then, at the second reading I felt a little embarrassed though I was never sure why. At the third reading I got bored, but it was a hot night and hard to concentrate.

When Sylvia opened the door, the sound of children yelling hit me. According to her journals, there was one child. The noise sounded like half a dozen. Sylvia looked terrible. She had been crying and her swollen red nose and eyes flamed up in her white face. The Nordic, oriental look was all twisted, as if the swollen, drawn parts of her face didn't fit together. Even before I smelled her breath, I knew she had been drinking. Her face was wet with sweat and tears, her thin-straw hair dry. But her body was erect and graceful as a swaying reed. Her movement looked familiar. Yes, she stood and moved just like India. She looked at me for a second as if she had no idea who I was or why I had come. Then she recognized me, tried to smile. "I'm putting the kids down for their nap now."

There were four of them. I stood just inside the front door watching them as they watched me. Sylvia went on talking while she picked them up or led them off to another room. I could hear her from any part of the tiny house. "This one's mine. The others I take care of so I don't have to leave her. Next year she'll be in school all day, so maybe then I'll get a day job. Right now I work two nights a week at Cutter Labs. I wanted to stay home with her and I wanted to write, so I tried it this way, but it doesn't work!" She glared at me as if I had told her it would. "The only time I have to write is when they take a nap and then I'm so tired, I fall asleep too. Late at night, when I can't sleep, that's when I work on the journal."

I was watching one of the kids, fascinated. He had pulled away, refusing to go to the bedroom. Then he leaned back against the couch and fell asleep standing up. Sylvia looked at him, shook her head, then left him there.

Piles of clean diapers covered the couch. The little kitchen was full of highchairs. I saw tears fill Sylvia's eyes as she looked around for a place for us to sit. So I sat down on the floor in front of a huge, unused fireplace that would have fitted better in Margot's mansion. Sylvia sank to the floor beside me.

"The police were here. Inspector Merino thinks I killed India!"

"Why would he think that?"

"Oh, he didn't say so, but...did he come to see you?" I nodded. "Oh. Maybe it was just routine. I don't know. I'm so mixed up."

"It's the shock. I'm still numb, aren't you? I mean, who could have wanted to kill her?"

She sniffed. "Maybe...Margot?"

"Margot?" I had just about ruled Margot out. "Why Margot?"

"If India found out about her affair with Reuben...no, that wouldn't explain..."

"With that old man?" I couldn't take it in. Sexy Margot and that little, ugly old man. An absurd, obscene image of him nibbling at her big breasts flashed on me.

"It didn't last long. I guess it was over already. But Reuben has charm, a way of looking at a woman and really seeing her, letting her be a person who...India describes it very well in the journal, didn't you read it?"

I nodded. "But I don't see how sleeping with Reuben gave Margot a motive for murder."

"No, I'm...I'm getting it all mixed up." I got another whiff of her breath and could understand why. "Reuben was Margot's revenge. For the film. I don't think she's ever forgiven India for that mess."

"Film?"

"About three or four years ago. That's how they met. Margot wanted to make a film of *Emma Pride's Journal.* Of course, India gushed all over her, welcomed her into the fold, just the same way she treated you, she treated everyone that way at first." There was pure jealous spite in her narrow, slanted eyes. "Told her she was full of talent. To India every woman was an undiscovered genius. So Margot borrowed a lot of money and started making the film. Halfway through, she ran out of money. Tried to borrow more, but no one would lend it to her unless she had the film rights. She asked India for them, and India, of course, had to say no. It was an awful film, I saw bits of it. Margot's an amateur. Besides, she has no taste. The journal is a hot property. India couldn't let Margot mess with it. But she was wrong to encourage her, she should have thought before she let Margot get in so deep."

"I guess India is...was too kind. Tell me, what did you mean when you said..."

"If you're going to interview me, we'd better get started before the kids wake up."

"Yes. Tell me about your work. I heard you read a few times, but I've never seen the whole..."

She rose from the floor gracefully, like a dancer, then walked unevenly to the couch, easing the little sleeping boy down to the rug as she passed him. She did it so gently—setting him to rest. All her anger seemed to have left her. Even her tipsiness looked like the soft vulnerability that men usually like.

For the first time I noticed the row of black bound books on a shelf above the couch. "I started these ten years ago, right after I read *Emma Pride's Journal*. I'd never written a thing, never dreamed of writing, never suffered the hardships India put into that journal. But reading it made me realize that I wanted to write, to make my deepest feelings live on paper, to touch the common sisterhood of women, bonded in our experience, our..." Her voice trailed off as if she'd forgotten the next word in a prepared speech. She smiled as she put one hand on the shelf, like a child, like my niece who is so used to being photographed by my father that she's always falling into irresistible poses. The only difference was that Sylvia's pale face was drawn downward, weary, as if, like the little boy on the floor, she might fall asleep just standing there.

She told me there were now thirty-eight volumes in her ten year journal and several publishers were interested in printing selections from them. She excused herself to go to the bathroom, then came swaying back with her eyes a little brighter, her breath heavy with mouthwash. My eighth-grade teacher was like that, disappearing every half hour to take a nip. Sylvia kept talking. She was editing, putting together excerpts to submit to publishers. It was a long hard job, especially because she was alone, supporting her daughter, with all the usual troubles. Her voice went on and on like that weather report you get on the phone, machine-like and cheery and automatic, while she looked distracted, not just absent-minded, practically absent. Like someone that an old-fashioned cubist would paint all in pieces.

At the first gap I slipped it in. "Free at last?" I wanted to shock her out of her act, and I succeeded.

"What?" She sank into the pile of diapers on the couch.

"You said 'free at last' when India died."

Suddenly tears were running down her face, but she sat up more erect as she said, "I bet you told the police that!"

I shook my head. I hadn't told Jim Merino that, but I would. "What did you mean?"

"Mean? I meant it's been like being...under a spell. I meant she ruined my life!" She kept smearing her tears away with the backs of her hands, shuddering and coughing so that her words came out in little clumps. "I was only twenty...my marriage was all right...can't remember what I thought was wrong with... started a journal...writing down every little problem, that's what did it...Dan didn't...he couldn't...we didn't break up all at once, took years...and the baby...can't you see...I was India. I started writing like her and thinking like her, and pretty soon I *was* her, living her life...the parts in the book...the book!" Suddenly she turned toward the wall and took a wide swing at the row of black books, but only two or three of them slipped and fell into the pile of diapers without making a sound. "Ten years...deepest feelings? I don't even know what they are...not me...I'm not me!"

She covered her face with her hands so I couldn't hear her for a while. I was thinking about that Oscar Wilde play where someone says "life imitates art." Then she let her hands fall into her lap and raised her head.

"Writers are liars." She wasn't crying, but her red-lined eyes were so narrow they looked closed. "You know Nancy Drater's book on creative motherhood?" I nodded. "Lies. She writes all about how she gets up at four a.m. to write for three hours before her kids wake up. She doesn't mention that the kids live one week with her and one week with her ex-husband. I just found that out. And Bethelee Lane? *Successful Womanhood?* She just doesn't happen to mention that her mother sends her housekeeper over three times a week to clean up and babysit. And you've read Aphral Woods' book about her thirty years of perfect marriage and motherhood." I nodded. "Well, she took that big paperback advance and walked out! She's in Spain!" I thought that was kind of funny, but when I started to laugh, Sylvia glared at me.

"India wasn't a liar," I said. "She told it like it is, how being a wife and mother stifled every..."

"India was the biggest liar of all!"

"What do you mean? Tell me how she lied."

Suddenly her eyes widened as if she had just woke up. "You're going to put all this in your article!"

I shook my head.

"You are, you are, I won't say anymore. No more."

Actually I was wishing she wouldn't. I'd already heard enough to keep me awake for a few nights. Sylvia had scared me. What she told about herself sounded too much like what had happened to me. I'd spent my whole life reading, and the last six years of it—since reading India's journal—writing. Was I like Sylvia, just acting out a character in a book? Maybe I was going to wake up at thirty or fifty or sixty-five and see that I wasn't a writer at all, that, like Sylvia, I had never lived my own life. I tried to put all that out of my mind and remember what I was there for. "Have you read India's new book?"

She shook her head, her eyes narrowing again with a bitter glint in them. "No, but I gather I'm in it. We're all in it. I'm sure she said my work was just imitative, unoriginal...well, when it comes out, it won't matter what you say about me in *Ms.*" Tears were oozing out between her eyelids again. "I wonder if she put in everything about Carla...and how she portrayed Reuben this time."

I started to ask what she meant, but the little boy on the floor woke with a howl, staring at the ceiling and waving his arms, lost and terrified.

9.

I didn't know I was on my way to see Jim Merino until I found myself rolling down McKinley Street toward the Berkeley police station. It was a quiet time of day, just before noon, when the high school kids were mostly still inside; traffic hummed over on Grove Street but was almost nonexistent here, just a block away. Or did people just tend to tiptoe past the police station?

I looped my bike chain around the slim trunk of a new tree in front of the station. It just fitted—another year or two and the trunk would be too thick, like the other trees. Someone was watching me—a big-jawed, blonde cop who sat at a desk just inside the big glass door and gave me a sour nod as I walked in. I asked for Jim Merino, and he pointed to the stairway. "Through the door at the top of the stairway, down the hall, turn left." He almost smiled when I thanked him.

The foyer of the station rises two storeys, with twin stairways curving up from both sides through dark wood paneling. Whoever built it must have been trying for a gracious entry, a good try defeated. Maybe too many depressing things had happened here; as I walked up the stairs I felt as if I'd meet a hooded executioner at the top. I followed directions and ended up at a dark counter where a woman buzzed for Jim. Right away he came through a door to my left, so close that he must have heard our voices louder than the phone.

"Hey, Jessie, what's happening?" He was smiling as if there was no one in the world he wanted to see more than me. He still wore a suit, but his tie was loose and some long gray-green thing was hanging from his arm. It looked like an old, sun-faded window drape, which it was. "Come on into the den."

I followed him into a room like a closet, with a table and a couple of chairs. A glass door and windows looked out into the murky hall by the counter. The air was stale, the walls dingy. On the table there were some blank forms with printed disclaimers that no rights had been violated "during the taking of this statement."

"Impossible, huh? No privacy. And the noise! No way I can do a successful hypnosis in here. That's why I got these old rags from over at juvenile hall. If I can rig up a pole across here..." He held the drapes up over the dark windows, then shrugged and dropped them into a box with others in the corner.

"Hypnosis?"

"Sit down." We sat facing each other at the table. "I went to an advanced seminar two weeks ago. I swear, I made two years progress in one weekend. The guy was fantastic. He brought in a psychic too. Some departments use them, but my chief's not ready for that yet." He laughed. "I'm not sure I am."

"You use hypnosis, here, officially?"

"Oh, all the time. On people who are willing. You can't hypnotize a suspect who racked up thirty burglaries and doesn't exactly want you to know it. Witnesses. People forget things. I help them remember...license numbers, speech patterns. Remember that missing girl who..."

"I thought you only did homicides."

"Felonious assault, homicide, missing persons." Jim sighed. "But now I'm doing some hypnosis for other departments too. We've just scratched the surface. If I could just get some money for. . . ." His voice faded out along with his smile and I realized that all the time he'd been talking, he'd been watching me too. "Did you come to ask me a question or to tell me something more?"

"I thought I'd better tell you that I've started talking to some of the people at the party." I kept my voice cool and assertive just in case he would try to tell me to keep out. "I've told India's husband the truth, that I want to find out who killed her, but I'm telling the women that I'm writing an article on women writers. Now, whatever objections you have. . . ."

He was shaking his head. "No objections. I think it's a great idea. I need you. Some of those women won't talk to a man, not the way they would talk to you. I started with Carla Neeland. I didn't know she was the editor of that Lesbian magazine. She talked to me like *I* was the murderer!" He laughed, but I didn't. I don't like easy laughs at women who stand at the extreme. He stopped laughing right away. I liked him for that. A person doesn't have to be perfect; he just ought to look and listen and think. "And that woman who lives with her?"

I shook my head. I didn't know who he meant.

"Little blonde with heavy eyebrows."

"That must be Pamela Righbottom. She's from New York, on exchange teaching at State. I guess she's going back to Eastward U. for the fall semester."

"So she said. But I told her not to be in a hurry. What was her connection to India Wonder?"

"None. Carla brought her to the party, I guess."

"Better ask around, make sure."

I nodded.

Jim smiled. "You really can help me, Jessie. I was thinking about asking for a woman officer, but that might make it worse. You'd be just right." I could see that wasn't the only reason he was willing to let me help. There's a way a man looks at you when he's interested, before he even knows he's interested, a kind of soft lift of his face, like waking up. He was looking at me that way. "What have you found out so far?"

"Well, I saw the husband, then Margot Stackpole, and then Sylvia March. I'm not too good at this, didn't find out many clear facts. One is, you know India Wonder had a new book coming out? Her husband says all these women are in it and they all resent it."

"Enough to poison her?" He looked dubious, like a man who isn't used to thinking words in books would hurt anyone, but he nodded for me to go on.

"Then I found out that Margot Stackpole was sleeping with him, and that she had once lost a lot of money because of some mix up over film rights to India's first book. But Margot just sold a novel for tons of money and moved up by the Claremont Hotel."

"That should cancel out old grudges." Jim nodded again.

"I just came from seeing Sylvia March. You scared her. She acts guilty, looks guilty, scared, mad at everyone, especially India. Sylvia's a kind of disciple—put India on a pedestal."

"And then she fell off."

"After ten years, a wrecked marriage, money problems, alcohol, maybe dope. She's in a bad way, mad at everyone. She could have done it, but if she did I don't think she'd have told me she hated India, she'd cover up."

"Sometimes they expose a lot. They want to be punished. Anything else?"

"Margot told me India was afraid."

"Of what?"

I shrugged. "She pushed me out the door before I could ask." Some detective, I thought he would say, but he only nodded again.

"Okay, now I'll tell you what I've done so far." He got up and left the room. I saw him through the window, opening a file cabinet, taking out a folder. In a minute he was back, leaving the door open so that some of the slightly less stale air from the hall might come in.

"Money," he started, as if he always started there. "Not much. Royalties were only a few thousand a year. The big money was in fees for lectures and reading; those stop with her death. The advances—she got several advances because the new book was taking longer—were about gone. Mr. Wonder says the potential in royalties, movie rights, was pretty good?"

"Unlimited. With paperback rights, maybe millions. She was a very..."

"But dead?"

I thought for a minute. "Her death might make her work even more popular. Look at Sylvia Plath." I could tell he'd never heard of Sylvia Plath. "Who gets the money? Her husband?"

Jim shook his head. "The daughter. Aurore Williams. What do they call her?"

"Georgie."

He nodded. "India made a new will about..." He looked at a sheet of paper in the folder. "...six months ago. Left everything to her daughter, to be divided among other family members as she saw fit."

"Maybe she found out about her husband playing around."

"Could be. He didn't know about the will. The daughter did." He looked at me as if I should be able to draw a conclusion from that. When I didn't, he did. "That leaves both of them with a possible money motive. The husband could have assumed he'd inherit everything; the daughter knew that she would. That daughter... Georgie. Strange woman."

"You talked to her? She wouldn't see me."

Jim nodded. "She answered all my questions, but didn't tell me anything. And when I brought up the will, she just...laughed." He shuddered as if someone had walked over his grave. "The body has been released to the family, sent to a funeral home. Tests supported the original judgment: cyanide. One interesting thing the pathologist said: the dose was just lethal. Usually people have enough in them to kill an army. But this dose was given by someone who knew poisons. Anyone at that party with medical training?"

"I don't know."

"Or access to drugs, chemicals?"

"Sylvia March works at Cutter Labs."

He made a note on the folder. I took the hint and pulled out my 3 × 5 cards, the ones I always carry for notes on writing. Under an unfinished poem I wrote, cyanide—lethal dose—medical training—Sylvia access.

"Then, aside from you, I've only seen Carla Neeland. You can imagine how far I got, being male *and* white. What do you know about her?"

"She edits a newsletter called *Herland,* and she started Women Writers United. She edited a collection of black women poets and one of excerpts from women's diaries—a piece from India's book is in it. Her play *Delilah* is a sort of feminist classic. Her poetry is..." I hesitated. This part felt like it was none of Jim's business, but I guess it was now. "I heard her read once, love poems. To a woman. The woman was India."

"Are you sure?" He looked disappointed.

"You couldn't miss the description of her—much older than Carla, thin, the long white braid of hair."

Jim stared thoughtfully at the windows as if he were still measuring them for drapes. I checked my cards and said, "There are four more: Celeste Wildpower, Yolanda Dolores, Jane Lee and Antonia Moran."

He picked up his folder again. "Do you know anything about them?" He held his pencil like a good student taking notes. "Celeste Wild...power? Her real name is McDougal."

"So what? She has the right to choose a name instead of just taking whatever man's name was tacked onto her!" Jim was nodding anxiously. I smiled, partly at that, partly at the name. It was kind of funny. We both laughed. "Celeste is a witch." I was glad he didn't laugh again. "Forget the old hags in fairy tales. That's not what a witch is. A witch is...it's a religious movement. I went to a meeting of Celeste's coven once. It was sort of...like a Quaker meeting. She wrote a book called *Dream Witch,* a fantasy about an island governed by people's dreams. It's a sort of underground best seller, really a good book. Well-written too. I think you'd like it, especially with your interest in hypnosis." I saw he was writing down the title. "She did something strange at the party, did anyone tell you? She pointed at India and...and that was when India fell, as if she'd..."

He was nodding. "Sylvia March told me about that."

"I guess you don't believe in..."

"I don't disbelieve in anything, Jessie. What about Jane Lee?"

"She's a great writer, almost as great as India. In her way." I hadn't really thought about this before. "None of her books grabbed me just the way India's journal did, but they all sank in and stayed with me. They're simple, but deep. Every time I reread one I get something I missed before. Novels, poetry, short stories, children's books. First book I ever read was *Good-bye Dragonfly.* Her latest is an adult novel about an old schoolteacher who gets mad and burns down the school."

"I never heard of her either. I guess I'm..."

"A lot of people haven't. But the ones who have—well, I judge literary people, readers, you know, by whether or not they've read Jane Lee." Jim looked sad, as if he'd just been judged illiterate.

"What's her relationship to India?"

"I don't know. Don't know a thing about her. I never saw her before the party. She's kind of a recluse. She looked...mousy. Shy. Like a little girl with glasses. But she's pretty old. Fifty at least."

"Yolanda McVittey? Dolores? Whatever her name is."

"I think McVittey is her married name. She writes nonfiction. She did one of the first articles on DES, you know, that hormone that's giving women cancer. Mostly she does literary muckraking. She exposed a phony agency that was charging writers a lot of money, with no hope of ever selling their work. Her latest thing was on this small press that had gone vanity—between taking money from authors and getting grants and nonprofit status, the guy was making a nice living without actually publishing very much." I could see that Jim was not as fascinated as I am by all this.

"You know her personally?"

"On, no, I never even talked to her at the party. I was surprised at how she looked. Her articles sound like some nineteenth-century essayist, formal, sharp-edged. She's plump and rosy, thick black hair and, you know, that rosy golden skin some Mexican women have. Not young, about forty?"

"Antonia Moran?" Jim was too busy taking notes even to look up.

"She was the oldest woman there. Older than India." Old, old, I kept calling everyone old. And I hate ageism. "One of those... elder Berkeley radicals. You've probably seen her picketing wherever ...the draft, farmworkers, everything. She wrote a book called *Seven Sisters Left,* about seven women who were heroines of labor, civil rights, peace movements, all socialists. Part biography, part personal reminiscence—she knows everybody in radical circles. She and India knew each other since they were pretty young. There's a section in India's journal where she's a communist until the Party tries to censor her writing. I guess the friendship with Antonia goes back that far."

Jim put down his pencil and looked at me for a long minute. "You sure have read a lot of books."

I didn't know whether to take that as a compliment or not. "Well, I'm a writer," I said, a little defiantly but almost apologetically too, and I could feel a blush spreading over me. He watched it spread, a soft smile growing on his face, and that made me blush more. Then, finally, my blush began to cool, his smile faded, and the soft look moved up into his eyes. They were brown, like mine, what Mom used to call my chocolate eyes, bittersweet.

10.

The papers said the funeral was private, for only family and friends; a memorial service for the public would be announced later. I wasn't sure if I qualified as a friend. But Georgie called, so I guess I did. "There will be a rosary at the funeral home the night before, then the funeral at Saint Joan's." I told her I couldn't come for the rosary—I'd missed too many hours in the restaurant already—but that I'd come to the funeral. Before I finished thanking her she had hung up.

Saint Joan's turned out to be a tiny old wood frame building in West Berkeley, not far from India's house. It couldn't have always been a Catholic church. I'd been to lots of different churches, though not this one, and it had a definitely Baptist look on the outside. Jim was standing near the curb when I rode up. He watched me tie up my bike to the wrought iron railing, then turned away. I pretended to look right through him as I went up the narrow five steps to the dark, open doorway.

Inside, the place was smaller than the restaurant and dark except for the dozens of little candles flickering on the red satin-draped altar. There were about a dozen narrow pews. On either side of them stood huge plaster statues of Mary holding crucified Jesus across her knees like the famous painting. In the back, near the doorway, assorted saints and angels stood crowded together like extras standing around on a set for a Biblical movie.

As my eyes got used to the dim light, I could see the back of Reuben Wonder's bald head in the front row. Georgie sat on one side of him and a big woman with brassy hair on the other—that would be Antonia Moran. Behind them sat a couple of younger men. Further back were women I recognized from the party, with some men mixed in, one next to Yolanda Dolores. I saw a space next to Yolanda and walked a narrow aisle around a winged angel to sit beside her. Then someone else squeezed in beside me. It was Jane Lee, her little body fitting in cozily as she whispered, "Neither of us takes up much space, room for us both?" I nodded and felt a thrill at having Jane Lee squeezed in next to me.

The closed coffin took up most of the narrow space in front of the altar. The priest came through a small door in the side wall, went through some rituals with his back to us, then started shaking something over the coffin as he spoke. I had heard that there were churches here and there that had gone back to the old forms, but I'd never heard a service in Latin before. It wasn't so hard to understand; I got most of it—holy spirit, resurrection, eternity. The altar behind him flickered flame on red satin and gold fringe, warm. This must have been what it was like for my mother when she was a kid and her Quaker parents took her alternately to Catholic church and Buddhist temple. This must be what it was and had been like all over the world for hundreds of years, in so many places and times, before the church was modernized. No wonder my mother, who became a Quaker anyway, kept a soft spot for the Catholic masses she remembered. If they had been like this when I was a kid, I might have become a Catholic. I watched the candles flicker, let those old words flow over me, and almost decided to convert.

Then it was over and we were walking out. I walked between Yolanda and Jane, and they talked over me. Jane thought the service was beautiful, but Yolanda said she wouldn't think so if she'd been forced into it. We were outside by then, with Yolanda explaining, telling about her childhood with "...nuns swooping down on me like vampire bats." She still had that musical lilt and just a slight flattening of "th" the Latino kids have. "I am surprised India went back to this."

"Oh, she probably came way around to it again from a quite different side," said Jane. "It's a kind of outlaw church, I've heard. All the old Catholic ritual but not under the pope."

"How Berkeley," said Yolanda.

The coffin was coming out now, carried by Yolanda's husband and some other men. "Carla wanted to have women pallbearers," said Jane, "but Georgie told her to mind her own business, which is going to be organizing the public memorial service, I understand." Yolanda said something in Spanish that I didn't get, but I didn't need to; the tone was enough to tell me she wasn't pleased.

Behind the coffin came two men in their thirties, Georgie between them leaning on their arms. These must be India's sons. Both looked like Reuben, square and short, with wide mouths and kind eyes. They were already pretty bald in front. Georgie held their arms tightly and swayed as if she was about to fall. Her face was still frozen, but her body was going limp on her. Behind her came Reuben, gripping the arm of Antonia Moran, almost leaning on her.

He looked shrunken next to her, and weak. She was holding onto him with one hand and lighting a cigarette with the other. Then she threw the lighted match behind her as if she hoped it would set fire to the church.

"Brava Antonia," murmured Yolanda. "She waited long enough." When I asked what she meant, Jane shook her head at me. "Just old gossip, Jessie." I was so flattered that she remembered my name, I almost forgot to make a mental note: something between Antonia and Reuben.

"Cop," said Yolanda, tilting her head toward where Jim stood at the curb near the hearse.

"How do you know?" asked Jane.

"He came to see me last night. Hasn't he gotten to you yet?" Jane shook her head. "You, Jessie?"

I remembered the old rule of lying, to stick to the truth as much as possible. So I nodded. We stood looking at Jim and at the coffin being pushed into the hearse behind him. Everyone was out of the church now. The family was moving into a big black limousine parked behind the hearse.

"This is incredible!" Carla Neeland's voice was not loud, but it cut through the silence. She was dressed all in white, stiff cotton like the hospital white interns used to wear, topped with a floppy white hat, so that her face looked deep black by contrast, silky, velvety black.

Pamela stood beside her, shrugging tolerantly. She wore the sacky burlap suit I remembered from the day in class when she dropped literature to talk fashion, complaining that she could have left her Guy Rudolfo suit back in New York for all that anyone in California knew about really good clothes. Her hair was skinned back so tight that her thick eyebrows were pulled up like wings at the outer edges. Sylvia March was huddled next to her in a tan coat that matched her straw hair. She bit her lip as she nodded to me. Her eyes were red with crying. Also glazed, not really focusing on anything. She'd probably had just enough of something to make all this bearable. Behind her, almost a head taller, stood Celeste Wildpower. This time her habit was gray, and she wore a gray transparent veil over her head that flattened her spikey red hair and blurred any expression that might be on her face. She looked misty, like an ominous cloud over Sylvia. "Incredible!" Carla repeated. "Nothing about the woman, the *person*. A half hour of that man mumbling and shaking water and swinging incense over what might as well have been an empty *box*."

I expected Yolanda to agree with her, but she said, "You don't understand."

"I most certainly don't. That's why it's in Latin, I suppose, to make sure we can't..."

"A few Latin phrases, everyone knows," Yolanda snapped. "To remind the living of our own mortality, of the brief span of life, of the glory of true eternal life *con Dios*."

"You *believe* that?"

"I understand it." Yolanda had turned away from Carla and was really talking to the rest of us. "When I was a child, I fidgeted through *muchos funerales*, too many. Now I see how humane it is to keep the ceremony detached, anonymous, even soporific." An interesting combination, her accent and her vocabulary, mixing formal English with a dash of Spanish here and there.

Pamela nodded. "Our ethnics in New York still go this way," she pronounced, like an anthropologist starting a lecture. "In fact, I've observed that..."

"Well, that's not the way *I* see a memorial service," said Carla. "I think I can get the big Unitarian Church in San Francisco, and people will speak about *India,* will testify. We all knew her in a different way. Each of us will have something to *offer* to..." As Carla's voice rolled on, Yolanda's black eyes turned hard, like two stones. Jane's went blank behind her round glasses; she wasn't listening. I couldn't tell what expression was hidden behind Celeste's cloudy veil. Only Sylvia nodded nervously at Carla, though I bet she wasn't able to make sense of anything she heard. I looked past Carla's bobbing head toward the hearse. Jim had disappeared. A strong wind suddenly came up, and Carla clamped one hand over her hat, holding it to her head as it flopped around her ears.

"*Bueno,* Carla, you'll have time to organize us all," interrupted Yolanda. "But right now, we'd better get on with this."

"It's not over?" Sylvia's eyes began to fill again.

"To the grave." I had hardly heard Celeste Wildpower say two words since that time I visited her coven. I had forgotten how high and quivery her voice was, no resonance at all.

"Yes," said Jane. "I think we're supposed to get into our cars and follow the hearse to the cemetery. Is that right, Yolanda?"

Yolanda nodded. Her husband had joined us now. He had put an arm around Yolanda's plump middle, giving her flesh a slight pinch, like a private, reassuring joke. His pale face stayed serious, composed, as veiled in its way as Celeste's. He held a sign that the funeral director had given him for his windshield, and he pointed to his car, parked behind the limousine. It was agreed without anyone saying it that Jane and I would ride with him and Yolanda, and that the others would go with Celeste.

11.

Dick McVittey smiled at me, then got behind the wheel and didn't say another word. Yolanda sat next to him in front, half-turned so that she could talk to Jane and me in the back seat. "So Carla has sunk her jaws into this memorial service."

"You don't like her?" I asked, with an innocent look that made everybody laugh, or maybe we just needed the relief.

"Carla is a good publicist, organizer. She's getting high fees now, and she earns them. But Carla—is for Carla. We had a big fight over a neighborhood arts project in San Francisco last year. When Carla wants something, she is like—well, I'm not going to tell that story again." Her husband gave a big sigh of relief. Yolanda laughed again and punched his arm. "She uses people. She used India."

"How?"

"Tried to use her," said Jane. "I think India slipped out of her grasp. She could do that. She was in some ways... elusive."

"How?" I asked again, but no one paid any attention to me. I guess this was old gossip too. I turned to look out the window. We were on the freeway now, heading north toward one of the cemeteries beyond Richmond. The houses were thinning, and the freeway cut through high banks of stiff, parched grass. It could rain any day now, but it might not until November. Through the long dry season from May till October, I wait for the rain, feeling dry and lonely, like missing a friend.

Suddenly I remembered something else was missing. "Where's Margot?" I had wondered if she would show up wearing her tight T-shirt. But she hadn't shown up at all.

"Probably home, licking her wounds," said Yolanda. She made a face to show that her position was uncomfortable, then turned around to face front.

I looked at Jane. Was this more private gossip? "I only heard about it yesterday," she said, "but I guess the word will get around fast enough." Still, she hesitated, shaking her head slowly. "Her book. The deal fell through."

I shook my head, but faster, not believing her. "She had an advance. She moved into a big house."

"I hope she didn't sign a lease," said Yolanda.

"You mean the publisher just...can they do that?"

Jane sighed. "I heard the story from my agent. Margot and I have the same agent, you see. Helen's been very loyal to me, but I think she hoped for a real moneymaker in Margot. You heard about the deal—a large advance, promise of big promotion. That's what we all hope for, real support behind the book." Her voice was slow and deliberate. It sounded like her writing—moderate, considered, low-key, expressive. Like her physical appearance, it could just fade out and be ignored unless you paid attention. "You'd think having put that much into the book already they'd carry it through, but anything can happen in this business. Once a publisher actually printed one of my books and...it never left the warehouse. They...shredded it." She shuddered as if describing a murder. "My agent finally got the rights back and Yolanda published that one through Para Todos Press, so it all turned out for the best."

"A good seller. Almost keeps us in the black." Yolanda turned to her husband. "Carla is telling Margot to sue. You think a case could be made, *amado*?" Her husband shrugged. I couldn't hear his answer.

"Oh," said Jane. "Maybe in this case it's also...for the best."

Yolanda burst out laughing and turned to Jane. "I detect a tone of satisfaction!"

Jane was blushing, just like I do, and looking young. Now that I was getting used to her face, I could see more in it. She had a way of peering through those little round glasses into a far distance where she searched her thoughts. A slow process. The blush had died away from her cheeks by the time she answered. "Not satisfaction. The anger I felt when the book was accepted isn't appeased by what they've done to her now."

"Anger?"

"Say envy. I've never had an advance that big. But perhaps it's better this way. For Margot. Because it was such a bad book. The publicity, the attention might ruin her for any really good work in the future."

"What work? Not Margot." Yolanda turned full around again, brushing her thick black hair away from where it had twisted around her neck. "Margot's no writer."

"Yes," I said, "she told me she considers herself an actress."

Yolanda shook her head again. "Maybe a movie star, born too late. Maybe she could be a rock singer. No, that's passing too."

I laughed but Jane only smiled faintly. "Margot...in her way ...works very hard."

"Then she didn't come today because she couldn't face us."

Jane shook her head. "I'm afraid it's worse than that. I think she may be bitter toward India. According to my agent, the publisher sent a copy of Margot's manuscript to India, for a jacket blurb. India refused, said the book was bad."

"Which it was," said Yolanda.

"Yes, but India always tended to lean the other way, toward being too kind."

Something didn't add up here. "When did they tell Margot the deal was off?" I asked. "She—I went to see her a few days ago— about this article I'm doing—and she didn't tell me about this."

Jane frowned. "She must have known."

"Even before...the party?"

"Oh, yes. I suppose she kept it quiet hoping for some change, perhaps another publisher."

I took a deep breath, then said it. "Someone told me she was having an affair with India's husband." No one said a word. Throughout the rest of the ride, no one spoke or looked at me or at each other. So I had plenty of time to theorize that India had learned about the affair, had used her influence to kill Margot's publishing deal, so Margot had killed India. It sounded fantastic, but murder for any reason sounds fantastic. If my theory was possible, Margot was a better actress than Yolanda gave her credit for. In fact we were all great actresses. Hadn't we been together for a couple of hours without anyone mentioning how India had died, without showing by any sign that each of us was looking around at the others and wondering who had done it?

12.

I had never been in a cemetery before. The only person I knew who had died was my New York grandfather, and after the service in the temple he'd been cremated. I guess I had seen too many old movies where people stand around the grave, watch the coffin lowered into it, then throw a handful of dirt after it. I even imagined that someone might break down and confess while we stood watching the coffin sinking, or at least that someone might throw an accusation across the open grave.

But there was no grave. The grave diggers had been on strike and were still catching up. When we got to the cemetery, we watched while the coffin was put on a rack and wheeled into a green nylon tent. Where it would go from there, I couldn't imagine and didn't want to.

We all crowded into the tent around the coffin, almost touching it. Reuben and Georgie stood together holding hands, Reuben's sons behind them. Antonia Moran had drifted back behind the priest, who stood at the head of the coffin. The only sound was the snapping and flapping of the tent in the strong wind. The priest began to recite in Latin. He was a very young priest. Up close he reminded me of a man I used to see playing the flute on Telegraph Avenue. Maybe he was the same man. I looked around at the green-tinged faces, made ghoulish by the sun filtering through the green tent.

I guess it was because everyone looked sick in that light that no one saw how sick Reuben Wonder was until he crumpled. Antonia Moran got to him even before his sons grabbed at him. The priest looked a little puzzled, but he didn't stop. The Latin phrases kept flowing from him like an unreeling tape.

It was Celeste Wildpower who took charge. Maybe it was that cloudy veil hiding her expression that gave authority to her gestures. Without saying a word she got the men to lay him out flat, to clear the tent opening, to lift and carry him out while she was already taking his pulse, checking his eyes and mouth, the same as she had done when India collapsed. The difference was that she bobbed her veiled head in a reassuring nod at Georgie as they followed the men outside. By this time the priest had speeded up to a finish and made a little sign over the coffin. Then he looked around at the rest of us, coughed, and edged out through the open tent flap.

"Celeste is a nurse," Jane murmured to me. "She'll know what to do."

Antonia Moran was the first to move toward the tent opening, but her way was blocked by Celeste coming back in. "He's all right. Too much standing. He'll rest in the car." Now I knew what her high, quivery voice reminded me of—the school nurse at Berkeley High, who always sounded as if her nerves were shattered, whether she was dealing with menstrual cramps or a stabbing, but who handled them both pretty well, and all things in between. A nurse. Medical training. I knew that was important, but I almost forgot why when Celeste suddenly closed the tent flap behind her, then spread her arms wide to gather us in close to the coffin. The motion of her arms was irresistible. Even Antonia Moran backed up and turned to face the coffin. We all stood close in, our bodies touching the cool sides of the coffin as we turned to look at Celeste, who now stood where the priest had been, at the head of the coffin.

Through her veil I could see that her eyes were closed. Her arms stuck out straight from her sides as if she were crucified on the air. Slowly she raised her arms until they were straight up in the air, parallel to her body, touching the sides of her head. Her gray sleeves billowed out, then fell across her face so that we could see nothing but her small, white hands trembling above her gray habit.

Then she stepped to the side, in a way that made Carla Neeland move a step, which forced Sylvia to move, and so on. She kept moving irresistibly, until we were all moving with her around the coffin, so many paces to the left, so many paces back to the right. Her arms were moving now, making passes over the coffin as we moved around it. A low moaning sound came from her lips, not her usual voice, a harsh, grating sound. Once she tripped on her skirts, and I had an impulse to giggle, but if I started to, I don't think the giggle ever came out.

What happened instead, I was never sure about. Something like a gathering of black mist whirled up from the ground around me. Something like the smell of deep-dug earth. Something like the muffled sounds of voices and bird calls and wind and the rustling of dry grasses far, far above me. And then a sinking, sinking through darkness toward a tiny pinprick of light, like a flickering star alone in a black sky, glowing and growing.

"Rest, sister. Rest. Sister India. Rest."

My hands were on the coffin. My forehead rested against its cool metal. Celeste kept repeating, "Rest, sister," as I raised my head. The others were all looking at me. Had I done something weird? Fainted? Had I said anything? I couldn't remember.

They looked at me only for a second or two, then turned and started moving out of the tent. Celeste Wildpower grabbed my arm, held it tightly, and led me out of the tent as if she were afraid I might get away from her. The men were walking back from the car where they had left Reuben Wonder. Only a minute or two had passed.

"What did you see? Tell me," Celeste squeaked at me. She pressed her face close to me like a thin, hungry girl pressing her nose to the window of a candy store. Her veil tickled my cheek.

"See?"

"Or hear? What was it? Anything at all. Can you remember?"

I shook my head, but she didn't believe me. I got my arm loose from her.

"How do you feel?" She grabbed my hand and began to take my pulse.

"I'm fine." But I stumbled, and I was glad she was holding my hand. I felt a little weak.

"Hungry?" Without waiting for me to answer, she started to nod as if she understood everything. She pulled me toward her car. Before I could stop her, she had rearranged all the passengers and was driving me alone toward her house in El Cerrito.

13.

As she started the car, she pulled off the veil, uncovering her red hair, which had flattened to kinky strings. Then she pulled open the glove compartment and put on a pair of thick glasses. She drove out of the cemetery, took quick turns into side roads, then onto the freeway, and I relaxed a little: she was a good driver. But she talked all the way to El Cerrito. How did I feel going around the coffin? Had I heard anything? Seen anything? What body sensations? Any vibrations near the throat? the toes? Lowering of body heat? Had anything like this ever happened to me before? Did I have any idea how lucky I was to have so thin a floor over my psychic levels?

She swung off San Pablo Avenue and headed up one of those winding streets that, compared to Berkeley, were incredibly neat. Every front garden looked as if it had just been gone over by the same Japanese gardener, who had not only placed every bush and tree, but had cut each blade of grass to a perfect level and arranged each pebble and chunk of tanbark.

She stopped in front of a pink stucco house spread across a corner. Celeste took off her glasses and put them back into the glove compartment, glanced into the rear view mirror and frizzed up her hair by rubbing her head back to front. Then she smiled and gave me a long, narrow-eyed, nearsighted look, a sort of hungry look. I realized that she must be a lot younger than I had thought, not much over thirty. I smiled back at her, but I felt a little like Gretel being taken into the gingerbread house.

I don't know what I expected to find inside, not what I saw. Deep white carpets covered with little plastic mats to walk on, like stepping stones across a creek. Shiny satin upholstered chairs. Tables with carved legs, their tops covered with little glass animals and ceramic dolls. Lamps with plastic covers on the shades. On one table there was a picture of Celeste, taken when she graduated from nursing school. Her face was plump and her hair was limp brown. I had to admit that now she did look more interesting.

The kitchen was all waxed wood cabinets and electric gadgets. I sat on a stool while she gave me a Twinkie and a cup of herb tea which she said I must drink in exactly seven gulps while she whispered incantations between gulps. Before she sat down with her own tea, she put an apron on over her gray habit, a flowered apron, pink daisies. I had expected to be taken into some kind of dark witches' haunt, and instead I was in a suburban house with too much furniture and a television set in every room. Maybe it was all a front? She looked at me across the counter and said, "When a person wants to know something, she should just ask."

"I...uh, you're a nurse?"

She shrugged. "I was. I hardly ever have to work now. My book royalties, offerings for leading rituals, seances, healings." Her face was very long; long nose, long chin, high forehead. Her mouth and eyes were just little cuts across that long face. "I'd rather you didn't repeat that, about the healing. No use giving them a good excuse for witch burning." Her voice was thin and squeaky, but she seemed quite calm while she assured me that she expected something like the Salem witch trials to begin again. "Unless they get me first for India's death. They'd love to pin that on me."

"For a minute I thought you did kill her, when you pointed at her that way."

"Oh, that!" she squeaked. She shook her head and looked disappointed in me. "Jessie, I never have done anything but white magic. Never. That you could even think I would...even you. With such ignorance, the burnings will come soon." Her voice dropped in pitch again, settling into a quiet calm, as if the thought of witch burning comforted her. "I was just angry. She was goading me. And after all I did for her, after the way she depended on me."

"I don't understand. Depended on you? How?"

"India came to me over ten years ago, when I was still just doing body work, massage. I taught her some relaxation techniques. Without me she couldn't write, couldn't keep that lecture schedule. Help me, she said. I helped. I learned more. Each new...each old part of the old knowledge I rediscovered, I gave to India, practiced upon her. Whenever she was blocked, she came to me. For money? No, for the discovery, the development of my calling. For the excitement of finding direction parallel to hers. In a sense we were doing the same work! My work is a logical extension of *Emma Pride's Journal.* That book states the suppression of woman power; my work is to release that power.

"I wanted only one thing from India: acknowledgement. As she became more known, more famous, more admired." Her voice was going thin and squeaky again. "As she had the power to help me, with no effort, to give credit where it was due so that I could go on to give my work to others..."

"You wanted some sort of endorsement from India? So that other writers would pay you for helping them?"

"But it wouldn't do, would it, for a famous writer like India Wonder to endorse a witch! Instead she went back to that church, back to its tradition, death to the old knowledge, burn the witch. That priest, of course, told her to repudiate me."

"Did she?"

"Not directly. She stopped seeing me. Then she began to ridicule me. You saw it, there, at the party, in front of them all, in front of Jane!"

"Why especially Jane?"

But she didn't answer me. She took a paper towel and began rubbing at a stain on the counter, murmuring that she would be blamed for India's death, everyone would enjoy burning a witch again. Saying that seemed to calm her down.

"But," I told her, "India died of cyanide poisoning, not from you pointing at her, so how could they blame you?"

"That's right. And when they search this house, they won't find any cyanide. There's nothing they can prove." Her face got longer and longer.

The more I looked at Celeste, the more she reminded me of my old school nurse, Miss Miligate, though she didn't look anything like her. Miss Miligate was much older, a sallow Mormon lady, with all her questions and all her answers squared off by sharp lines into boxes she moved around like hopscotch. I once overheard my English teacher saying that Miss Miligate's faith surpassed her opportunities, that she was like a missionary among tribes who paid her the ultimate insult, humored her, instead of at least cooking and eating her. Maybe that was why Celeste looked comforted when she talked about witch burning; at least it meant being taken seriously. I tried to reassure her. "You don't need India's recommendation," I told her. "You have your own following. Why, some people I know look at your book *Dream Witch* as a kind of Bible. When you write your next book. . . ."

She didn't look pleased at all when I said that. She swept the paper towel across the counter as if wiping out everything we had said. She looked at me. "I brought you here for only one thing, to know if you are serious."

"Serious?"

"About your powers. Don't you realize. . . I could train you, save you years of misdirected energy. It's best this way. You know nothing, no one has tampered with you, you have been unaware, we start fresh. I wouldn't charge you a penny, if that's what worries you."

"Look, Celeste, I just forgot to eat breakfast this morning, so I felt a little faint. That's all."

"Why isn't anyone serious? You must be *serious*."

"I. . . well. . ."

"It is god-given. Don't you know that the deepest sin is to let a talent lie undeveloped? All you need is direction. I offer you that

52

direction." She reached out and grabbed my hand. Her voice had gone into a thin whisper.

"I...I don't know." I pulled my hand free, wondering how I could get out of there.

She stood up. "I'll drive you home." She had read my mind, and when she saw I was surprised, she gave me an impatient look, then a smile. "Oh, skeptics are the best in the long run." She took my hand again. "We could give you a little awareness exercise to practice at home, and then when you come back..."

"Well, not today, I think..."

"Not today? Not even to build a little on what you did at the cemetery?"

I shook my head. "But I'll think about it."

She squeezed my hand once before she let it go. "You must be serious. It would be a sin not to."

14.

Luckily the restaurant is closed on Wednesdays. When I got home, Mom and Dad were still scrubbing the stove. Joe, one of the high school kids they hire, was doing the windows, hauling garbage, moving the furniture so I could start mopping under it. By five o'clock everything was cleaned up and we were ready for our usual day-off dinner: fruit and yoghurt. Sometimes my half brothers come by with their wives and kids, but on this day they were all busy. I was glad that we three could sit quietly at a back table while I told them about the funeral. When I came to what happened at the cemetery and how Celeste tried to recruit me as a witch, they didn't laugh. They just listened.

The phone rang. It was Jim. "How about going out to dinner?"

"I've already had dinner."

"Well, then...maybe take a walk? I'd like to hear what happened today, compare notes."

"Okay." I went back to the table. "That police inspector, Jim Merino, is coming. I'm working with him. Asking people questions. I'm pretending to be working on an article about women writers." I don't know why I hadn't told them before. I felt shy about it, silly.

My dad nodded and stroked his beard. It was thin, fuzzy and gray. He was starting to look more and more like one of those skinny, ascetic sinners in a story by I.B. Singer. He loved a puzzle. "Can anyone play this game?" His eyes sparkled. I nodded.

My mother was shaking her head. "I don't see how it could be any of those women. You say they all loved her. You told me everyone loved her." I'd been telling Mom that for years. I had once pushed India's journal on my mother, but she hadn't gotten very far with it, and I had been too impatient with her to ask why. That was back in the days when I felt that everyone had to read whatever I was reading.

I nodded. "But it's not that simple. Margot and Celeste were. . . ."

"Wait, wait a minute," said my dad, and he grabbed an old menu where he began writing the names of the women across the top, making columns where we could fill in facts about each.

"There's the daughter too," I told him. "Georgie, named after George Sand." My mother smiled. "And the husband, Reuben."

My father nodded. "The only male suspect?"

"The only man at the party," I said. "It was a women's party— he was serving drinks."

"Like a good wife."

I just laughed. The one thing Dad didn't want was for me or Mom to be a "good wife." I gave him information to fill in under each name: age, appearance, type of writing, what I knew so far about their histories. Without intending to I'd listed them according to age, from the youngest on up. Margot first, then Sylvia and Celeste, on up to Yolanda and Jane (I guess Georgie would be squeezed somewhere between them) and ending with Antonia.

"Didn't you leave someone out? That visiting professor whose class you audited? The daughter of Murray. . . ."

"Pamela Righbottom. I keep forgetting her. She just came with Carla. She's been. . . living with her, you know. But she didn't know India before."

"Did she know Carla before? How did they meet? From what you say I wouldn't think Righbottom's daughter was exactly Carla's type." So we squeezed Pamela in between Sylvia and Celeste, figuring she was in her mid-thirties. "Is she as good a critic as her father?"

"I don't know. All she ever did in class was read from his book and from her introduction to it."

"He's dead now, isn't he?"

I nodded. "Died last year."

"I didn't think he was that old, only about my age."

I nodded again. "Heart attack. He was in the middle of a book on O'Neill. Pamela's going to finish it."

I heard a light tapping on the front door and saw Jim through the glass. I let him in and brought him to the table. He was wearing jeans and a T-shirt that showed his broad chest, firm, not too muscular, not bulging, just right. He looked very off-duty, very young, and very different from my father. As they shook hands, I saw them eyeing each other, measuring. My mother asked Jim if he wanted some tea and fruit. Jim shook his head and glanced at the columns of facts my father had made.

"We were talking about . . . "

"That's very helpful." Jim nodded at the notes on the menu. "Sometimes I put things on cards and then lay them out, move them around. It helps me to think." The same as I did when I was writing. I didn't like the idea that other people used my method for less . . . creative kinds of work. God, I was not just ageist but a rotten snob too.

I pointed to a chair, but Jim didn't sit down. My dad picked up his notes, looking eager, but Mom poked him. "I think Jim wants to talk to Jessie alone. Too many cooks . . . "

"What's that?" grumbled my dad, "an inscrutable old Japanese proverb?" He shrugged and gave Jim another measuring look. "It's dark for a walk, but I guess Jessie has good protection. Do you carry a gun off duty?"

"Sometimes. Not tonight."

We walked out up University Avenue and turned north onto Grant. Jim said he liked my parents. Then neither of us said anything. Well. It was time to get it said and done with.

"I expect to be taken seriously."

"What? Sure, I . . . "

"I mean about this investigation. Do you really want me to help you or is that just an excuse to see me?"

"Well, I . . . what makes you think . . . "

"There was a look between you and my father. Him sizing you up. He wouldn't bother to unless he sensed something . . . some interest in me. What about it? Am I wasting my time or are you taking me seriously?"

He took a deep breath. "I'm taking you seriously," he said, looking at me and nodding, looking anxious but looking pleased too. Men are intrigued by opposition, by a response they didn't expect. But it doesn't always mean they take you seriously. It may just mean they find a challenge interesting. "Find out anything today?"

I nodded. "Celeste Wildpower is a nurse. Is that enough medical training to know about poisons?"

"Could be."

"I went to her house for a while after the funeral." I decided not to tell him what happened at the cemetery. "She says she expects to be arrested, persecuted because of being a witch. Her career—her witch career, I mean—really got going when she started working on India."

"Casting spells?" Jim wasn't smiling. "I meant to look her up in the cult file."

"Cult file?"

"We've had some pretty ugly incidents—where have you been? You heard about the Honeybile case didn't you?"

I shuddered. That was an occult-torture story from two years ago that I'd managed to forget. I didn't want to remember it now. "Celeste insists she does only white magic."

"If that's true, we won't have anything on her."

"I think she does mostly massage and hypnosis, ritual and prayer, to break writer's block. She said that after years of coming to her, India dropped her, went back to the Church, started to make fun of her."

"Motive." Jim nodded. "If Celeste Wildpower's career as a witch ends, she has to go back to emptying bedpans."

"I can't believe it. She's too conventional even if she is a witch. Her house. Stuff like electric can openers and plastic on the lampshades."

"One case I handled," Jim said, "was a woman who stabbed her kid for tracking mud across a newly waxed floor. Did everyone come to the funeral?"

I was glad to change the subject. "Margot Stackpole was missing, probably because the big deal for her novel fell through. At first I thought it was the shock. But Jane Lee told me Margot must have known even before the party, and that India might have caused it. She told the publisher it was a bad book."

"Motive," he nodded again. "Margot was sleeping with Reuben, so India messed up the book deal, so Margot..."

"That reminds me. Antonia Moran. Did you notice the way she held onto Reuben Wonder at the funeral?"

"Old friends."

"More than friends. Yolanda dropped a hint, but wouldn't give me any details."

Jim laughed. "Old Reuben gets around."

"He collapsed at the cemetery. He really looks bad, sick with grief. I can't imagine he..."

"Most murders, the killer is grieving because he killed the person closest to him."

"Is that true? Is it always the obvious person, the husband, the wife, the lover?"

"Used to be. Now we get more of the unconnected ones. I used to think it was awful that people killed their lovers. Now they kill people they don't even know. What's worse? I don't know."

We turned on Virginia Street and headed west. "I have an appointment to see Jane Lee tomorrow. I rode with her and Yolanda Dolores. Yolanda can't see me till next week. I should be able to get to the others before then. What have you done?"

"I've been trying to get a copy of the manuscript of the new book. So far Georgie has put me off. My people have been through India's stuff, but they don't really know what to look for. I don't even want to show too much interest, scare anyone. Maybe you could do something on that?"

I nodded. At Sacramento Street I turned left so I'd be bringing us back to University. He saw the walk would soon be over, so I knew he would say it. "Look, about taking you seriously, that doesn't mean that more isn't possible. Yes, I take you seriously and yes, I want to see more of you."

"Aren't you married?"

"Separated."

"Children?"

"Three."

"You'll go back."

He shook his head. "Never. Look, I'm not just one of those husbands on vacation. I like my work, my kids. I have no time to play around. I'm interested in a real relationship, with someone I respect, no one-night stands, I'm stable, I'm..."

"I'm not!" I said, backing away.

"You look scared of me."

"I've seen you three times, and it sounds like you're proposing marriage!"

He shrugged. "I can't say anything right. You don't want a married man playing around, you don't want a stable relationship. You want to be taken seriously, you don't want me to be serious. What do you want?"

Just at that moment I wanted to throw my arms around him and feel those hard chest muscles against me and breathe his good male odor. But I wasn't going to tell him that. Then we'd both be scared. "I don't know."

"I'll call you tomorrow."

"Okay."

I hurried into the dark restaurant and upstairs to Mom and Dad's bedroom, hoping they wouldn't be asleep yet because I suddenly had something very important to tell them. They were sitting up in bed. Dad was reading and Mom was writing a letter. "Look," I said, sitting on the edge of the bed. "If I could work in the restaurant six days a week and not pay any rent for one more year, I could save enough to live on for at least two years. Then I'd go away to Europe or South America or somewhere and begin to see the world, something beyond Berkeley that I have to see before I can write anything good."

Mom and Dad looked at each other, then back at me, nodding. "That sounds like a good idea," Mom said mildly, then went back to writing her letter. Dad yawned, but I saw him watching me. I got up and left the room, telling myself that something important had been settled, but not feeling very sure that it had.

15.

I found Jane Lee in a sagging duplex in north Oakland, just beyond the Berkeley line. It looked like a one-family house, which it probably was before being split down the middle. The two doors on the front porch didn't match, and the older, scratched-up door had the number Jane had given me. A little note said Bell Out of Order. As I knocked, I thought I must have the wrong address because an established writer like Jane couldn't live in such a shabby place. Yet, if a woman answered the door, would I know if she wasn't Jane? A crazy question. Jane looked...I couldn't picture her. I'd never known the true meaning of the word, nondescript. But that's what Jane was, nondescript, a blurr, a blank, so ordinary she just faded out like an overwashed shirt.

Of course, when she opened the door, I knew her, and I tried to memorize her features. Medium size, medium build, medium gray-brown hair, medium complexion, middle-aged, glasses. Nothing to hang onto. I gave up.

"Come in, Jessie." The narrow front room had a couch in one corner near a small fireplace, but the rest of it was her workroom. A round oak table near the window was covered with papers. A typewriter sat on a metal stand beside it. Two cardboard boxes filled with bits of paper sat on the floor underneath, and bits of paper were taped to the walls near the window.

"So this is where you work." I could hardly believe it. I forgot my real reasons for being there. I was seeing the place where Jane Lee had written all those books. "Have you always lived here?"

"Just the past ten years. When my husband died and my son left, I moved into the smaller apartment. Before that we lived on the other side. It's bigger, has bedrooms upstairs. Now I rent it to a couple."

"I thought...." Of course, I couldn't say it.

She motioned me to the couch where we sat side by side. I was beginning to see that she had one distinctive feature, her mouth. It made a clean, even line, with lips that were generous but not full, a mouth used for shaping words that counted. I sank into the couch, a soft old thing covered with an Indian bedspread. "You thought what?"

"I thought you'd have a better house."

"Why?" Her mouth made a slight, ironic twist, not a smile. She seemed to know the answer to her question.

"You're a successful writer. A famous writer. I've read everything you ever wrote, and I...the critics say..."

"Did you buy them?"

"What?"

"Did you buy my books, all twenty-three of them?"

"Oh, no, I got them from the library." As soon as I said it, I began to understand, but I still couldn't believe it.

"And how did you start to read my books?"

"Someone told me, in a writing class I think."

She nodded. "That's how my readers find me, one by one. No sudden best seller—so my books don't go into paperback, no big advance. They don't translate easily into film."

"And that's where the money is?"

"That's where the money is." Her mouth formed her words slowly and deliberately. "I've been writing all my life and I've never been able to earn a living."

"That's not right! That's awful, why, when you're dead you'll be a classic, you'll be. . ."

"Dead." She looked away from me, her eyes going blank, taking that faraway look that made her face fade out. "I collect some royalties, enough rent to pay taxes and keep a roof on the house. Some free-lance editing, like helping Antonia with her book, but the pay is bad and it takes writing energy. Sometimes I teach a class. But I'm not a good teacher, that's an art too, not my medium. I worked this summer at a pickling plant in San Leandro."

"A what?"

"A pickling plant, a cannery. You know."

I shook my head. I couldn't believe it.

"I may have got something out of it." She almost smiled. "Something. . .usable."

"Material for a story? Are you working on. . ."

"I never talk about what I'm working on." Her voice was sharp, almost scolding. She looked at her watch. "I hope this won't take too long. I hate interviews. I'd have refused, but you caught me at a weak moment."

"I've been a fan of yours for years. I wrote you a letter once." I laughed. "You never answered."

"Were you hurt?"

I thought about it. "No. I didn't really expect an answer. I thought you were busy with a brilliant life—fascinating friends, travel, literary parties. . ."

"I never go to parties. India's party. . .even if it hadn't become a tragedy. . .a party costs me at least a day's work. Too many people, too much talk. I have to guard against disruptions. Oh, in the beginning I tried to answer letters."

"But they took too much time." I was nodding eagerly.

Jane's lips moved into a slight, ironic curve. "And I couldn't afford the stamps."

I felt a blush of shame start to creep over me. Why hadn't I thought of that?

"What I have to give is in my books. I need my energy for them. To demand a personal note when I've already tried to give them the best of me..." Her voice had gotten quieter but harsher. Light from the window hit her glasses, hiding her eyes. "What do they want? Isn't what I do enough? Can't they leave me in peace to do it? Do they want blood? Bunch of vampires. Why don't they find their own work instead of feeding off me?"

I didn't know what to say. I couldn't look at her face.

"You're shocked. You think an artist should enjoy every expression of admiration, should be above caring about earning a decent living. You're disappointed too. What I write isn't enough for you either. You want me to fit your romantic image of the artist."

I shook my head, but I knew she was right. I was angry at her for being angry. I felt cornered, and I had no answer for anything she said. I wanted her to be gentle and wise, not implacable behind her ordinary...oh, God, I even wanted her to look different.

"Put that in your interview if you like." Her voice was softer now, almost kind. "Come on, Jessie, ask your questions. I won't snap at you again."

"You said you never go to parties. Why did you go to India's?"

Her mouth made a little smile, as if she enjoyed a joke on herself. "Well, when India calls—it's somehow like a royal command. Even the summons. She never makes a phone call herself. It's always her daughter or Reuben who relays messages, invitations, whatever."

"Why is that?" We were talking about India as if she were still alive. Maybe it was a way of not thinking about what happened at the party.

"She always said mechanical things disconcerted her. She never even used a typewriter. I think she liked letting Georgie take care of things like that. Having someone else do your phoning and typing —that means power, like a corporation executive or..."

"She wrote to me in her own hand!" I defended her.

Jane touched my hand solemnly, a gesture which took back nothing she had said, even if it acknowledged my feelings. "And you were ecstatic when her letter came. I know. That's how I felt the first time."

"When was that?"

"Oh, years ago, seventeen, eighteen years. My first two books had come out. . . to a great silence. Then came the note: India wanted to meet me. Lunch with five other writers I'd heard of but never met. India presided, Reuben cooked, I made a couple of valuable contacts. Then India called my publisher, offering a jacket blurb for the next printing—if there ever was to be a next printing. There wasn't. My publisher was ready to drop me, but her interest made them try again. My third book sold just enough to make them go on publishing me. She tried to get me to do readings, lectures with her. But I couldn't. I'm no good at that. I owe India a lot, so you're wondering how I could ever say anything unkind about her. Well, I've written twenty good books and can't make a living, while India's one book keeps snowballing—fellowships, lectures, prizes. She's made enough on movie options to support me for a lifetime."

Jane's face had gone expressionless again, but her mouth looked a little pinched. "You're thinking envy is an ugly sin. You're right." She looked at her watch again. "I really can't give you much more time. I've got to write a review of three very bad books. That's another way I earn a few dollars."

So I asked her when she worked on her fiction and how she got her ideas, the usual general, safe, unimportant questions. She showed me the rest of her apartment, the tiny kitchen, bath and bedroom. All the walls were covered with her own pen and ink drawings. "Not good enough to show anywhere; doing them just trains me to focus more sharply, see more clearly." When we went outside onto the back porch and looked at the garden, she pointed out the remains of a vegetable crop. "That's where I get my ideas, digging." We stood looking at dried-up berry vines and bean stalks, and I turned our talk back to India again. It was easy because Jane didn't like talking about herself.

"I can't see how anyone there could have killed her," I said, expecting silence or mild agreement.

Instead, she shocked me. "At the moment India fell, I think everyone must have been mentally strangling her." She smiled at the look on my face, just a slight, firm curve of a smile. "You didn't catch it, because you don't know everyone. Those introductions, India's speech. That was all double-edged. India had a way of stroking people and tripping them at the same time; uplifting and undercutting."

I shook my head. "She said I was a serious writer. She didn't. . . ."

"Oh, not the first time, not until...she knows you for a long time."

"For instance?"

She thought for a minute, the faraway look dimming her face. "For instance, Yolanda hates to be compared to Jessica Mitford, hates being called the Chicana Jessica. Both she and Mitford are muckrakers and neither had any formal education, but there the resemblance ends. Mitford has the assurance of an aristocrat; Yolanda was poor. Their styles are utterly different. Mitford is devilishly witty, Yolanda . . . well, someone once called her an 'earnest Mitford.' Yolanda felt patronized. The whole thing is subtle and complicated, but India understood it, rubbed it in. But she was much worse to Antonia Moran. Remember?"

I shook my head.

"India talked about her 'consistency.' They were in the Communist Party together years ago. India left, but Antonia stayed, became a pathetic figure, still out on the street corner with leaflets, scorned by the new left and by everyone else."

"In her journal, India quoted Emerson, remember, about consistency being 'the hobgoblin of small minds.' Remember?" I was just proud that I had remembered something.

"I remember," said Jane, "and so did everyone else. Then India reminded everyone that her daughter is named after the most prolific of women writers—poor Georgie, who's never done a stroke of creative work or even had any life of her own, a typist and messenger for her mother, and not a word of tribute for that. Sylvia, of course, she called..."

"The disciple." It was all coming back to me now.

Jane nodded. "Which is what's wrong with her writing. It's an overblown imitation of India's style, which could stand a bit of deflation itself." I didn't like hearing her say anything against India's style. Probably that was envy too. "Can you remember any of the others?"

"She called Carla Neeland, Delilah, and Margot Stackpole a... a tap dancer?"

Jane nodded. "Tap dancer, that's a New York expression. You can guess. It means someone who knows how to present herself, get attention, get success. It must have been a double dig, since both of them knew all the time that Margot's publisher had dumped her. As for the Delilah bit . . ."

"That's just the name of Carla's play."

"Yes, but that was double-edged too. Delilah the seductress and betrayer. Maybe you don't know how Carla used India—used a relationship with India to promote herself and to punish India."

Jane was looking at me now, waiting to see how much she had to explain. I nodded quickly to let her know that I knew about the love poems Carla was always reading. "If there was all this bitterness between them, I don't see why India invited her to the party, or why people like Antonia and Carla came."

Jane sighed and looked far away again. "What you have to understand about India was that she was both generous and mean. Actually I'd say she never held a grudge, yet she never forgot something she could use to needle you. Once you were her friend, you were her friend forever. Even though she never forgave you. It's very complicated. She was. . . very complicated."

"What did she say that made Celeste so mad?"

Jane waited for a minute. I think she was remembering the awful moment when Celeste pointed and India collapsed. "She referred to Celeste's book as produced by alchemy, by the fairies, by heavenly spirits. Do you know the book?"

"*Dream Witch*," I said.

"What do you think of it?"

"Well, the plot is standard science fiction, but I think the book goes beyond. It really touched. . . something very deep in me. And the writing is excellent."

"Thank you." Jane smiled slightly, with only one side of her mouth. "I wrote it.'"

"You!"

"I've ghosted several books. Mostly nonfiction." She named the autobiographies of a couple of movie stars. "When things have been desperate or we've needed something. My son was going away to college. Celeste needed a book, to enhance her reputation, legitimize her. A book can do a lot for a non-writer. It confers prestige, especially among people who don't care about books. She came to me with the idea. I wrote it. Of course, it took longer than I thought it would, so I really earned that money." Suddenly she laughed, a deep laugh that sounded as if it came from a much bigger person. "It sells better than any of my other books. She'll get a fat movie contract on it yet." She laughed again.

"Did everyone at the party know you wrote it?"

"Oh, yes, that's why Celeste was so furious. She doesn't like to have it mentioned, but you can't keep anything like that secret among writers."

"Then...you're saying the only people she didn't offend were me and Pamela Righbottom."

Jane just looked at me. "Pamela Righbottom. Pamela worst of all, I suspect."

"Pamela? But she never even saw her before. Pamela just came along with Carla. She..." I decided I'd better just keep still and listen.

"Do you remember what India said to her?"

I nodded. "Called her Doctor, brilliant scholar, it runs in the family."

"Meaning?"

"Her father. Why should that offend her? She still worships her father, worked with him when he was alive, now finishing up his book on O'Neill. That's all she talked about, him and his work, in class, except when she was complaining that California had no seasons."

"How long is it since you read *Emma Pride's Journal?*"

I thought. I was sixteen. "Six, seven years."

"Do you remember when Emma goes back to college? Takes a course from a brilliant professor, falls in love, is seduced by him?"

"Of course. And he turns out to a real nurd. Pompous, impotent ...that was the funniest sex scene I ever..."

"Do you remember the character of Professor Hightop? What he looked like?"

A slow, faint, dim memory was dawning. "Not..."

"Murray Righbottom spent a year teaching here, just as his daughter has done, but years ago. India took his class. I don't know if there was an affair. The whole thing became such a joke that now there are a dozen conflicting stories. It was, of course, before I knew India. The version I consider most reliable is that Righbottom detested India's writing, ridiculed her in class, and that in revenge she put him into *Emma Pride's Journal* just as you described him, pompous, lecherous, impotent, absurd. Read it again. The description of him is unmistakable, even to the slight lateral lisp he had when reading aloud. A famous man, at least in the literary and academic establishment. And then, a famous description. More famous every year. I'm told that India's book dogged him, hounded him, as it became more and more famous. It was quite a joke in academia. And Murray Righbottom was never noted for his sense of humor.''

It took me a minute to digest that, to realize that Pamela's presence at the party, even her coming here to teach for a while after her father's death, might not be coincidental.

"What about you? Did India...undercut you?"

Jane's mouth thinned out, pinched at the edges. "No one likes to be called underrated—neglected, unread, unsuccessful. India knew how I felt. She knew just how to rub salt in, how to arouse ugly traits...like envy. I'm sure that's how I'm portrayed in her new book—neglected, bitter, envious.'' Her frown set hard, petulant lines all around her mouth. I thought what an awful expression it was, how unworthy of all her wonderful talent. Then I thought, who am I to judge her?

"Have you read it? The manuscript?"

Jane shook her head. The ugly lines were fading. "She hasn't let a soul near that one. She just dropped hints."

"Could she have shown it to anyone...someone who...this sounds crazy, but if someone killed her because of the way India had pictured her in that book..." I expected Jane to laugh at me or to disagree or to tell me people didn't murder over a bunch of words in a book. But she didn't say anything for quite a while.

"She was afraid." Jane's face had gone all vague, and lineless again, her eyes far away, blind. "I don't think she'd have been quite so cruel that night if she hadn't been afraid, afraid for a long time." She blinked, then turned abruptly and led me back through the apartment to the front door. "I really have to get back to work now." She opened the door. "We'll see each other soon, I'm sure. And then you can tell me what progress you're making with... your article."

The door closed behind me, and I knew from the tone of her voice that I hadn't fooled her. She knew what I was really looking for.

16.

It took me over an hour to get to Antonia Moran. I took the bus across the bay to San Francisco, then the K car through the tunnel, coming out on the edge of Saint Francis Wood. It had been sunny at home, but it was foggy and windy out there, and those huge white stucco houses stood like tombstones on the lawn of a silent, gloomy-gray cemetery. What was a "consistent" communist doing in a place like this?

A brick path wound through the front lawn to a tiled Spanish doorway. I rang the bell and waited. And waited. It was a big house, and she might be coming from the other end of it.

Finally the door opened and she stood there scowling at me. She hadn't wanted to see me, insisting that she wasn't really a writer and had nothing to tell me. Her thick makeup made her skin reddish brown, dark next to her golden-bleached hair. A cigarette hung from her purple lips. Her pants and shirt matched her lips. Over them she wore a white apron. She closed the door very softly behind me, beckoned me to follow her, then walked soundlessly across the oriental rug, then the hardwood floor. For such a big woman she moved lightly. I knew by the way she tiptoed that this wasn't her house; she worked here. She pushed a swinging door and we walked across a huge kitchen. "You know who owns this place." The name she murmured is a legend in San Francisco business and politics.

"I thought he died," I said.

"Not yet. Bedridden for two years. There's a nurse too and a cleaning woman who comes in. But I live in. Six years now. It's almost over, he's dying." Beyond the kitchen was a little white room. We sat down on metal chairs at a glass-topped patio table. Otherwise the room was bare; our voices echoed. I could see an open doorway, a bed, on top of the bed an open suitcase. "I know," she said. "Ironic, me working in the house of an old capitalist devil like him. What else could I do? A lifetime in the Party, no skills. No children—my husband used to say all the workers were our children, no time to have our own. I don't even get social security because I never worked at a job except when I helped my mother clean that twenty-room mansion in Boston. She came over from Ireland when she was sixteen, brought over to be a domestic, at least until she married. But my father was a labor organizer, blackballed everywhere, so my mother never could stop working. There were seven of us kids—she was a good Catholic too—and she never got out of other women's kitchens. Patrick was in my father's union. I married him, and we were going to change all that for women like my mother. But here I am, full circle, a domestic like her."

"A writer too," I insisted. "I read your book, *Seven Sisters Left.*"

"You did?" She seemed surprised.

"It was inspiring, those women, especially in those days. But I think I need to read some more history to be able to understand some of it, like the Palmer Raids, the general strike..."

"Oh, for people your age, even the fifties are ancient history, and anything before that is prehistory, paleolithic. Don't deny it. I'm seventy, that's nothing, no time at all, I'm seventy and there are kids being born now who'll get Abraham Lincoln and Martin Luther King all mixed up together and the Spanish Civil War confused with the Vietnam War."

"Well, your book will help to educate..."

"That's what I thought! What a comedy." She wasn't laughing. "It was supposed to be published by a women's press. It was all typeset—and they declared bankruptcy. So that old devil..." She pointed her cigarette toward the ceiling. "...said he'd use his influence; two phone calls and he had a publisher for it. But all they did was print it—you think the capitalist press would sell this book? They suppressed it. Not one review. They never intended... probably were using it for a tax write-off.

"Then Imogene sued for libel, about the way I wrote about her role in the Scottsboro Case. Senile, she was senile, for God's sake, couldn't they see it? All of a sudden, everyone taking sides, attacks on me in all the left press. She died before we came anywhere near court. But by that time, the publisher had withdrawn all but the few books that had been sold, shredded them. The advance they gave me had gone into attorney's fees. And too many hard words had been spoken between me and people on the left. We were through. I was through. For good. They made me wish I hadn't left some things out of that book. I should have put it all in. Then they'd have something to sue!

"I'll tell you something, that old man dying upstairs treated me with more decency, I'm in his will, a small pension. The old devil laughed when he told me. He knew it wouldn't change my convictions, I'm a socialist to the end, consistent, as India said. Consistent!" she hissed, then took another deep drag and held the smoke in so long that my chest began to hurt.

"Are you going somewhere?" I looked through the doorway at the suitcase on the bed.

"I'm going to Reuben. Now she's finally gone, I'm going to him." She inhaled. "That's something to put in your article. Ha." Smoke rushed out of her mouth and nose. "He's sick, he needs me, he's always needed me, now she can't keep us apart anymore. That's why she left the Party, you know, not the lies she put into that book of hers. Lies."

"I don't remember that part. Was it..."

"You forgot because political commitment means nothing to your generation, so you skim over it. Don't you remember how her Party group read her journal and told her it was not politically correct, called a meeting and told her, stop writing that way, if she wanted to write, they would assign the book, like a child's life of Lenin?"

"Yes, yes." I nodded. It had come back to me "And so she left the Party after..."

"Lies. It didn't happen that way at all." Antonia lit another cigarette. Now there were two of them smoldering in the ashtray. She ignored both of them. "It had nothing to do with writing. No one knew she was writing, if she was, I doubt it. That came after, I think, after they threw her out."

"The Party threw her out? Why?"

"Because of me. Me and Reuben. We were in love. From the first. We understood each other. Both of us committed, both political, from political families, not on-again-off-again-left like India, even the same age, but we met too late. My husband had become a high party official, I couldn't embarrass him. Reuben's boys were babies, he couldn't leave them. We were careful, but lies weren't in our nature, we...someone found out. There was a meeting."

"A what?"

"Oh, what it was like for us, you can't understand. We were radicals about economics, but, about sex, in such matters we were very conservative. All the comrades said no divorce, impossible, because of what it would do to my husband, to his authority."

"You mean they had a meeting? They took a vote?" I tried not to smile, but I was losing the struggle.

"I knew you couldn't understand, in those times when there was purpose beyond the individual life, when personal life had to be subordinated to...oh, what's the use, your generation has no idea." She looked at the two cigarettes smoldering in the ashtray, then carefully snubbed out both of them. "It had to end. They decided. I was necessary to the group, to my husband, so they had to leave, and she started writing those lies, how everyone stopped her from writing, the Party, her children. All lies. She was writing all the time, not books, leaflets, going on picket lines while Georgie took care of the boys, and Reuben too. At night he worked in a restaurant, a cook. In the morning he was up taking care of the kids, then nursery school, school. Georgie took over when she got home from school. India was too busy making the revolution, getting in our way mostly. Unless there was a big demonstration coming up. She was useless for the real work, the meetings, the canvassing, she got bored, it had to be dramatic, a strike, a demonstration. India was always getting arrested, she loved getting arrested. Until they threw her out and she wrote all those lies."

"But..." I wanted her to talk, to tell me everything she knew, yet I didn't want to hear what she was saying now. I certainly couldn't believe a word of it.

"But what?"

I gulped when I looked at her fierce old eyes, makeup cracking at the edges so that she looked like a hard old statue. "She had a terrible time. Working in that old people's home, scrubbing floors. Leaving Georgie with that babysitter who turned out to be alcoholic and..."

Antonia just shrugged. "That I don't know, it was before I knew her. When I knew her Reuben took care of the kids. A father to Georgie. He worshipped India, she was beautiful, yes, at her best. With that long hair, already gray like those eyes, and skin like cream. And I looked like I always looked, strong, like a football player in drag! But I could love like a woman, which was more than she...oh, ancient history. She's dead, let her lie, let me forgive her, never forgive her." Tears had smeared her mascara, but she didn't look funny to me, even after saying she looked like a football player in drag, which she did. Yet, she had begun to look very womanly to me, very passionate, full of courage and a nobility that was something like beauty.

"You can't forgive her for keeping you and Reuben apart."

"No, no!" She shook her head. "You can't understand! That was only personal, only my personal happiness, not what mattered. I can't forgive her for that book, for saying the Party wouldn't let her write. Never, we never, if she was writing then, we didn't know it. And when that book came out, in the fifties, it was the worst time, with McCarthy and the FBI and, you were a baby then, you can't know. Her book was the final blow, one more kick when we were down. Everything broke apart, and there was no group anymore to save, to sacrifice for." She put another cigarette between her lips but didn't light it.

I shook my head. "India's book came out long after, when it couldn't have hurt your group one way or. . ."

"It was in the worst time, when everything we built had been cut down and no new movements started, no anti-war, no counter-culture, nothing yet, no hope. We were down and she kicked us."

There was no point in arguing with an old woman who got her dates mixed up. Somehow her bitterness about Reuben had made her telescope events so that India became the central devil in her life, right alongside the FBI. She dabbed the edge of her eyes with her apron, looking at the black smudges.

"So what are we talking for? You came to interview me about writing? I don't know anything about writing. If it hadn't been for Jane's help I never could have pulled that book together. And now Yolanda nagging me to expand it! I'd rather walk ten picket lines. Graveyard shift. In the rain. You're wasting your time talking to me. Both wasting our time." She lit the cigarette, took one puff, then set it down in the ashtray. My head was starting to ache from the smoke. And I was afraid she would tell me to go.

"Do you have any idea who could have wanted to kill India?"

I was too blunt. There was a slight blink, a more attentive look in her eyes. "Besides me? I guess Georgie had even more reason to. . ." She clamped her mouth shut, looking hard at me.

"Georgie? Why?"

Long silence. "Ask her." Her rush of words was over for good now. She stood up, still and watchful. She wasn't fooled by me anymore. I was the FBI now.

"What about her husband?" I stood facing her across the table.

"He worshippped her."

"But you said that you and he. . ."

"Old women imagine things, get things mixed up. He worshipped her." She turned abruptly and went through the doorway to the kitchen. There was nothing to do but follow her as she strode, strong and fast, to the front door. She swung the door open wide as if to let out a fly or moth that had got in by accident.

"About the new book India was writing...."

"More lies!" Then her mouth clamped tight and, as she swung the door shut, she threw her cigarette out after me.

17.

Since I was at the southwest end of town and it was getting near commuter rush hour, I took a bus to the Daly City Bart Station where the trains started and I would be sure to get a seat. That was a mistake. There was another of those mysterious slowdowns, then some problem at the Oakland West Station, so that my train—now jammed full—sat in that tube under the bay long enough for my imagination to write a complete scenario of our watery death. After ten minutes everyone had that look of numb, shifty-eyed doom, which wasn't improved by the driver's voice mumbling "routine procedure" over the microphone. Finally the train started up with a humming lurch, and we all let out our breath in a sigh of relief, then buried our noses in books, newspapers and private worries.

I got home half an hour late and the restaurant was full. Mom and Dad didn't even look look up when I rushed in. I mumbled "sorry" a couple of times as we rushed past each other. As I took orders I told the people there might be a wait and it was my fault and I was sorry. They all sighed like the people on the Bart train. People will put up with a lot if you just tell them what to expect.

The rush didn't stop until 9:30 when all at once it was over and only a couple of tables were still occupied with late tea and beer drinkers. Mom and Dad were cleaning up the kitchen while Joe washed dishes. I told them I'd help as soon as I made a couple of phone calls. Then I ran upstairs to use the phone where it was quiet.

The upstairs phone was attached in the hallway on a long cord that reached into either bedroom. I sat on my bed and looked at my list made from India's address book. Four more to go: India's daughter, Georgie, Yolanda Dolores, Carla Neeland, and Pamela Righbottom. I was tired, and I was less excited about talking to well-known writers. Georgie made me nervous. Carla and Yolanda were tough and smart; they might see through my story about doing an article for *Ms.* I wasn't sure the others hadn't already seen through it. Maybe I should change my story.

Carla Neeland answered the phone with a quick, "Hello!" then went on arguing with someone who must have been across the room. ". . . not unless my people get a percentage. Hello!"

"Yes. . .I, yes, this is Jessamyn Posey." I explained and described until she remembered me. "They said you are organizing the memorial program for India Wonder. Can I help?"

"Can you help? Sure, you called at just the *right* time. We're meeting at my place Saturday, ten o'clock, *all* day. A long list of things to plan, to work on, mainly the *mailing.* See you Saturday," she said, and hung up.

When I called Yolanda I was answered by a machine. "If you want to talk to Dick McVittey or Yolanda Dolores McVittey, wait for the beep, then leave your message." It was Dick's voice. I left my name and number. Then I called Georgie.

The phone barely rang once. Georgie answered very softly, almost in a whisper. "Yes."

I took a deep breath and started talking fast. "Georgie, this is Jessie Posey again. I've tried not to disturb you, but it's important that I see you. I plan to work with Carla on the memorial program for your mother. There's also a possibility I will write an article about her work. I've been interviewing people who knew her. There are some questions only you can answer, especially about the new book. I'd like to see the manuscript." I got it out all in one breath before she could hang up on me. There was a long pause. "Hello?"

"Reuben is ill and I don't want him disturbed."

"I promise I won't. I'll come any time you say and I'll be very quiet."

"I don't want to talk to you."

I opened my mouth to beg. Then I thought of Carla and tried to make my voice like hers, fast, strong, coming down on certain words like a fist. "Miss Williams, I'm working with the *police.* Inspector Merino thought you might *prefer* talking with me." It didn't come out very strong, but it came out anyway.

She sighed, unimpressed, maybe even bored. "Reuben told me."

Hadn't he told me not to tell her? "Can't you just leave things...
all right. Come tomorrow morning. Nine-thirty. Don't ring the
doorbell. Reuben doesn't sleep well, he might be napping. Just
come, I'll watch for you and open the door."

I ran back downstairs. Jim was there helping my father put the
chairs up on the tables, pretending not to notice me while he talked
about another case. "They injected him with Drano, strangled him
with three ropes and shot him three times in the head. Sharing
responsibility. Each to cover for the other. Execution. We knew
who they were but had nothing to build a case on."

"What happened?"

"Oh, we got them on a burglary-murder a few months later.
They're serving life."

"Fascinating in a gruesome way. Reminds me to ask you, Jim.
About Jessie—in helping you she couldn't be placing herself in any
danger?"

Jim didn't answer right away. Then, solemnly, "Mr. Posey, I
wouldn't insult your intelligence with an absolute guarantee of
safety. I'd be stupid to think it. But, believe me, if I catch the slight-
est sign she's in any danger, I'll pull her right off. Why, it's like my
own life, more than my own, why, that girl is...oh, hello, Jessie."
It was so carefully casual that my father couldn't hide his smile.
My mother had her back to us as she folded napkins, but I could
feel her smile all over the place.

"Hi."

"I came by to see what progress you've made. I think I probably
should every night." I didn't have to look at either Mom or Dad to
see if they were still smiling. "I've made a list of common uses of
cyanide. I thought we might go through it and see if anyone close
to India Wonder had easy access." We moved into the kitchen so
that Joe could mop the floor under the tables. Mom brought the
stack of napkins. She and Dad and I folded them while Jim leaned
against the refrigerator and read aloud.

"Used as a poison, of course, by fumigators, pest control, in the
form of gas. Like exterminators who get rid of roaches. Used that
way for grain storage too. I guess no way that would apply. Several
industrial uses, extracting gold or silver from ore?" He looked at
me and shrugged. "Silverplating. Used for hardening metals, pol-
ishing metals. Here's a good one. Pickling. You know, in can-
neries." He started to laugh, then saw my face.

"Jane Lee worked in a pickling plant last summer."

"Oh?" He made a little note, but didn't seem very interested. "Photography?"

"Margot Stackpole is a film maker. How much of the technical stuff she does, I don't know. Yolanda Dolores publishes books, maybe some with photography."

Jim nodded and made more notes. "Then, of course, any drug company or place where various chemicals would be used, manufactured?" He looked at me and waited again.

"Cutter Labs," I said. "Sylvia March works there part time. And Celeste Wildpower is a nurse."

"That seems to cover most of them."

"Except Carla and Georgie. And the husband. I've seen him, but I haven't seen Yolanda yet." I could tell Jim was nodding at me, trying to get some response besides my short answers, trying to get me even to look at him. I didn't want to. "And Pamela. That reminds me." I sighed. The Pamela connection would be a long story.

"Uh. . . you seem tired. Getting fed up with all this?"

I turned to him, on him. "I don't see how you can do it. I heard you talking about that other murder when I came down. It's disgusting. Why do you do it?" I knew why I was attacking him, but I couldn't stop myself. I couldn't figure out how to handle his feelings or the mixture of feelings growing in me.

"Oh. Why? That's easy. It's about the highest ranking job in my . . . profession. It pays the best. It carries—believe it or not—some prestige. For me, that's something. I don't have your talents, Jessie. After seven years I'm still just plodding toward my B.A. There's no family business like this one for me to work into. I'm just doing the best I can."

Damn him! I felt so ashamed. And I even had to be grateful that he didn't leave me in my red-faced silence.

"Listen," he said. "I left my wash in the laundromat across the street. It's ready for the dryer."

"If it isn't gone by now," said my mother, shaking her head and smiling at him. "It's best not to leave anything."

Jim nodded happily. "Want to walk over there with me, Jessie, so I can keep an eye on it while you tell me what you found out today?"

Well, I had to go if only to make up for being so nasty. Dad and Mom looked tired, ready for bed, for quiet. Sounds drift up from the restaurant. Better if we talked somewhere else. Dad was already turning out the lights. "I'll lock up, Jessie. You come in the side door."

Jim and I crossed the dark street to the brightly-lit, yellow-walled laundromat, all glass like a fish bowl. It was narrow and long, running clear through to the street behind, with washers lined up against one wall and huge dryers on the other. No one else was there. Jim took his clothes out of four washers. Every sheet, towel and piece of underwear he owned must have been there. He scooped them all up and dumped them into a dryer.

"How often do you wash?"

"I let things go for a while. I just. . . these places are so depressing, and the first time I did it the machine almost ate everything up."

"Simple machine."

"Yeah, but I'm not used to them."

"I read somewhere about a high suicide rate among recently separated husbands. You think it's because you men can't learn to work the washing machines?" I was starting on him again. I shook my head. "Don't mind me. I'm in a bad mood."

"You sure are." We sat down near the dryer watching the clothes lift and fall as it spun. "Has it anything to do with the investigation?"

"I think so. I went to talk to Jane Lee today and Antonia Moran. Both of them hated India. Not hated her, exactly, but. . . held things against her."

"Like what?"

"Jealousy. Jane of her success, Antonia of her husband. And even more because of politics. But that can't be motive enough to kill someone. Can it?"

Jim shrugged. "Nothing is motive enough to kill."

"Jane says that India was taking digs at everyone at the party. Even Pamela, the one I said just came with Carla? Something about her father. Jane says India was kind one time and cruel another. And that she was afraid of something or someone. Jane's the third person to tell me India was afraid. Antonia is going to live with Reuben now that India is gone. They had an affair thirty years ago and India got thrown out of the Communist Party, and that's not the reason her book said."

"You've seen the book? Did they let you take the manuscript?" Jim leaned forward raising his voice slightly over the hum and swish of the dryer.

"Not that book, not the new one. I mean the first one, *Emma Pride's Journal*. You know, I think I'd better read that book again. I don't seem to really remember any of it. I thought I did. It's the most important book I ever read, it made me know I wanted to be a writer, but I think I remember the feeling it gave me instead of the content. People mention things in the book, and I can't remember them. And what I do remember from the book, they say, isn't true!"

Jim scratched his head, and a little lock of black hair fell over his forehead on one side, almost brushing his sideburn. It made him look tired and vulnerable. "Seems to me the current book would tell us more."

"I'm going to Georgie about it tomorrow."

"Think she'll let you have it?"

I shook my head. "It'll be worth a lot of money now, to collectors, libraries. I'll ask her to let me read it there. I'm a fast reader." I sighed, watching the clothes twirl upward and fall back, upward and fall back, lighter and slower as they lost moisture. I felt like them, getting light and dry, rising and falling, rising. "So much anger. I guess I don't want to know the things I'm finding out. I thought that artists—people who wrote books, painted pictures— knew how to live. The older they got, the more they knew, that they had solved...life. It isn't true, Jim. You know, I think that you can get old and never solve...." I don't know how he came to be holding my hand, but I noticed it just as the dryer stopped, so I got up and away from him.

We stood on opposite sides of a table, folding the clothes, not talking. He folded slowly because he knew that I would go home as soon as we were done, and he didn't want me to. I tried not to look at his face because I knew he would wear that nobody-to-go-home-to look, trying to get my pity.

But when I folded the last pillowcase and looked up at him, he surprised me. "You've had a hard day and so have I," he said briskly, smiling, firm in the jaw. "But I hope you won't get discouraged, because you're doing a great job, learning things I could never pry out of those people." Well, I'm a sucker for praise, so I smiled back.

He walked across the street with me, carrying his basket of laundry on his head like an African woman. That made it impossible for him to get too close to me, let alone try to kiss me in the shadow by the side door. So I relaxed and said, "Sure," when he told me he'd be back tomorrow night for another report.

Up in my room, I searched until I found my old paperback copy of *Emma Pride's Journal.* I planned to sit up in bed and reread at least the first twenty pages, but before I got through the first two, which I knew by memory anyway, I fell asleep.

18.

By the next morning my grumpy mood was gone. Standing on the front porch of India's house, I expected to feel sad, but the sun was bright and a brisk wind had blown the sky blue, so that instead of remembering India's death, I felt that sudden rush of beauty into me, filling me the way it always does, with a joy like froth, like bubbles (like gas, my mother says). Still, I was nervous, expecting a hard, hostile session with Georgie.

The door opened and she motioned me in, nodding quickly at the inside stairway as if to tell me Reuben Wonder was still asleep up there and we must be quiet. I handed her India's address book and she put it down on the arm of the couch as we walked through the living room. I was relieved that we would not sit in that room. She was leading me to the kitchen.

It looked different from the way it had at the party. Then I had noticed that it was old-fashioned, with an old tile sink and stove and refrigerator lining the walls and an old round oak table in the middle. Now I saw a skylight above the table, letting in bright sunlight. The kitchen extended beyond the second storey, back into the garden, so it was the lightest room in the house. "We can talk here without the sound traveling upward." We sat down and faced each other across the broad table. A slant of sunlight turned the grainy wood golden. "Now, is it the article you want to start with or the police work; do you want to question me about my mother's life or about her death?" She wasn't exactly friendly, but she was not as tense or forbidding as I had expected. Maybe the pale rose shirt she wore softened her looks. Maybe the sunlight warmed even her.

Again I was startled at how much like India—a dark India—she looked.

"I've always wondered what it would be like to be the daughter of a famous writer. You must have some interesting experiences to..."

"Are you suggesting I should write about them?"

"You might."

She shook her head. "One writer has been quite enough for this family." Her head was still now, her face expressionless. I wondered how long it had taken her to learn that control, or if she had been born that way.

"People have been telling me that your mother's journal wasn't strictly accurate. I remember the part about you being the daughter of a famous black writer who deserted you and how your mother struggled to..."

"It is understood," she said, "that anything you write will be approved by me before it is printed."

"Oh, yes." I'd read her all wrong. She actually wanted to talk.

"Put that in writing."

So I took out one of the 3×5 cards I always carry and wrote a couple of sentences, then signed it and handed it to her. She read it and nodded.

"*Emma Pride's Journal* hints that I'm the illegitimate daughter of Richard Wright, conceived when my mother was sixteen. He isn't named, of course, but you noticed how all the details add up to Wright. Mother was a great fan of his, but he wasn't my father. My father was a dishwasher who wanted to be a tap dancer, but was usually unemployed at either, and he married her, which in those days wasn't doing her any favor. Unemployment and prejudice and their own differences split them up. The hardship afterward, the hand-to-mouth jobs, her going hungry to feed me, that part of the diary was true, I think, for a little while. It was still during the Depression.

"You remember..."

"No, I was just a baby. All I remember is my grandmother, my father's mother. India left me with her." Georgie's mouth took a tight twist, almost a smile. "My mother tried to go into a convent— she always said she should have been a nun—but they wouldn't take her because she had a living child. Me. They told her her first duty to God was her duty to me. So she went back east; World War II was already creating jobs in Washington. She stayed there until the war ended. That was where she met Reuben. He was the one who insisted they come back to California and get me. I was almost ten years old by then. I hardly knew what India looked like. But I had letters. She wrote me every week. I still have them." Her face softened a little. "Sometimes I think they would have made a better book."

"Why didn't your mother publish them?"

Her face went tight again. "She never knew I kept them. Besides, how could they be explained without contradicting the famous diary? The suffering years of devotion to her daughter. The art sacrificed to maternal duty."

"Did your father..."

"I never really knew him either. He joined the army in World War II and stayed in. I guess it was the first and only job security he ever had. He was killed in the Korean War. Reuben became my father. Even after the boys came along, he always made me feel that he loved me the same." Her face softened again. When it was hard, it looked fierce but when it softened, it was sad. "He knew what loneliness and cruelty did to people. He tried his best with me. Used to make such a fool of himself, trying to make me laugh." She smiled just a little at me, as if she knew how hard it still was to make her laugh. I was beginning to have...a feeling for her. I wouldn't say I liked her, but I had a feeling for her.

"Antonia Moran says that you and Reuben took care of the boys while your mother..."

"Oh, Antonia!" she said impatiently, shaking her head, then giving a short cough, something like a laugh. "Yes, that's right. Reuben awoke my mother's political conscience, introduced her to radical movements, and she threw herself into strikes, demonstrations. She was a great campaigner. She helped start the first campaign to save these houses back in 1960?"

I nodded. "Reuben was the political one?"

"Yes, that's why he couldn't get a job. He was a physicist, that's why the government let him in, but he flunked his security check. That was all right with him; he didn't want to make bombs. So he became a cook." I was beginning to see similarities between Reuben and my father—both Jewish, both leaving an intellectual discipline to feed people. I wondered if they would like each other. "Between Reuben and me, we took care of the boys. Mother was always out, always busy."

"Until her Party group expelled her? Antonia Moran says. . ."

"I know, I know, that it wasn't over her writing, but because of Antonia and Reuben. She's gotten an awful lot of mileage out of that old affair. She's trying to use it now to move in here with us, but I won't have it. I have enough to do without another old person to nurse. Mother called her consistent, but she's not even that, just. . . just tenacious, hanging on to whatever she wants to believe. The truth is, yes, she was Reuben's first affair and Margot Stackpole was his last, and there were many in between." Now she really smiled, a soft-lipped, affectionate, amused smile. "Reuben is irresistible to women!" Reuben Wonder, irresistible? That squat, square-headed, bald, ugly old man? Georgie laughed as she saw the look on my face. Her mouth spread wide when she laughed. She looked less pinched and less like India. Was it from her father she got that wide mouth?

"Yet he stayed with your mother."

Georgie shrugged. "He loved her."

"You mean they had one of those 'open marriages' where each had other. . ."

"No, my mother never had any other. . . man." I knew she must have hesitated because she was thinking of Carla Neeland, and I knew I should try to find out something about her, but I was getting too angry thinking what Reuben must have subjected India to.

"You mean it was a. . . European-type, old-fashioned marriage, where the husband plays around but the wife is expected to be faithful and just put up with. . ."

"Oh, you're such a child!" Her mouth was narrow and thin again. "It wasn't like that at all. You don't know anything at all about their relationship!"

"I think I do," I insisted. I searched my memory for whatever bits of India's book I could remember, and plenty came back to me. "I understand, from The Diary, Reuben's problems—nightmares, heavy drinking, threats of suicide—his body and mind wrecked by the concentration camps and then by the killing he did with the British commandos. He drew strength from India, she kept him from going over the edge, gave him her strength." I stopped to let her comment, but she just waited for me to go on, and I assumed she was agreeing with me. "So you're saying he couldn't help it, he needed other women too. It was part of his emotional dependency, his lingering illness, the horror branded into him like the number on his arm." I was a little annoyed with myself for getting literary toward the end of that sentence, but sometimes I can't help myself.

She didn't laugh. She just shook her head. "Right and wrong. You're right, but you're all wrong. When she met him, yes, he was like that. In Washington, right after the war, during their first year together. When I knew him, he was all right, an occasional nightmare, but not taking that constant care and watching, that constant emotional drain. It was the other way around."

"What do you mean?"

"I mean she was the one who demanded!" Her voice rose at the end of that sentence and stayed loud. "Reuben took care of the house, us kids, because she was busy saving the world. Then, when the Party threw her out, there was her writing. Everyone had to be quiet so she could write. For days at a time no one could speak to her. She had to have a room of her own. Reuben insisted I must have my own room, so the boys moved in with him, and my mother slept in her work room, her room-of-her-own. You understand what that did to their relationship? That and the crazy hours he had to work? And still, it was never enough, never enough quiet or time, never the right conditions. A noise from the street and her concentration was ruined for hours. Any little upset, bad news on the front page of the paper, the ring of the telephone, using the vacuum cleaner at the wrong time. Can you understand that Reuben had to have something else, some warmth coming in? And even with those women, I think he gave more than he got."

"She didn't mind?"

"I don't think she ever noticed." Georgie's voice was tight and cool again. "She was too self-centered even to guess or to care about it if she did. She was . . ."

"Georgie, huh-uh, let it go, Georgie." Reuben Wonder stood in the kitchen doorway. He wore an old robe that looked like an American Indian blanket. Little wisps of fringe hair above his ears stood out. He was pale, and his eyes looked tired, but his voice was gentle and soothing. I thought of Antonia Moran and Margot Stackpole and . . . the others. Could it be that gentle voice?

"You shouldn't be up."

"Should lie there and wait for bed sores?" He smiled at her and shrugged. "I'm better up a little." Then he smiled at me.

I thought I'd better grab this opportunity since he was up. "You told me Georgie has the manuscript of the new book." I turned to Georgie. "May I look at it?" She looked at him, then back at me. Then she shook her head. "You won't let me just see it? I'll be very careful, I won't..."

"No, I just mean...I don't have...my mother wrote in long-hand. Then I typed it for her and gave it back to her to correct before sending it to her publisher."

"Oh, so you gave it back to her?" She nodded. "Then it must be up in her room. Could I..." I could see her stiffening again. Was there something in that manuscript she just wasn't going to let me see?

"Sure," said Reuben. He smiled at me. "Help yourself." He shrugged at Georgie, but the shrug turned into weaving, stumbling. Luckily he just bumped against the door jamb, blinked, and stood leaning against it, turning even more pale.

Georgie was next to him in a second, patting his shoulder, then taking his arm. "You're tired, see? Why don't you go back to bed for a while?"

He sighed. "I think I will."

19.

India's room looked just as it had on the night of the party. If Jim and his staff had moved anything, they had put it all back where they found it. There was the same pile of papers on the desk, the cardboard boxes on the floor, the file cabinets with boxes and folders stacked high on them. For no good reason, I went first to the cot and read the titles of the books on the shelf above it. This was what India read before she went to sleep, as she rested back on the four pillows, which someone had puffed up neatly, smoothing away the dents and wrinkles, the last signs of India as a living body.

The books were all new: fiction, biography, criticism by women mostly. They all had rough paper covers, and when I opened one, a slip of paper saying this was a review copy fell out. So these were just the latest books sent to India in hopes that she would give a few words for an ad, a review, a jacket blurb. Looking across the room at the file cabinets, I noticed that most of the books piled up there had the same kind of covers. I guess every woman who published a book sent one to India Wonder, hoping for a phrase, a sentence, that would insure big sales.

I went to stand at the desk where I could see out the window to the backyard, which had been neatly patterned in flower beds and vegetable beds, blurred now, overrun by about two years' weeds. Whoever did the garden had given up. Another year and it would be wild.

I started sifting through the papers on the desk, picking up sheets at random—letters. One asked if India would read at a benefit for battered women. Another was from a woman who was editing an anthology and wanted an excerpt from *Emma Pride's Journal.* Another was a pure fan letter, so much like the one I had written that I felt as if someone had robbed me of my feelings, or as if I had borrowed someone else's feelings without even knowing it. One letter was from India's publisher, encouraging her to meet their October deadline so that her new novel could be on the fall list for next year. Did it really take a whole year to get a book into print? Another fan letter read as if the writer thought India's journal had just been written, by a woman her own age, thirty-three. The longest letter was from a student who had enclosed a long list of questions about India for a term paper. Most of the answers would be in any library. Didn't he have any respect for India's time?

One of the boxes on the floor was labeled GEORGIE. It contained more letters, but these were clipped to answering letters in India's illegible backhand printing. I guessed that after India had written her answer, Georgie took care of envelopes, stamps, mailing, getting rid of the letters. The larger cardboard box was filled almost to the top with unopened letters. While I was looking at them, Georgie came into the room and dumped a dozen more letters into that box. She didn't need to tell me that the mail had just come. "We were always going to change this system," she murmured. "I was going to read through the mail first for her and sort it, eventually take on answering some of them." She looked at the overflowing box for a minute, then silently left the room.

I moved to the file cabinets and checked the folders sitting on top. My guess was right, they were manuscripts written by other people, mostly journals, mostly by women. Some were typed, but many were just roughly written in loose-leaf binders, smudged and illegible. There were some boxes of poems, envelopes containing short stories. Once I'd come close to sending part of my journal to India; now I was glad I hadn't.

The folders piled on the file cabinet nearest the door each contained a note, a few sentences in India's backhand. These were the ones she had read and was ready to send back. Did she really read all of them? I read a couple of the notes. They were pretty specific. She had read enough of each of them to make a direct comment on the content. One more thing I noticed because of my talk with Jane: some of the folders contained stamps, but most of them didn't. The postage alone, for these and for all those letters, must have cost India plenty. Enough of this, I had to find India's work before I wasted the whole day.

I pulled open the file drawer nearest me, but found only more letters. This was where Georgie filed them after mailing India's answers. I slammed that drawer shut and tried the next, and the next. I kept finding letters. Some were in folders marked by the year; this year's letters already filled seven folders. Some folders were labeled with a name, for an ongoing correspondence. A few of the names were almost as famous as India's, but most of them I never heard of. I was about to close the last drawer when I saw a folder marked CARLA.

It was a thick folder, full of tiny sheets of stiff yellow paper, covered with tiny, tiny handwriting, smaller than type, but completely legible as soon as my eyes got used to it. I wasn't surprised to find that they were love letters.

Not the first few. Those were like the letter I had written, like the letters everyone wrote to India. In Carla's case they were just more intense because "as a black woman and a Lesbian, I must be a member of the smallest minority, most threatened, least understood, most isolated, least vocal, most torn by conflict." The first few letters were dated only days apart. Then came a long letter ecstatic with reactions to India's reply. Then more daily letters asking to meet India. Another long one after their first meeting. Then daily letters, some just a few sentences, others long, spaced like poems, heating up gradually till they were love letters, passionate description of India's body and soul.

The love affair must have been short. Less than a month after the first erotic letter came complaints of not seeing India, then demands, then accusations. Then a long letter full of rage, written in script that was smaller than ever, condensed, cramped down into an intensity that even scared me. "You told *him* about us? You desecrated the purity of our love by speaking of it to him?" Reuben must have called Carla to ask her to stop writing. "That I was upsetting you? You, sick with worry about how to handle this! So I am this, a thing to be handled, this. And he is to protect you from me, from this. As if anyone could protect you from the consequences of such betrayal!" That letter was followed by two more which threatened India's life. "Not suddenly, not tomorrow, not in a week or a month, but when you are least ready, when you have most to live for, when you are surrounded by all the adulation you crave. In time. I have plenty of time, which you do not, and I have ways."

I was shivering when I finished that one, and when I heard a sound behind me, I jumped. It was just Reuben again, leaning in the doorway the same way he had downstairs. I didn't know how long he had been standing there, watching me, shaking his head. From across the room he must have recognized the yellow paper. "India could refuse no one, that was the trouble. That Carla is so aggressive. I finally had to threaten to turn her letters over to the police. That put a stop to it. Did you read the one where she says they will go away together and be like Gertrude Stein and Alice Toklas?"

I nodded.

"Only I don't think Carla would be an Alice Toklas, eh?" He gave me a weary smile. "India was so upset. Out of kindness she ... got involved so deeply and didn't know how to... so I had to put a stop to it."

"Did you... did she often...?" I just didn't know how to ask him about India and love affairs.

He was shaking his head. He knew what I was trying to ask. "No, India was not interested in love affairs. No, no, this was the only time."

"So India was afraid of Carla. And this letter is dated..." I looked at the last letter again. "... over a year ago. Did India ever write to her again?"

"Yes, a few times. Christmas cards, a note of congratulation when Carla's play won an award."

"Did India ever ask Carla to stop reading those love poems about her?"

"No. Georgie wanted her to get a lawyer to write a letter to Carla, threaten to sue, put a stop to her using India that way. But India said no, never would she try to stop the expression of an artist. I think she invited Carla to come, have a talk, be friends again. It hurt India for anyone to be angry at her."

"Did Carla come?"

"Not until the party. That was the first time they had seen each other since..." He pointed to my hand holding the stiff yellow sheet.

"You know that Carla is organizing the memorial program for India?"

His weary smile was only a little ironic. "She'll probably do a good job."

"I want to keep this file for the police." He nodded. "But this isn't what I'm looking for. There's nothing in these files but letters. Where are India's things, her manuscripts?"

He tapped on the open door. For a minute I didn't know what he meant. Then I realized something was behind that door, in the wall, a closet door I hadn't noticed before because it had always been hidden behind the open door. It was a low door, like the entrance to a dwarf house, pulling open to the series of narrow shelves, with gray manuscript boxes stacked on them like coffins. I counted about twenty. "I don't know what I'm looking for. Did India tell you what the new novel was about?"

I couldn't read the expression on his face. He nodded, then seemed to change his mind, shaking his head and turning away from me.

"You've read it."

"No, no, I never read anything." I was sure he was lying.

"She told you what it was about, then," I insisted.

"Uh...about her life, her friends."

"But not another journal."

He shook his head.

"I heard it was a satire." I looked into the little closet at the rows of manuscript boxes. "I heard it was a satire that some of her friends wouldn't find funny." I turned back to see his reaction, but saw only the open doorway. Reuben Wonder was gone.

20.

Two hours later I was hungry and tired. My eyes and shoulders and head ached.

I had been through every box in that closet, reading through dozens of fragmented scenes packed into the boxes in no particular order: a girl at piano practice dreaming visions of Indian goddesses; her father appearing after long absence, bringing her a strange porcelain locket from some far-off place; the girl trapped in her own screaming tantrums like a nightmare from which she was trying to wake herself; a cramped wood-frame house surrounded by rows of grape stumps like gnarled, sinister dwarfs; a train rushing through green slopes to the sea; the girl drugged by heavy incense and hypnotic candles in a huge, dark church.

So, whatever fact and fiction had been mixed in the patched, tattered, almost illegible fragments that usually broke off in mid sentence, I could deduce that India had grown up in the Napa Valley, had been rebellious, emotional and religious, and—if one fragment was true—had run away at sixteen during a trip to San Francisco with her father, who had an import business there.

The manuscript of the new book wasn't there. I looked at my watch. Almost time to go to work, and I had accomplished nothing. I tucked the folder of Carla's letters under my arm and walked out into the hall.

"All done?" Reuben Wonder's door was open. I could see him sitting up in bed with a tray across his knees. I went to the doorway, and he beckoned to me, gave the bed a little pat, and before I thought about it I was sitting on the edge of his bed.

"I didn't find anything but some old sketches of India's childhood." He was nodding at me. "The new book must be somewhere else. Where else would. . ."

He shoved the tray toward me. "I'm not hungry," he said. "Go ahead." Suddenly everything on the tray—the little custard, the applesauce, the toast—looked and smelled wonderful. I couldn't resist. While I ate, Reuben talked. "She read me some of those, oh, years ago. Bits and pieces, but still India, the beginning, the potential. . . passion, feeling, it's all. . . but you knew her too late, you really can't imagine."

I disagreed, shaking my head, then nodding and mumbling something about the journal, my mouth full of custard.

He shrugged as if to dismiss that. "I have been thinking so much of the early days, when I first knew her, when I first came to this country. I had escaped from the camp, fought with partisans in France, made it to England, joined an English commando troop, dropped into Italy, then worked my way north with the invasion force until...I collapsed. They sent me to Washington. To die. I was already dead. After losing everyone. After what I had seen.

"Then I met India. India Crawley, her name was then. A girl like a reed vibrating in every movement of the air, sensitive to all feeling. You saw it, all those letters, answering, always answering the cry, the need. My need, my silent cry for help. You know how she put it, how she came to live with me? She said, 'If you're going to kill yourself, you shouldn't be all alone when you do it. I'll sit with you.' Perfect. Perfect understanding. And she was only about your age. How old are you?"

"Twenty-three."

He nodded. "I was a thousand. Thirty, but an old man, trying to die. She saved me. At first only the offer to be, to sit and watch me die. Then, when I was stronger, she held...the means, promising to give it to me when I asked. So we lived together all that year. Nothing in it for her, nothing but work and sitting up all night with me. I couldn't even...I was impotent, of course, for a long time. All she said about that was, 'I always wanted to be a nun anyway.' Even when we married, I couldn't. She insisted she wanted to marry me, '...so when you're ready, I'll be an honest woman.' I laughed. Finally she made me laugh! And saved me." He pointed to the toast, and I took a piece. What he had told me was all in the journal, where it made up their whole life together, not just the first year or two.

"Georgie said..."

"Oh, Georgie." He pointed to the rest of the toast, and I reached for it. "Georgie can't help it. Poor kid. To be bitter is..." He talked about Georgie as if she were still a little girl with an ugly affliction like acne, instead of a middle-aged woman stiffened with old grudges. "I tried to spend as much time as I could with Georgie and with the boys. India was out a lot, when she wasn't writing.

"Georgie doesn't understand. I loved it! Enough excitement, enough extremity, enough drama I had had. The routine that drives you women crazy—the cleaning, the diapers, the cooking. I loved it. Boredom was a luxury I could never afford before." He handed me the dish of applesauce. "There are people, like India, who answer the cries of suffering, but who cannot abide the daily, ordinary needs of people. No use expecting them to. They are made for the extreme, the crisis, the cry of the soul—for all those women who write to her. You can ask the utmost of someone like India, but..." He smiled his sad smile. "...if you say, pass the tea, she won't hear you." He poured some cream into the cup of tea and handed it to me. For a minute or two he was quiet, looking down at the sheets, smiling at memories that, I guess, were just for him, not to share. Then he looked up at me again, watching me as I looked at him over the teacup. I was feeling better, less achy, almost drowsy now that I'd gobbled up all his food. "And are you writing about all this?"

I hesitated, then nodded. "In my head, I guess."

He nodded and kept looking closely at me. "And how are you going to make a life to go with all this writing in your head?"

It wasn't really *his* question. It was as if he had read it in my eyes or had looked through them into my head and seen that question rolling round and round. I started to talk. His old, tired eyes reflected me, held a tiny image of me, one in each eye, as I said all the things about what it meant to be an artist, and a woman artist, and how I meant to make my choice and how the choices were scaring me, trapping me.

"That's good," he said, nodding his sad smile at me. "Trapped by choices, yes, that's good. Not many people your age know that. How did you find that out?"

"I borrowed that from my mother. You'd like my parents." I started telling him about my father. Now I understood what Georgie had meant when she called him irresistible to women. He listened and heard. He looked and saw. He gave all his attention to trying to grasp who and what I was.

And then suddenly he looked tired to death. I didn't see myself in his eyes anymore. I don't think his eyes saw anything. I reached out and took his hand, said he was tired. He just nodded and I let go; he looked too tired even to stand being touched. I got up and turned to leave. That was when I saw Georgie standing in the doorway, waiting for me. Her eyes were glistening, and she turned away as soon as I looked at her, so that I wouldn't see her tears.

90

I followed her downstairs to the front door. There she turned to me. "What Reuben said about my mother is true, she was what she was, and I stopped resenting that, didn't mind working for her. I chose it. The most important work I'd ever have found, better than taking dictation from some banker or lawyer. I only resent the way she demeaned my work."

"Demeaned? You mean the way she wrote about you in the new book? Look, I couldn't find..." There was a sound from upstairs. She jerked the front door open and turned to go upstairs, all in one motion. "Is he very sick?"

She turned around on the stairway and looked down at me. Her mouth was stiff and controlled again. "Cancer. He won't last the year."

"Does he know?"

But she had turned away and was hurrying upstairs. So I left, shutting the front door behind me, taking with me a lot more unasked questions, and realizing that the two of them had managed to get rid of me without showing me the manuscript.

21.

That night I sent Mom and Dad to bed as soon as the last customer was served. Then I cleaned up and turned off the lights. I was locking the front door when I saw Jim's car stop right in front. He got out slowly, peered at the dark door, saw me through the glass. I let him in, then locked the door again. He was still wearing a suit, pulling his tie loose as if he couldn't breathe. "I'm still on duty. Have to go back." When I asked him what was wrong, he shook his head. "Just another case. You don't want to hear about it." His face, which was usually such a good dark tan, looked yellowish, and he was wearing glasses. "When I'm tired, I need them."

We left the lights out and sat down in one of the booths, side by side, so we could keep our voices low.

"I went to see the priest at Saint Joan's, Father Sterling. I thought he might know something about India Wonder's state of mind, or maybe she told him something."

"Did she?"

Jim shrugged. "He said she seemed troubled. Afraid? He wasn't sure. Finally he admitted that she only came to confession a couple of times, mostly just came and sat in the church. He didn't even know she was a writer. She was just one of the old women who like to come to his church because of the old-style ritual. That's what really interested him. He kept talking about this antique altar cloth he wants to buy." He took off the glasses and rubbed his eyes. "Did you get anything today?"

I shook my head. "I wasted the whole day searching India's files. I couldn't find the new manuscript. I did find this." I handed him the folder of letters from Carla Neeland. "Someone else for India to be afraid of." He took the folder but didn't try to look into it. He couldn't have seen anything in the dark anyway, so I told him what was in it.

"Do you think her husband was jealous of Carla?"

I shook my head. "Unless he's a good actor. He said India was always getting in too deep with people because she couldn't refuse them help. The letters support that, I think."

"What about his love affairs? Could he have wanted to get rid of his wife, marry someone like Stackpole?"

"No, no, he sounds so. . . you should have heard the way he talked about India. Besides. . . he's a very sick man. Cancer. His daughter —stepdaughter—Georgie says he hasn't long to live."

"Does he know it?"

"I think he does. So he wouldn't be likely to make plans with Margot or any other. . . ."

Jim shrugged. "Sometimes that's when they do odd things like that. Denial. Have you read Kubler-Ross? She explains it. An escape from death." He surprised me. Just because he didn't read the things I read, I had thought he didn't read at all.

"I know now why women like him so much." I told Jim about sitting on Reuben's bed and talking. "Men don't, you know. Don't look at you like a person, don't look at women that way." I felt Jim looking hard and steady at me, but it was too dark for me to see just how he was looking at me, if he was just trying to imitate what he thought I meant. He raised one hand from the table as if he wanted to touch me, but stopped himself and put his hand down again.

"Did you pick up anything that made you think India might not be the only target?"

I shook my head. "What do you mean?"

"I saw Celeste Wildpower today. She says she's gotten some strange phone calls. Silence, waiting, breathing. Just like someone checking to see if she's there, hanging on long enough to make her uneasy."

"Things like that happen all the time."

"Yolanda Dolores called me too. Same kind of phone calls. Could be coincidence. Anyway, let me know right away if you get one."

"Me? Why should I... if someone's after famous writers they'd skip me."

"You said you weren't good at fooling people about why you were asking questions. If you start getting close to anything, you could be... well, just let me know if it happens."

It had never occurred to me that I could be in any danger. The thought shook me so that, without thinking, I reached out and grabbed his hand. He held mine like a tired swimmer, gratefully. It would have been cheap to pull away, so I left it there, our two hands on top of the table, holding.

"I tried to hypnotize Celeste Wildpower. She asked me to. What a failure. She's a terrible subject, no concentration or too much will, or both. But I think she was so pleased that I couldn't do it, she offered to conduct a seance for us."

"A seance?" I giggled. We were both used to the dark now and our faces were close so that I could see Jim's face perk up with a smile. Good, he didn't look quite so old and tired as when he came in.

"It'll be a good way to get everyone together again, in a situation where feelings, tensions... might bring something out."

I guess that was true. My giggle had been a little bit nervous at the prospect, and I didn't believe in seances, or anything like that. "That makes sense, but you don't believe in contacting the dead." He didn't answer. "Do you?"

He shrugged, slightly lifting our clasped hands, then letting them rest on the table again. "I see so much on the lowest level of the human mind. Maybe I like to think that on the higher levels, there could be... only trouble is she won't do it for a whole week, next Saturday night. Full moon."

We both giggled, then hushed each other, Jim pulling our hands up to his lips to say, "Sh-h-h!" then keeping my hand against his lips. They were warm, and he held my hand to them as if its coolness soothed a fever. He held very still, not looking at me, waiting, as if he expected me to pull my hand away, loosening the grip of his hand on mine so that I could slip my hand out of his if I wanted to.

I didn't. I waited too, until he could tell that I wasn't going to snatch my hand back. Then I waited again to see what he would do about it. He did nothing. And I waited again to be sure he wasn't playing a game, that he wasn't going passive on me to throw me off balance and then just reel me in. He probably could have, the way I was feeling toward him just then, but either he wasn't that smart about sex or he didn't want to play games. It was both. I could tell by the awkward way he held onto my hand, and by the way he was afraid to look at me, that it was both, and I was glad.

I took my hand out of his and touched the side of his face. It was as if I switched on a light. He turned his face to look at me; he looked like a little kid facing a happy surprise. We didn't open our mouths, just touched and brushed and pressed lips before we touched with our hands.

The back of his neck was all taut ropes that I smoothed and stroked, slipping my hands under his shirt. His hands were bigger than I thought, the two of them almost going all around my waist as he held onto me, his thumbs almost touching under my breasts. We kissed lips again. Then he rested his head on my shoulder, lips touching my neck as my hands smoothed his.

His head dropped forward on my chest. I took my hand away from his neck and unbuttoned my blouse to let his head rest between my breasts, then let my head drop onto his shoulder. His hands tightened around my waist and held me firm as I pillowed his head.

After a while, he sighed.

"You have to go," I said.

I felt him nod against my breast. Then he raised his head to look at my face, frowning as if he was worried, until he saw me smile, and he smiled back, and sighed again.

I buttoned my blouse on the way to the door, and I kissed him full and open-mouthed before he left. Then I locked the door and went up to bed with that sweet, aroused feeling that smoothed out into a warm glow and rocked me to sleep like a baby.

22.

When I saw the newspaper in the morning, I understood why Jim had been so tense and pale. A blind woman had been forced into a car on Telegraph Avenue, driven to some place in Oakland, gang-raped, then dumped on the Emeryville mud flats. She was in the hospital now and police were "still looking for the men responsible." That was the kind of thing I usually skipped when I read the paper. This time I read the whole story, looking for Jim's name, finding it, and thinking that he couldn't skip this but had to penetrate every horrible detail. In a way, I thought, that's something like what a novelist does. Hadn't Auden written a poem about that? I knew where it was but had no time to look it up.

The address Carla Neeland had given me was one of those little roads off Euclid, high up in the hills. Pumping up those roads was hard, sweaty work, probably slower than walking, but it felt good to pump and gasp up there where the air was fresh. Luckily it was Saturday, nobody going to work and still early for shoppers, so there was less chance of a car barreling down to knock me off into the ruts and gullies on the side near the trees. My reward, after seeing Carla and Pamela, would be to push off and sail downhill, like ten years ago, like a kid again.

I found the address on a wooden stump, but to reach the house I had to go through a gate and down winding paths of steps between other houses and tall trees until I found an old rustic stone and shingle place growing out of the downside of the hill, someone's old summer cabin added onto and rebuilt by succeeding owners, now worth hundreds of thousands of dollars, a woodsy-Berkeley classic. You don't see many black people living in houses like this. When they get that much money, they want a big house out in Moraga, with a pool and with floors that don't tilt downhill.

This house had a screened porch with a door going into a sunroom, all glass. The door was open and I could hear women talking. I could see through the sunroom windows to the big front room beyond it, with more glass looking out across the trees, across Berkeley to the bay, across the bay to San Francisco. Three women were sitting on the floor around a low table, but the light was behind them and I couldn't make out who they were. The voices got louder, and I recognized Carla's voice.

Someone was bent over a box in one corner of the sunroom. As she straightened up, I recognized Pamela Righbottom, wearing an apron over baggy gray slacks. She turned, saw me, and her eyebrows flew up for a moment, like startled black birds. Then she crooked her finger at me to come in. She bent over the box again, one of several she was stuffing books into. "The planning meeting is in the living room. Go right in."

"Aren't you going to. . ."

She shook her head without raising it. "I'm packing whatever I can to send on ahead. I'll be back in New York before the memorial service, thank God."

"Oh, can you. . ." I almost asked if Jim had told her to stay for a while, but an instinct told me not to bring up the police or the investigation just yet. I had to find some other excuse to talk to her alone. I looked around and found the excuse on the walls, old photos of fishing boats, of huge logs behind harnessed oxen, with bearded men posed stiffly beside them. "What are these?"

She looked up over her shoulder. "Carla's family. The white side." She came to stand beside me, pointing to a blurred figure in the bow of a fishing boat. "That is Carla's great-grandfather, a Maltese fisherman who went out from Crockett, through the Carquinez Straits. He never married Carla's great-grandmother, but he did settle some property on her, and this house finally came down to Carla. She only put those up recently, along with the black ancestors." She waved her arm toward the rest of the photos covering the walls, stiffly posed formal portraits, most of them, heavily retouched, everyone dressed like black royalty. The more recent photos were less formal. One of them showed Carla and India together, smiling, Carla's arm around India's shoulders, squeezing her tightly.

I had to say something before she would turn back to her packing and ignore me again. "So you'll be glad to be going back east."

She looked at me and raised those eyebrows as if there were no words to say how glad she'd be. "Where are you going to graduate school, Jessie?"

"I don't know. I thought maybe I'd take some time to write. I'm not even sure if I want to go to. . ."

"Listen, you must go to a good eastern school. I'll be happy to write a recommendation for you."

"Thank you."

"...must be the climate here or something. We must get you in touch with some good minds. You've never been to New York? Oh, Jessie, you'd love it."

I nodded. "I'm sorry you're not staying for the memorial service. I'm sure they would want you to speak."

"Me? I didn't even know the woman."

"But you knew her work, as a scholar, a critic, a..."

She was shaking her head. A wisp of hair slipped out and she pressed it back. Her face looked so naked, so exposed and puffed out, with her hair slicked back that way. It didn't look severe or intellectual, just naked and faded except for the eyebrows. "I'm too busy finishing my father's projects to bother with current melodrama."

That made me mad enough to say it. "I thought you would have read *Emma Pride's Journal* anyway."

"Can't imagine why." She was huddling over one of those boxes again, but she looked stiff.

"For personal reasons, I mean." She didn't answer, didn't move. "Isn't your father a model for one of the characters?"

"I don't know what you're talking about."

"Oh, I just heard..."

"Ridiculous."

"Maybe it was a mistake."

"Who told you that?"

"Uh...I can't remember...let's see..." She was still frozen over one of those boxes. I couldn't see her face, but the tension in the room was so bad, I started edging toward the door, toward the voices arguing in the living room. Pamela straightened up and turned to look at me. Her eyes were slits. Her eyebrows had almost come together over them.

I edged through the doorway, through a small kitchen, and into the living room. Carla saw me and waved me down to a pillow on the floor beside her.

The women with her were Margot Stackpole and Sylvia March. Margot was wearing her T-shirt again, with the title of her book meandering over her big, uptilted breasts. Sylvia kept biting her lip and shaking her head. Her eyes were clear, but she looked drawn, ravaged. Hungover? "You can't read those poems at the memorial," she was saying in a weak, shocked whisper.

"Why not, if *you're* going to read from letters?" Carla turned on her, and Sylvia flinched.

"That's different," she moaned.

"Why? Because it's safely *straight?* And *white?*" Sylvia winced each time Carla came down on a key word. "Look, some women will be there just *because* of my poems, just because she stepped over that line, just once, just *because* of this sign that she loved a *woman.* These are women I *delivered* to India, just as I brought her to them." Carla was all in white again, this time a rough muslin gown slit down the front to her waist, showing the slight swelling of firm, dark breasts. Her bare feet sticking out below the hem were long and velvety smooth. Her head, uncovered, was shorn tight to the scalp, and was perfectly shaped, like a statue.

"Look, first of all," Margot said, "we should agree on what part of India's journal should be read. Now, I've marked a couple of places..." She pulled out a paperback edition like the one I owned.

"And who should read," said Sylvia.

Margot's eyes narrowed. "I'm the one with dramatic training. You know I read better than any of you."

Carla made a hoarse grunt. "It ought to be someone famous. I think I can get Maya Angelou."

"Why? She hardly knew India. Just because she's..."

"It should be someone close to India," said Sylvia, touching her head as if it were sore and raw. "Wallace Stegner would be more..."

"No men," Carla said.

"But it...."

"The only reason you want to ask him is to *flatter* him so he'll get his publisher to take your book, the same reason why Margot wants to read, to *revive* interest in hers." They both blinked rather than meet Carla's eyes. "No men. India's readership was *women.* She spoke to and for us. And women should read her work and speak about her at the memorial. Right, Jessie?"

It was the first time she had looked at me since I sat down. "Yes," I said. "Yes, I think it should be women. Unless her husband or her sons..."

"They don't want to," said Carla. "The sons can't fly out again, won't even be there."

"But," said Sylvia, "I'm sure some men will fly out for the memorial. Saroyan is an old friend. And that critic, what's his name, on the *New York Times?*"

Carla set her jaw, took a deep breath, then shrugged and compromised. "They can sit on the platform, with the distinguished writers, friends of India, the mayor. Silent."

Margot nodded. "Okay, but by the same token, it doesn't have to be a famous woman writer. That's not what India was about. Her journal touches the hidden women, the unheard, the shy, forgotten..."

"Of which type you are an example?" Carla said, looking Margot up and down. But she was smiling.

Margot smiled back at her. "I can look that way if you want. I'm an actress, after all." There was just a slight tone of begging in her voice, an actress fighting for a role.

"No, I wouldn't..."

"But I'm the..."

"Wait!" Sylvia closed her eyes and put her hands over her ears. "Wait." To my surprise, they did, while she spoke very slowly and very quietly, like a woman who is about to throw an hysterical fit. "I think we ought to decide about these mailing lists first. Scheduling what will be on the program comes after."

Carla agreed. "We have to get a mailing out this week or it'll never get to people in time."

That was how I learned that they had agreed on at least one thing, the date, a Friday evening, two weeks off. Now that Sylvia had turned them away from the actual program, they were able to argue productively for the next two hours, working their way down the list of decisions Carla kept in front of her. She had listed questions that would never have occurred to me, and she knew most of the answers. During that time, Pamela came in with a bottle of wine and glasses. She sat down across from me, never saying a word, never looking at me, just looking cool, slightly amused, above all this wrangling.

By the time we came back to the program again, everyone talked as if they had agreed all along. Antonia Moran could speak about India as a political organizer, Yolanda as a supporter of community arts. Carla would read one poem as a general tribute to India, and Sylvia could read a selection from India's letters. Margot would round off the program with a reading from *Emma Pride's Journal*. Celeste Wildpower could do a short opening and closing ritual.

"What about Jane Lee?" I asked.

"Jane never speaks in public," said Sylvia. "We'll have enough trouble just getting her to sit on the platform."

"Well, that's about it," said Carla. "Now there's just getting it *done.* I'll contact organizations and schools." Margot took on the press releases and media people. Sylvia was to design a flyer and gather mailing lists. I volunteered the restaurant for an addressing session on Wednesday night. We were doing fine until Margot brought up the question of photographs.

Sylvia looked ready to cry. "We can't allow cameras in the church! Those flashbulbs. . . ."

"They don't have to use flashbulbs, do they, Carla?" Margot brushed back her hair as if she were already getting ready to have her picture taken. "You're the expert, with your photo lab. Explain to Sylvia how. . . ."

I made a mental note about Carla's photo lab, cyanide access, while Carla and Margot ganged up on Sylvia. I knew neither of them would pass up a chance to have their pictures taken. "In fact, it ought to be televised, *live.*" I couldn't tell whether or not Carla was serious or just enjoyed watching Sylvia squirm, but I couldn't stand this two-against-one battle.

"I think you should ask the family before you plan anything," I said. "This is one thing they should decide." Sylvia nodded, grateful but exhausted, while the other two shrugged, not too sullenly. Margot drained her glass and got up. "That's it. I'm leaving." Sylvia trailed behind her for a ride home.

As soon as they were gone, Carla said, "That Margot, she'd speak naked and standing on her head if she thought she could get into the newspapers."

For the first time since sitting down, Pamela reacted, laughing, reaching forward to give Carla's knee a squeeze, looking amused and superior and affectionate at Carla all at once. ". . . threatening to overwhelm a shrinking violet like you." Carla's power lust was something else Pamela could laugh at, but it looked like the one thing among all of us that she respected. Carla smiled and grabbed Pamela around the waist. I thought I was in for more love scenes like the ones at the party, but Pamela shook loose and frowned, shooting a cold glance at me.

"You think Margot is just doing this for publicity?" I asked.

"Sure," said Carla. "Not for *love.* India wrecked her chances to get that *awful* book published. Now she must be hoping to be photographed reading from India's book. Maybe get another publisher interested. God, you don't think she'll wear that shirt! I'll have to *tell* her." She made a note.

"And Sylvia?"

"Oh, Sylvia." The shrug that dismissed Sylvia would have wiped me out. "Sylvia just doesn't have any life, doesn't *exist* without India. Even if she *hated* India, she has to hang on *somehow,* to *something.* "

"You think she hated India?"

"People always end up hating anyone they get too dependent on."

"What about you, Carla?"

"What *about* me!" She'd made her voice rough again, giving me a look that would keep people like Sylvia on edge. I wanted to cringe too, but I knew I just had to meet her head on. I knew she wouldn't be sounding so tough unless I had said something that worried her.

"You hated India too. I read your letters to her."

Carla took a deep breath, but her voice came out soft. "She kept those letters?"

"I think she kept every letter she ever received."

"Oh." Carla looked disappointed. She bent over to look at her elegantly long second toe and began rubbing it with one finger. "Would I be reading those love poems to her all the time if I hated her?"

"Well, I guess you couldn't very well read the hate letters in public."

She kept rubbing that toe, stretching it out, her long, slim body folded, coiled over her foot. Then her head moved just slightly so one eye could take a quick look at me. "How did you get to read those letters?" Then she was looking at her foot, as if nothing else mattered. I thought I'd better change the subject.

"Did you ever try to publish those poems?"

"Ummm." Her face was hidden. "Never got past the legal departments."

"What?"

She raised her head and looked at me. "A couple of publishers wanted them, knew they'd be a sensation. But they were afraid India would sue."

"And now?"

"Now. India's dead. No problem. I'm expecting a call from my agent any time. I'll be able to announce forthcoming publication when I read at the memorial program." Her mouth opened into a wide, hard, biting smile. "How come you read those letters?"

"I...uh...I was looking for the manuscript of India's new book."

"Georgie let you into India's room? She never let anyone *near* India's work! How come she let *you?* "

Now I was the one who was trying to hide my face from inspection. "I told her you'd want to read from it at the program."

"So did I. But she didn't let me see anything. Did you read it? Are we *really* all in it? Me? Letters and *all?*"

"I don't know. I couldn't find it."

She kept looking at me, and one eyebrow went up as she said, "What are you up to, Jessie?"

"I think Jessie is playing detective," said Pamela, "Like a cheap old Hollywood movie."

"Oh?" Now they were both staring at me.

"She is theorizing," Pamela went on, "With the third-rate mind of a laid-back Californian, that I murdered India Wonder out of revenge for the damage her book did to my father."

"Oh, tacky," said Carla to me. "And watch that *laid-back Californian* bit," she said to Pamela. "I told you before, that's gotten *boring.*"

Pamela slicked back her hair with both hands, sighing, as if she were trying to wipe away a headache. "It must be catching," she murmured. "Everything here is so boring."

"Well, you won't have to put up with it much longer, will you?" Carla glanced toward the sunroom where Pamela's boxes were stacked. She didn't look at Pamela, turned toward me instead. "Actually, your theory isn't a *bad* one. Pamela got tenure, and her father died. Cause of death, wounded pride, from being laughed at in India's book. So Pamela arranges for a year of teaching here so she can get revenge on India."

Pamela was slowly lowering her hands to her lap, watching Carla quietly and arranging her eyebrows in a careful lift of contempt. "Be careful, Carla. What India did to my father is no joke, and he was worth ten of your..."

"Oh, spare us, Pam. I'm really *sick* of your father." She went on, still not looking at Pamela. I wondered why she was pushing at her this way. "So, Pam sets out to kill India. But she doesn't even know her. How can she get to her? She's heard of this black Lesbian poet who loves India. She becomes a groupie of that poet, follows her from reading to reading, until she finally seduces her, moves into her house, all so she can get to India, poison her, then run back to New York."

"A poor theory," Pamela said with a superior look, but her voice trembled just a little. "There are more direct ways. I didn't need you to get to India Wonder."

"Then what did you need me for?"

"And who seduced whom?"

They were glaring at each other now, and I think they had forgotten all about me.

"What did you need me for?" Carla repeated.

Pamela spoke so softly I hardly heard. "I've told you what you... what this has meant to me."

"Okay." Carla got up, standing very straight and still. "I'll start packing too. I'm going back with you."

"But..."

"You're right, New York is the only place to live. And we won't have to be separated."

"Carla, I don't think you..."

"You don't want me to come with you?" Carla stood over Pamela. "You don't think your colleagues at Eastward U. would like me?"

"All right, Carla, all right, I'll admit I did want to get to India through you. But then I came to genuinely care for you, and forgot all about India, and when I did finally meet her, someone else..."

"Liar!" Carla pulled Pamela up, jerking at her until she was standing, facing her. "You'd rather be suspected of murder than of what you really are. Daddy's girl, rigid, frigid, man-dominated biddy. The only orgasm you ever get is when the male head of your department says you might get a full professorship in ten years! Riding in on Daddy's name, finishing Daddy's work. Safe and sure. But then you weren't so sure that was the way to get it. Times are changing. Some academic women are even cashing in on going *Feminist*! Better hedge your bets. Safely. Take a vacation in California—teaching here is a *vacation*, right? all those sunny laid-back minds. And while you're dropping in, dropping out, have an affair with a woman. It's an experience every Feminist Critic should have once, no telling what *depth* it would add to your next paper on Virginia Woolf."

I could tell Carla had hit something, because Pamela was standing loose, like a rag doll shaken by Carla, everything shocked limp, except her eyes, fixed on Carla with fear and... respect. "I love you, Carla," she whispered. "You're... wonderful."

Carla let go, pushing her away. "You love me just at this moment because I see *through* you. Bitch. Bitches, all of you. *I'm* called the seducer, the *promiscuous* one. But it's you, it's all the women like you who drop in on Lesbian Land for a short visit, a new experience, a vacation from struggling with men. And it never occurs to you that you have some responsiblity toward me!"

By this time Pamela was stiffening up again, putting the superior lift into her eyebrows again. "Oh, come, Carla, you're becoming positively operatic, and you're miscast as Madame Butterfly."

"You used me the same way India did."

"You're projecting again, Carla. You used India."

Carla grabbed her arm again, then reached back as if she was going to swing at her. But Pamela pivoted and threw one hip against Carla, throwing her off balance. I just sat there, watching them edge closer to the big windows. I don't know what would have happened if just at that moment the phone hadn't rung.

They froze.

"The breather again?" Pamela hissed.

"I'll get it," said Carla. "If it's that creep again..." I got up, nodded and waved as casually as I could, then got out of there. As I hurried through the sunroom to the door, I could hear Carla. "Hello! Oh. Hi, Yolanda. Yes, we just finished the meeting, everything's all set. Listen, I've been telling Margot she ought to sue Doubledom for reneging on her book. Does your husband think..."

I unchained my bike and flew down the hill, getting to the restaurant just in time for our first customers.

It was a usual Saturday, busy from one o'clock on, never a minute to stop until late closing at ten. I didn't hear from Jim, but I didn't expect to. I knew he would be busy on the rape case.

After we cleaned up, I went up to my room and pulled the television out of the closet. The eleven o'clock news started with local headlines, and for once I was glad that the violent news came on first. "Five men who kidnapped and raped a young blind woman were caught by ingenious police work involving hypnosis." I waited for Jim's name to be used, but I guess he had kept his name out of it. "Under hypnosis by a trained police inspector, the woman recalled a combination of sounds—traffic, streetwork, music—which helped police locate an apartment above a bar on a corner in West Oakland. There they found all five men along with clear evidence, the woman's handbag and some articles of her clothing." There were movies of the men hiding behind handcuffed hands, walking between policemen, but no sign of Jim. Just as the news switched to an accident on the Carquinez Bridge, the phone rang. I knew it would be Jim.

"I was looking for you on TV," I said. "It was you, wasn't it, the hypnosis and all?"

"Yeah."

"Maybe now they'll give you a better room to do it in."

"Maybe." He sighed. "I haven't been to bed since I saw you. I'm half asleep. Going to bed now. Look, I'm going to have my kids tomorrow, promised to take them to the park. Want to come?"

"Sure."

"I'll pick you up around noon."

"I'll have to back by five, dinner shift."

"Okay. See you." His voice drifted off as if he had already fallen asleep.

23.

On Sunday morning my mother woke me up and said Jim was already there with his three kids. I dressed and hurried downstairs, where I found them sitting at a table with a pot of tea, holding little cups and listening to my father explain how sushi is made. The two oldest were boys about seven. The little one was a girl about three. They were fair and small-boned, with fine blonde hair which, in the boys, was already turning dark like Jim's.

Jim looked exhausted and grateful to see me. I just felt resentful. He wanted me for baby-sitting help, but I didn't know anything about handling kids and didn't want to learn. I drank some tea and ate some melon. Then I was in a better humor, so we piled the kids into the car and headed for Oakland.

The two boys sat in the back seat and I held little Jenny on my lap. She snuggled in right away with her fine hair brushing my cheek, while I resisted all the maternal feelings welling up in me.

"I thought we'd take the kids to Fairyland, where they can play around the little castles and stuff, and you and I can talk."

It took a long time to find a parking place and a longer time to walk back to Fairyland, Jim carrying Jenny most of the way and the boys, Mike and Max, running ahead, lagging behind, whooping and punching each other, as if they were afraid to lose our attention for even one second.

When we reached Fairyland, Jenny had to go to the bathroom, so I took her while Jim stayed with the boys and let them into the place. By the time we got back, they were tired of that "kid stuff" so I played tag with them for a while until Jim had taken Jenny through the little paths and around the steeples, and she'd gotten bumped by kids climbing around, knocked down twice, and had had enough. We walked around Lake Merritt until we found a playground with swings and slides, where Max and Mike did all right, but Jenny kept chasing after them trying to use equipment that was too big for her. I pushed her in a swing for a while, but what she really wanted was to hang from the jungle gym while I stood below ready to catch her because it was too big a drop for her. Jim kept pulling stuff out of his pockets: raisins, nuts, chocolate bars. Chewing moments were fairly quiet.

Just when I'd given up hoping for anything but the passage of time, they let go. The boys got into a kickball game and Jenny squatted down by the side of the lake, pulled off her shoes, and started pushing pebbles around her toes with a total concentration I'm never able to get while writing. Jim and I sat down on a bench where we could keep an eye on her.

"Beautiful kids," I said.

"Yeah."

"Well. Yesterday I went to a meeting to plan the memorial for India. Carla Neeland's house. Pamela lives with her, but was packing up to go back to New York."

Jim nodded. "We don't have anything strong enough to make her stay."

"She admitted that she wanted revenge on India because of her father, but she said she didn't kill her. But, Jim, after the meeting she and Carla had this terrible fight right in front of me."

"What about?"

"It's too complicated. And they didn't say anything that would prove either of them killed India. But...watching them, I thought they were both capable of murder."

"Both had motives. They could have done it together."

"And then had a fight that way, right in front of me?"

"Who else was at the meeting?"

"Sylvia March and Margot Stackpole. Margot and Carla spent most of the time fighting over who was going to be the center of attention at the memorial program."

"Who won?"

"Carla, I think. Or she will win in the end. There's something relentless about her. Scary. Did you read those letters she wrote to India?"

He nodded. "Pretty strong threats. Almost indictable."

"And while she was writing those letters she was going around reading erotic love poems to India, partly to embarrass her, partly to promote herself. For a whole year she did that and never saw India, never spoke to her. Want to hear a murder theory?"

"Go ahead."

"Carla takes her revenge by pretending there's this hot love affair going on still, by reading the poems in public. She tries to get the poems published, but can't because of possible libel. Then she hears how India's new book will tell a different version of their love affair, deflate it and the poems. So Carla goes to the party. She steals the manuscript from India's room, then slips the cyanide—taken from her own photo lab—into India's drink. There's only one thing wrong with my theory."

"What's that?"

"Just as I was leaving the house, the phone rang and she said something about receiving those phone calls like the others, so. . . ."

"That doesn't kill your theory. Whoever is making the phone calls could be lying, pretending she has been called, to divert suspicion."

"Why would she make those phone calls? Is she really planning to kill others, to. . . ."

"Wipe out the competition?"

We both laughed, but it didn't sound as crazy to me as it would have before I went to India's party.

"What are you thinking about?"

"The party. There's so much I didn't notice because I didn't know these people. All I saw was India Wonder surrounded by adoring, brilliant women. Now all I can see is envy and malice, a bunch of swelling egos!"

"Let's get back to the manuscript. You think someone went into her room and just took it, without being noticed?"

"Well, I was in there alone, a complete stranger. I could have gone through everything. So I guess someone else could have, especially someone who knew what she was looking for. People were up and down the stairs all night. The bathroom was up there, coats were left up there in the other rooms."

"You don't remember seeing anyone coming out of India's room carrying anything?"

I shook my head. Then something came, then slipped away again. "I don't remember much about anything except when India fell. It's like. . . that wiped out everything else."

"Maybe we ought to try some hypnosis."

"Now?"

Jim shook his head. "It has to be quiet. No distractions." He nodded toward Jenny, still busy pushing pebbles around her toes. "Maybe I could take you through the whole thing again under hypnosis, and you might come up with something that's been overlooked, something subliminal. You saw it, but it didn't register."

I nodded. It sounded like a good idea.

"What are you doing tomorrow?"

"I'm seeing Yolanda Dolores. She's over in the City so it will take me a while to get there and back; then I have to work."

"Is she the last one?"

I sighed. "The last."

"Maybe we can get together Tuesday and try hypnosis. I go off Tuesday for a few days. I'll have time."

Just then Max ran by, kicking up sand and startling Jenny, who fell over and started crying. Mike, standing on the edge of the lake, made himself stumble knee deep into the water, then waded out looking pleased with himself. Jim picked Jenny up and we headed back to the car.

By the time we got there, Jenny was sucking her thumb and whimpering, and Mike was whining that his wet feet were cold. He and Max started tumbling around the back seat, yelling and laughing as they tried to pull off the wet shoes and socks. When Jim put Jenny into my lap so he could drive, she scowled, let go of her thumb, opened her mouth, took a deep breath and got ready to howl.

In desperation I started to sing. I sang "This Old Man," which I couldn't remember ever knowing. By the end of the first verse the boys had joined in, and Jenny's thumb lay on her open but quiet mouth. After that, the boys called out titles, all the same old songs I had sung when I was their age and hadn't really forgotten. Jenny sat up straight and bounced in time to our music. Jim added a tuneless bass sound, the words all faked and mushy.

We drove up to the restaurant, parked, and finished the last phrase of "Row, Row Your Boat." Jenny kissed me and the boys said, "Hey, you come next Sunday, okay?" I got out, waved, blew kisses, and escaped into the restaurant, going straight to the kitchen toward a big, lovely, quiet pile of vegetables. I took my mother's knife away from her. "I'll do them."

"You're early."

"Yeah, well, the kids were tired."

Mom smiled at me. "You look a little tired too."

I put the knife down. "Mom." I looked at her, so little and brown and bright. "Mom, I don't know how you did it."

She knew what I meant. She didn't say anything, but she stopped smiling as she picked up another knife and started slicing yams.

"Well, I'm never going to. Never. I'm going to get my tubes tied or something. I'm not going to have my life just sucked away, eaten up, taken from me, so that I never get a chance to use my talents, to find my identity." I chopped onions in time to the words I wanted to emphasize: talent, identity, growth, education, art, creativity. I was talking like Carla, underlining all the words, until finally I stopped because my eyes were stinging, filled with onion tears.

After a while Mom sighed and said, "You mustn't belittle me." That reminded me of something. Georgie. She said India had demeaned her life. I hadn't understood her either.

I was shocked. "Mom! I meant you were great! I meant you're a hero. You know, if you put all the effort you put into us kids, if you put that much energy into developing your own talents..."

"That's what I did." Mom was still slicing rhythmically, quietly, and her words came out the same way, in Quaker-Asian-contemplative style. "For you, no, you have a talent for writing. Perhaps some day you will have children too, but..." She shrugged, nodded, kept slicing. "I know that if I put the effort for you children into something else, some other work, I would have done it well, but...what other work? Raising human beings. It was the finest work to do with my life, and I did it very well. I missed doing some other things, as you will miss doing some things in order to write. I gave my best to the most important work I could find. No one could do more."

I don't think I had ever heard my mother make such a long speech. She never looked up from her work, but was still cutting elegant, thin slices of yam. I looked up to see my father standing in the doorway, his eyes closed, the fingers of one hand stuck into his beard. He opened his eyes, looked at me, smiled and then sighed as he swung open his arms into one of those gestures of wonder, of contentment, that can't be expressed in words. And I thought, if Jim wants to hypnotize me, let him take me back to relive this moment over and over again.

The Sunday crowd was thin, so that we were done and in bed by ten. When the phone rang, I jumped up to get it before it would wake Mom and Dad. "Hello." There was no answer. "Hello. Hello."

I don't know why it took me so long to realize that I was getting one of those phone calls. When I understood that, I stopped saying anything. I just stood there waiting, like my caller. I began to feel that we were breathing in the same rhythm, though I couldn't actually hear breathing. I couldn't hear anything. I waited. And waited. My bare feet began to get cold on the wood floor. I waited.

Finally the voice came, a faint whisper, so faint I couldn't tell whether it was man or woman, old or young. Just two words, "You next," then a click and the dial tone.

24.

The F bus got me over the bridge to downtown San Francisco in twenty minutes. The second bus ride, out to where Yolanda Dolores lived, took longer. A few blocks of sleazy hotels behind Market Street, a few more blocks of warehouses, then a half-turn south under the freeway and we were in the Mission District, lurching past Mexican restaurants next to big chain stores, huge old movie houses hollowed out at the bottom to make parking lots, furniture stores with windows full of puffy-glittery junk, brand new bank buildings and empty old store buildings. The first time I took the bus down Mission Street, they were planting little palm trees along the sidewalks. The trees were still there, but they hadn't grown much. They looked dry and stunted, pathetic little gray-tan poles. I got off at Twenty-fourth Street.

If I turned right, as I usually did, I'd be going uphill, past the library and bookstores. But this time I had to turn left, down the part of Twenty-fourth Street where most of the signs are in Spanish, and the stores mostly sell household things, for families, poor families. Some boys on the corner eyed me and made cracks in Spanish. They thought I was one of them, a little, dark girl they could force to walk tightly with her eyes pointing front.

After a few blocks I turned right again, crossed Army by the school, then cut across the park and started looking at house numbers. I spotted the sign on one of the store fronts before I saw the address. R. McVITTEY LEGAL OFFICE on the store window to the right of the door. On the window to the left, a sign was pasted: PARA TODOS PRESS. That window was full of books and pamphlets. I'd seen these books before, the time Yolanda visited a writing class I was in, and talked about independent publishing. Until then I hadn't any idea that I might not, within a year or two, be published by Doubledom or some other big publisher, with my picture on the cover of *Time Magazine*. Yolanda had wiped out a lot of my favorite illusions. I stood there for a minute looking at the books and listening to the whoops and yells from the yard of the building next door. It was a community center, full of little kids for day care. I caught a glimpse of Yolanda through the glass door. I tried the handle. It was locked, but she saw me there and came to open it.

"We can't leave this door unlocked. Lost a typewriter last time we did. Come in, Jessie." She was wearing a long green smock over a peasant skirt. The smock was streaked with black ink splotches that matched her hair, which hung loose and long, blackest black, all tangled around her shoulders, in and out of the collar of her smock. Her plump cheeks reminded me of those striped, golden-rose apples that come in season during late summer. *"Momentito."*

She walked across the concrete floor to a big table where a girl was working over a light box. The table was covered with papers and scraps, rulers, cutters, electric tools. The girl bent over the light box, her long, straight hair falling forward, hiding her face like a monk's hood. While Yolanda talked to her, I walked around.

It was a narrow store building, deep, with a concrete floor and windows close to the ceiling at the very back. Since the building backed up against the Bernal Heights hill, the yard of the community center was on a level with those windows, and I could not only see the little kids running around, but could hear them screaming as if they were right in the store with us. Yolanda didn't seem to notice.

Aside from the big table where she and the girl were working, and a big desk near the front window, and a squatty old printing press in the far back corner, the place was filled with boxes of books. They were stacked in order, several boxes of one title, with the top box open, then a space of two or three feet to the next stack of boxes of a different title. A thin white partition separated all this from her husband's law office. Another partition was marked PHOTO LAB: KEEP THIS DOOR CLOSED!

"We've got thirty-four titles now." Yolanda had come up behind me. "Including the one we're pasting up. We'd have thirty-five if I could get Antonia to update and expand her book on left-wing heroines. But every time I bring up the subject of reissuing it, she delivers an oration on capitalist publishing, huffing and puffing like a dragon gone *loco*."

"You do everything here, printing and all."

"Not yet. We just got that old printing press. I have to learn how to run it. So far I only print myself!" She laughed at the black streaks on her smock. I noticed one on her chin. "But we do our own typesetting, keep the machine locked in Dick's office. I hope you don't need him for your interview. He's in court today."

I shook my head. "Just you." I loved listening to her voice. There was not quite an accent, just a softening of all the consonants, a broadening of the vowels, and a sort of tough tone that probably came from the way she blunted her "th" sounds.

"You say you're writing for *Ms.*? Who are you dealing with?"

"No special person, I. . ."

"I thought you said you had a commission from them."

"Well, I do in a way." She stood waiting for me to explain, her big, black eyes fastened on me. I kept trying to avoid looking right into them. She knew all about the world of magazine publishing. Nothing I said would fool her.

"I just don't want you to do a lot of work *por nada*. You should get something firm. I know the woman who handles these features for *Ms.* and I've been trying to get her to do something on western women writers, but. . ."

"Were you born here?" I asked, in a desperate attempt to change the subject. "After I do some traveling, I'd like to settle here. It must have been exciting, growing up here."

"Exciting?" She gave me one slow, ironic nod. "No bookstores or galleries, no store-front politics, no neighborhood arts, no poetry in the community center. Just poor people like my parents coming in to build ships for World War II. Old Europeans on the west side of Mission Street, Latinos on the east, blacks north of Market, all growing up to converge on Mission High School and fight it out. Yeah, exciting."

"How did you manage to avoid all that?"

"I didn't." I followed her to the back of the place, where she picked up a dark rag and started wiping around the gears on the old printing press. "By the time I was fourteen I was head of the only Mission girls' gang. We tough Latino girls were not very tough, usually a year of cutting school, then pregnant. I didn't want that kind of trouble, so I got into worse. Burglary. The fence raped me. I put a knife into him. Then I stole a car and drove until I ran out of gas. I kept going, hitchhiking, all the way to Canada."

"You were only fourteen?"

"Fifteen by then. I was big, I looked older. I got a job waiting on tables in Victoria. All the people looked so different from what I knew, all...Scotch, little schoolgirls in plaid uniforms. It was another world. I was so lonely, I started to read. That's all I could afford, library books and, in those long winters...well, I read a lot."

"How could you stand it, alone?"

"Well, I was hiding out. I thought I had killed that man. I had..." She laughed. "...a very exaggerated idea of my importance to the San Francisco police. I expected them or the Royal Canadian Mounted Police or the CIA to show up any day and take me back. So for almost five years all I did was wait on table, afraid to talk to anyone, then go to the library and get books. An old-fashioned library, few new books, dark-bound sets of Emerson, Hazlitt, Ruskin, Montaigne."

Suddenly I understood why Yolanda wrote like a nineteenth-century Englishman, but talked and looked like a waitress in a Mexican restaurant.

"Everything changed with Vietnam. I answered an ad for a cook in a boarding house. It turned out to be a half-way house run by Quakers for American draft evaders. I met new kinds of people, all kinds of people came there, not just the men escaping the draft. They taught me not to be ashamed that I never got past the ninth grade. They were my school, my university. I wrote a newsletter for them, my first writing. I met Dick. He came up to counsel men who wanted to come back home. I was ready to come back home too. I'd been away almost fifteen years. My folks were out in Daly City. The Mission had changed, not just the book stores, Jessie, money moving in. Pretty soon poor people won't be able to afford to live here. If we hadn't bought this building when we did..."

"So you came back and started a publishing house!"

"Oh, no, when I came back, I had no idea...I started a little writing workshop at the community center. You see, life on this side of Mission Street is still the same for a lot of kids, especially for girls. I wanted to help them see they could do more. It was when

I tried to get their writing published...so, one thing led to another and..." She put down the rag and looked at the old machine, shrugging and shaking her head.

"What about your own writing? How did you first get published?"

"India. She got me published. After that I never had any trouble. I started writing about my workshops, but then got into other problems of publishing, writing."

"I loved your hatchet job on that phony agency."

Yolanda laughed, making almost no sound, but her plump body shook all over. "I shut them down," she said proudly.

Just then the screams coming in through the windows above us got louder, and even Yolanda noticed. "Maybe we should go upstairs and talk. Peggy, you're okay without me for a while?" The hood of hair hanging over the light box bobbed up and down a couple of times, so we went out the front door, locking it behind us, then around to a stairway on the side of the building.

The apartment upstairs had been remodeled. "We did it ourselves, took about four years." She showed me two tiny rooms in the back, studies for her and Dick, full of books, files, more old school desks, another even smaller room with their bed in it. Then the rest of the place, with walls taken out, all kitchen, dominated by a long table under sunny windows. "For meetings, meals, whatever. And that little room..." She pointed to a door in the corner. "...is Armando's room. I keep saying he should have the back bedroom, but he wants to be where it's happening, he says."

"You have a son?"

She nodded. "Almost eight years old."

"And you can do all this...writing, publishing..."

"Well, it's easier now, he's in school. And Dick helps." She smiled, tilted her head and grinned as we sat down to the table. "Marry a WASP, that's my advice, if you want children. WASP men help. Fewer macho-mama hangups."

"What about a Jew?" I was ready to defend my father.

She thought about that, then gave me a slow nod. "*Quién sabe*? Most are as bad as Italians. But when you get a good one..."

"Like Reuben Wonder?"

"Well, you won't find one that perfect very often!" She started to laugh, but then she must have remembered, and her smile disappeared.

"Why did Reuben say that? When India collapsed, I mean, he said you did it." I tried to watch her face carefully for reaction, but she had turned slightly to one side.

"It was my article, I guess."

"What article?"

"Criticizing India. She was hurt. Angry. Upset. At that moment when she died, he thought it was her heart, so he blamed me, I guess."

"I don't remember any article. If you had written something about her, I'm sure I would have seen it. Where was it published?"

"It wasn't." She was looking at me again, and her lips were tight. "No one would touch it. After trying the national magazines, I tried the little literary quarterlies. One of them sent a copy to India. I guess she was furious. Scared too."

"Scared? Of something you wrote? What could you. . ."

"Want a copy? You can have it." She shrugged. "It'll never be published anyway now."

"Why not?"

"The necessity is gone. India is gone."

"I don't understand. Are you telling me you wrote something destructive to India? Something to hurt her? How could you. . ."

She just looked at me for a long time, the way she had when I said how wonderful and exciting the Mission District was, the way you look at someone who has such a long way to go that you get tired just thinking about all they have to learn. "Look, Jessie, I loved India. When I wrote to her ten years ago, about my work here, she came right out. Those kids had never seen anything like her. She hugged them. She cried. She set those wild gray eyes on them and told them they were all pure divine fire inside, burning to get out. Have you ever seen her do that number?" I nodded. "It was great, just what I wanted, what they needed. Then she got my article about the workshop published. She gave us a jacket blurb for the first book we published.

"I owe a lot to India. That's why I held back my article on her for almost a year. I knew it would hurt her. I didn't know it would make her mad enough to screw our whole project." Yolanda's face changed in front of me, going from sadness to fury, dark and heavy and grim, and more scary than Jane's anger, even more scary than Carla. She bit her lip and blinked as if she had said more than she meant to. Then she shrugged and went on. "In the past month we lost two of our grants. Not renewed, after years of getting them. We counted on them. There's less money, I know, so maybe there's no connection, but..."

"Connection? With India? How could there be?" She shook her head at me as if she couldn't believe how far I was from reality. "How do you think decisions are made? Boards controlling funds contact literary people, teachers, critics, famous writers. India had become very powerful. It wasn't a lot of money, but without it... I can't ask Dick to put more of what he makes into...if she did it...." Her eyes had turned a hard, shiny obsidian black, and one of her plump hands was clenched into a fist. Suddenly she got up, scraping her chair as she pushed it out of the way and left the room. I just sat there thinking about what she had said.

When she came back, she was carrying a big envelope. "Take my article home and read it. You can keep it. I have no more use for it." She didn't sit down again, just stood there looking at me, and when she spoke again, her voice was gentle enough, but cold, and all the Spanish sounds didn't sound soft anymore. "I guess you have what you came for."

I hadn't fooled her either, not for long. While she watched me, I stood, and I had to look into her face. When I did, and saw the way she was watching me, I understood how she could have been head of the only girl gang in the Mission District.

25.

Monday night is usually quiet in the restaurant, and this one was quieter than usual. So when Jim showed up before nine o'clock, Mom and Dad said I could quit early and go out with him if I wanted to. We walked outside, but I wasn't sure I wanted to be with him. I was in a bad mood, and the easy way he put his arm around me only made it worse. "Where shall we go?"

"Well, unless you have more laundry to do or want to sit in your car or walk in the rain..." It wasn't really raining yet, just dropping a sprinkle now and then, not enough to wet the streets. "...I guess we'll just go to your place. I thought I'd suggest it and save you the trouble of working up to it." I was really feeling mean.

"Okay," he said, dropping his arm. We got into the car, and he drove down Grove Street. It took me a minute to realize that we were going to the police station. He parked in the lot, then took me in through a side door and up the stairs to a back office, then through that to a smaller room where I saw a sleeping bag on the floor behind a row of file cabinets. "My place. I've been trying to find a room I can afford, but so far this is it. Want to see my etchings?"

I almost laughed, loosening my hold on my bad mood a little. Then I went behind the file cabinet and sat down on the sleeping bag, my back propped up against the corner wall. Jim came and sat beside me. We stretched out our legs, and he flopped part of the sleeping bag over mine. It was dark back there, and we could hear office sounds all around us, phone rings and ratchety office-machine noises and sometimes voices.

"What happens if your superior comes in and finds us?"

"I'm off duty." He certainly was. He wore a striped T-shirt under a wool sweater, a tan, bulky, soft thing that made him feel like a pillow to sink into. "Now tell me what I did to make you mad at me."

"Nothing. I'm not mad at you. Just mad. Bothered. I saw Yolanda Dolores today. She gave me an article to read, about India."

"What does it say?"

"I haven't read it yet. I could have read it on the bus. Or even at work tonight; the restaurant was quiet. But. . . I keep putting it off."

"Why?"

"I must be afraid of what it will say."

"Nasty, eh? I've heard sometimes writers bitch at each other like. . ."

"Not Yolanda Dolores. No malice. She writes cool and plain. Earnest, they call her. Like Emerson." I wasn't sure whether to tell Jim how Yolanda learned to write that way. I'd forgotten to ask Yolanda if she'd squared everything with the local police. "But effective. She wrote an article about a famous poet once, demolished her. Everything Yolanda writes is so carefully. . . reasoned and documented, so like a. . . a final verdict. I felt sorry for that poet, even though I guess she had it coming."

"India Wonder didn't. . . have it coming?"

I hesitated, trying to figure out my own feelings. "Well, you have to write whatever you think is true, of course, but it doesn't seem right to...after all India did for her..."

Jim put his arm around me, and this time it felt good. "Are you afraid you'll agree with whatever she says?" I didn't answer. "By the way, I called Wonder's publisher today to see if we could get a look at their copy of the manuscript. They say they haven't received it yet. Have been expecting it, thought it would be there by now. They're putting a tracer on it. You know the post office."

Nodding, I brushed my cheek against his fuzzy wool. "I might as well be telling these people I'm working with you. I don't seem to fool anyone. Yolanda wasn't fooled. Not for long. When I start asking the real questions, it must be written all over my face."

"Did you find out anything?"

"A motive? India knew about the article, maybe stopped it from being published, maybe stopped Yolanda from getting some grants for her publishing house."

"Could India do that?"

"According to Yolanda, yes. She had a lot of power."

"Anything else?"

"I forgot to tell you. I got a phone call. Whisperer. Said 'you next.' I couldn't recognize the voice." Jim didn't react at all, just kept fingering a lock of my hair. "Did you hear me?"

"Mm-hm." I felt him nodding against the top of my head. "You're fired."

"What?"

"Off the case. I don't want you to go around asking any more questions."

"Because of one phone call? The others got phone calls too."

"I know. Maybe whoever it is, is after everyone. Maybe not, maybe only one or two, trying to confuse things by calling everyone. Maybe only trying to scare you off. You said you didn't fool anyone, they all knew you were working on the case. It's hard to figure out. Illogical. But murder is illogical. Maybe there's no danger. But I want you to lay off asking questions for a few days. Let me do it."

"But I'm just beginning to learn enough to know what questions to ask."

"You'll see everyone again at the seance. And didn't you say you were having all of them to the restaurant to work on a mailing?"

118

"Right. Wednesday night."

"Okay. So Wednesday night at the restaurant, Saturday night at the seance. Keep your eyes and ears open and your mouth shut. Especially, stop asking questions about the manuscript of the new book."

"Why?"

"If the phone call was meant to scare you off...from what? From asking questions? From locating the manuscript? I've been assuming that the killer took it from India's room that night. But maybe not. Maybe the killer is still trying to locate it, afraid you will first. If that's possible, my guess is that it's either in the mail on the way to her publisher or India hadn't mailed it yet, and it's hidden somewhere."

"Hidden?"

"You said she was very secretive about it, wouldn't let anyone see it. I guess it's time to have a crew go through that whole house, top to bottom. Maybe it's a waste of time, maybe the killer already took and destroyed it. But I'll give it a try. And you...you're fired. I don't want you to seem like the least bit of a threat to anyone. I want you to lose interest in this case, as far as they know. Just forget about it."

"Okay." I sighed...with relief. I hadn't realized how much I wished I could do just that, forget about it. That was why I had felt so bitchy. I was fed up with all the anger and malice running through the relationships of India and her friends. If this was the life of a great writer...I thought back to the night of the party to compare what I knew now with what I thought then. But I wasn't thinking then, I was feeling, and I couldn't feel those feelings. They were gone.

I raised my head to look at Jim. His face was quiet, attentive, waiting. I guessed he wanted to be kissed, so I did. Twice. Three, four times, soft and short.

"I have an idea," he said.

"I'll bet you do."

"No, I mean...could you take tomorrow off? That's Tuesday, then Wednesday the restaurant is closed, right? I know someone who has a place up on the coast, near Jenner. You could go up there tonight and stay until Wednesday, come back for the mailing party."

"Am I in that much danger?"

"Probably not, but if you were up there I wouldn't worry."

"I don't have a car."

"Wait a minute." He got up and left the room. I leaned back against the wall, listening to the buzzing and scraping in the adjoining offices, drowsy sounds. He was only gone for a few minutes, but I had almost dozed off by the time he came back.

He pulled me to my feet. "Let's go."

"Where?"

"Back to tell your folks while you pack. Then we'll come back here and get a city car for you."

"And I go to Jenner tonight?"

He nodded. "You can be there in less than two hours. I have a map, keys, everything. I go up there a lot. No one ever uses the place, but I called my friend just in case. It's clear now."

Back at the restaurant I let Jim explain to Mom and Dad while I stuffed a pack with clothes and reading material, including Yolanda's article. As an antidote to it, I put in *Emma Pride's Journal,* so that rereading it would bring back some of the inspiration I'd lost in the past week. Of course, I put in my own journal; I would have a lot of thoughts to sort out and write down.

Mom and Dad tried not to look worried, said they had just the girl they wanted to try out in my place. Jim told them, "I'm going to try very hard to get this thing settled before Jessie comes back." They nodded and gave me a hug before we left.

At the police station lot, Jim put my pack into the car and handed me the keys and the map.

"You forgot something," I told him. "You were going to hypnotize me. Maybe I saw something important that I can't remember, and the killer knows it."

Jim nodded. "I'm going to drive up tomorrow afternoon, soon as I get the search crew started on India's house. I'll hypnotize you then." And he gave me a funny smile. Anticipatory. I drove away wondering if all this was partly a way to get me to a beach house where Jim could join me for a romantic night.

If that was his plan, it never worked out that way. As I was driving out of the parking lot, a report was coming into the station. A sniper stood on the roof of the Wells Fargo Bank on Shattuck Avenue. It took two days to bring him down, with Jim and every other cop in the East Bay on duty the whole time.

26.

THE EMPRESS HAS NO CLOTHES
by
Yolanda Dolores

Nearly twenty years ago India Wonder's first and only book was published. *Emma Pride's Journal* is a novel, a work of fiction written as the journal of a woman who desperately struggles against obstacles which stop her from writing. These obstacles are economic, social, political, psychological. Indeed the book dramatizes almost every hindrance to the survival and expression of talent in the artist, particularly the woman artist. This fact is both the strength and the weakness of the book. Like *Uncle Tom's Cabin* it is a melodrama, presenting the many facets of struggle, a catalog of abuses against humanity, a political tract. Like *Uncle Tom's Cabin* its passion and conviction lift it above its faults. Indeed I want to state unequivocally that the first forty pages and the conclusion of *Emma Pride's Journal* stand above *Uncle Tom's Cabin* and equal to the best in American literature.

One impressive quality of *Emma Pride's Journal* has been its continuing immediacy. Over and over again, I have heard young women, freshly discovering the book, insist that it is new or (since India Wonder's name has been truly a household word for some time) that it was published four or five years ago at most.

Another false assumption is that the book is not a work of fiction but an actual journal, India Wonder's journal. This mistake, like the continuing freshness of the story, could be a tribute to the art of the author. It is also attributable to the first person narrative, which gives an immediacy and intensity which readers sometimes mistake for "real" experience. Furthermore, as in the case of many first novels, there are elements of Wonder's actual life, used as points of departure for characters and incidents, which undergo exaggeration, rearrangement, or even drastic change. Probably some confusion of fiction with autobiography in the minds of unsophisticated readers is inevitable.

That it should become crucial is a peculiarity of our times. I do not write fiction, but I am sympathetic to the complaints of writers like Jane Lee who tell me they are constantly correcting readers' assumptions that a work of fiction parallels the author's life. Writers like Lee gradually make their point and lessen their identification (in the mind of readers) with their characters, as they publish further books. Probably the same would have happened in the case of India Wonder, had she published more.

What has happened is quite the reverse. The book has become generally accepted as an actual journal, detailing the facts of Wonder's life. This error has been spread by insistent readers, but could not have survived and grown without the compliance of Wonder herself. Surely her identification with the thwarted heroine of her book was already complete when I met her over ten years ago, and I have never asked her certain questions. Did she try to deny this identification in the beginning and only gradually stop denying it? Did she forget and become convinced that her life and her fiction were one? Or did she find the rewards of total identification with her fictional heroine were too tempting to pass up?

Consider the rewards. India Wonder has received more cash awards, fellowships, honorary degrees and prizes than any other living woman author. A bibliography of interviews, graduate theses, critical studies, profiles, eulogies, excerpts in anthologies and references to her book in studies of contemporary American literature would be hopeless to compile (though no doubt some graduate students are making the attempt at this very moment). Indeed, the more time elapses without further production from India Wonder, the more honors she gathers.

What is wrong with this? Am I envious of her ability to manipulate the system which dispenses literary honors and money? If she is a "woman of one book," what is wrong with honoring her for that book? Furthermore, has she not used her power to benefit people like me, to help other writers, and most of all to recognize the long-suppressed creative potential of women?

The answer to this last question is a resounding yes. My first contact with India Wonder came ten years ago when she brought her inspiring presence to my Mission Writers' Community Workshop, used her influence to get financial support for it, and arranged for publication of my first articles. I am one of many writers who owe an enormous debt to her.

Nevertheless, it is time, past time, I think, to point out the less beneficial effects she has had on writers and readers, especially women. One obvious problem has been her virtual monopoly on attention and support which might be spread among other worthy writers.

A more serious disservice Wonder has done to young writers is as a model of style. As a first novel *Emma Pride's Journal* has many virtues, imbedded in stylistic excesses, particularly in the latter half of the book, which is overwritten, sentimental, self-indulgent prose which some good editor might have deflated and trimmed, to the benefit of readers and imitative writers. I have no intention of naming writers who are disciples of Wonder; it is unnecessary to point specifically to the many loosely conceived and carelessly executed books written clearly under the influence of Wonder's early prose style and printed by publishers hoping (so far in vain) to create more best-selling clones of the famous "journal."

But these are nothing compared to the unpublished imitations. I am tired of fighting with the young women who come to my community workshop, each carrying her copy of *Emma Pride's Journal,* each writing her own sloppy, self-indulgent imitation of its worst faults, in unconscious parody of them.

I used to believe such imitation was a necessary stage in learning to write. I believed Wonder's book would liberate young writers by raising their consciousness about the forces which had been suppressing their own creative powers. I believed the fad for the book would wear itself out. But years have gone by and the book continues to be presented to me as a new discovery, packaged in the fulsome praise of the literary establishment, and therefore legitimizing sloppy writing, making it impervious to criticism. That is why I have decided to speak out strongly, to state the weaknesses of Wonder's first, uneven effort, lest it become a standard which will damage the work of a whole generation of writers, if it has not already done so.

It could even hinder the production of any work, of whatever quality. Again, I speak from my experience with the young people who come to my workshop. Again and again, I must remind them that we come together to examine each other's work and that of great writers, to help each other to write better, to talk about writing— not to talk about not-writing. Again and again, discussion veers off into complaints about obstacles facing the woman artist, sprinkled with quotations from Wonder's novel. Within limits, such discussion has value, but like all consciousness raising, it has no use unless it leads to action, to change. Prolonged, it becomes what it complains of, an obstacle, a waste of precious time and energy.

Ultimately I see these complaints creating an ugly mood among women, one which, as a Latin woman, I recognize all too well. It is an ancient mood of bitterness grown out of attempts at resignation, the mood in which a woman devotes herself wholly to the service of others, service given with an air of self-sacrifice and resentment that poisons whatever she does, crippling those she serves with guilt and anger and the sense that nothing they do can ever make up for the sacrifice of a human being (as indeed it cannot). The new women's movement, I thought, was to free women and their families from this terrible trap. Are we instead to have a new version of it, in which women are silently (or not so silently) telling their loved ones, especially their children, "I could have been a great artist, but for you"?

This attitude is not only ignoble, it is simply, in the vast majority of cases, false. Most women (and men) would not become artists regardless of what helped or hindered them. Few of the young people who come to my workshop will make writing the center of their lives. My hope is that they will learn more about themselves and their world, that they will sharpen their perceptions, that they will touch in themselves that universal talent which makes them kin to the artist, and that they will enjoy some moments of what India Wonder's heroine (in the quite beautiful conclusion of the novel) called "the play and prayer of the word."

There are other important things to do in this world besides writing books or painting pictures or dancing or making music, though I would wish people to have some experience with all the arts. It is out of respect for all the other necessary functions of living that I most strongly condemn the enshrinement of India Wonder and whatever her book stands for in the minds of so many readers. There is something in this idol worship that denigrates the very people Wonder's book is supposed to inspire.

I spend much of my time with these people, women with hard lives and few opportunities. I wish I could change the world to broaden their lives, and I do work for change. But until great changes come, the most creative work, the greatest power these women have, lies in the rearing of their own children. To tell them that they could all be artists, but for their children, is to denigrate what may be their best opportunity, the most meaningful work they are allowed to do.

It is a lie, and it is a betrayal of the function of the artist, who should act as a voice for people. To set that voice above what it expresses is a perversion of art.

Can we blame India Wonder for this perversion? She only wrote a book. She did not hold a gun to the heads of television interviewers, literary critics and foundations. She did not force women to read the book and to identify with it so closely as to lose themselves. She only wrote a book. Who did the rest?

The literary and media establishment is owned and run by men. In a recent article in *Literary Review* ("Broken Wing Prose: Still Putting Out for the Boys") I explored the work of two of our most promoted and reviewed women writers, pointing out similarities of style, tone and content, stories of edge-of-sanity drifters written in a style I called Cracked Female Macho. My thesis was that these women were honored for their appeal to the diehard prejudices among those men who ultimately decide what is to be published and promoted.

If this thesis has any validity, it casts new light on the sacred position of India Wonder. What more appealing candidate (to threatened men) for fame as a woman artist than the woman who writes a novel about not being able to write at all, then becomes the living embodiment of her own heroine by producing nothing further after this first eloquent cry of pain? What more comforting confirmation of all the prejudices about the "weaker sex" than this evidence of the battle lost, the woman whose only creation is her admission of defeat?

Yet, if the male publishing establishment places anything above its prejudices, it is its profits. And its power does have limits. It can create a reputation overnight, but it cannot sustain it for twenty years. It is the market, the women buyers, who have sustained and inflated Wonder's reputation, and it makes me sick to admit this, for I must conclude that this worship is a sign of a failure of nerve in women, a turning of obstacles into excuses, into a female Walter Mitty daydream, into yet another soap opera to drug women into self-pitying passivity.

If women are to recognize this danger and turn away from it, India Wonder herself must stop accepting her false position.

Wonder could simply call herself a "woman of one book," acknowledging the fame she has achieved and asserting her happiness in using it (as she surely has) to help other artists. This would

mean she must speak out and admit that for the past twenty years
she has received every possible encouragement and help, yet has re-
mained unproductive despite her freedom from the adverse conditions described in a novel which, paradoxically, was written under
those very conditions.

But, as a matter of fact, Wonder is not a woman of one book.
Everyone knows that she has been working on another novel for
some years, a book that has been scheduled and rescheduled for release, but which at the last moment, she has always withheld for
further revision. We have heard enough about this book to know
that it is very different from *Emma Pride's Journal*, though it
draws again on the author's experience, that it is said to be a biting
satire on the world of women writers. I wonder if it might not even
say some of the very things I have been writing here. For those of
us who know India Wonder personally know that beyond the
yearning "Emma Pride" identity, there is a complex, witty, assertive, even contradictory person, capable of writing books very
different from *Emma Pride's Journal*.

What really has held back publication of this second novel? I
cannot indict the male publishers; I am sure they want to cash in on
Wonder's popularity. Rewriting is an easy excuse for holding back
a book— one could rewrite indefinitely.

Could it be that India Wonder is afraid to publish this book?
Second novels seldom gain critical acclaim, especially when the
writer takes chances, goes off in a new direction, not simply repeating an earlier success. The higher the praise for the first novel,
the more likely the second is to be panned if not damned. And who
stands higher than India Wonder? The temptation to leave things
as they are, to go on as the symbol of the thwarted woman artist,
to avoid risking what may be a terrible fall—I think I do understand her fear.

But I also think India Wonder underestimates her admirers.
Surely some will be disappointed, some will even say that she has
betrayed women with her satire. She will be misunderstood—
again. But all this will be nothing to the benefits she can give to
those who are ready to receive them, ready to go beyond *Emma
Pride's Journal* and look at another part of the truth.

126

27.

After I read Yolanda's article, I went outside and stood near the edge of the cliff. The ocean was bright blue and white under the lighter blue sky. A stiff wind blew. Hot sun, cold wind. The two of them together, burning and chilling. I looked down at the water and couldn't tell whether the tide was coming in or going out.

The night before, I drove up there in the dark, found my way inside the cabin with a flashlight, crawled onto a wooden bunk, and fell asleep. During the hours around midnight the ocean brought itself in with a roaring and rumbling like a movement of the earth. It would happen every few minutes, a slow, gathering roar that built up and up, but then lost its force in waves that scattered on the rocks below.

Now I looked down the cliffs, through all the gouges and gullies and jagged rock left from the tearing of the waves, and thought that long ago the ocean had roared in and in and in like that and had taken away what it could. Now it went on gathering itself up and roaring in, but the land that was left was out of its reach. For now. For last night. Maybe this winter, maybe tonight, it would build up the great wave that could reach out and take another chunk of land, maybe this whole piece.

Before coming out I had checked the original publication date in my copy of *Emma Pride's Journal*. Yolanda was right, Antonia Moran had been right, it was first printed nineteen years ago. I was one of those readers Yolanda said discovered the book as if it had been written yesterday. Did that matter? Yes, for this book, it did matter.

What about the rest of Yolanda's article? It gave me too many things to think about. I couldn't seem to pick one at a time. They floated around in my ignorance like noodle letters in alphabet soup, slipping away when I tried to arrange them into words that made sense.

I turned away from the ocean, walking between the tool shed and the outhouse, past the water pump, back to the cabin. It was only one narrow room, with one small window, a table, two chairs, three bunks, and a wood stove that was starting to get good and hot. Plain shelter, built small and snug to keep out the wind off that ocean. I heated water on the stove, found a jar of instant coffee and a can of applesauce for my breakfast. Then I set a chair under the window and began to reread *Emma Pride's Journal.*

It began with Emma at sixteen (the same age I was when I first read it) running away from parents who discouraged her writing. The black man she fell in love with had parts of Richard Wright and Paul Robeson all mixed up with Heathcliff and Othello. Their life together was all burning passion, till it burned out, or exploded, and she was left alone with her daughter.

Next came the struggle for survival, the Depression, and my favorite scene. It made me cry just as it had the first time I read it: Emma, with her baby wrapped in an old coat, haunting the back of a warehouse where bits of crating might be dropped, filling a sack to bring home and burn in the stove in their basement room. Then the succession of jobs, the pain of leaving her daughter with a stranger, the humiliating time as a servant, slave really, in a house where at least she could keep her daughter with her.

Then the war, better jobs, and her marriage to the Jewish refugee, brilliant but crazed by horror, carrying his suicide pill with him from his days as a commando, his "ticket out" just in case he should decide that tomorrow was the day to die. "One man deserted me, but this one will never leave me, God help me."

Political work gives him something to live for, and he draws her in. She believes, she works hard. There is the housekeeping, the two more children, the endless meetings, picketing, petitions. She tries to revive her writing by taking a class, where the professor encourages her only in order to seduce her, feeding his own vanity before dropping her for another conquest. She begins again, but her aging parents write for help, and she takes a part-time job. Later, other jobs pay for orthodontia, music lessons, endless therapy for her husband.

Persistently, at night, when everyone else is asleep, she sits awake and tries to write. Until the day her party group tells her that her writing is politically incorrect and that she must write something "useful." A leaflet. A child's life of Lenin. She tries, rebels, is expelled. But writing remains "that which I do in the dark hours, an unspeakable self-indulgence, doomed to fragmentation by divided attention, interruptions, fatigue, guilt, done with the remnant of feeble breath left after the seizure of my best energies to

feed the lives of others.'' The journal stops abruptly at her for-
tieth birthday when she leaves her husband and teenage sons, ''in
the perhaps vain hope that there is something left in me to salvage,
to develop, to recreate.''

It took me all day to read it. I read slowly and attentively, sometimes going back over parts. I read aware of structure. I read checking points of it against what I now knew about India's life. I read
with a lot more reading and writing experience than I'd had at
sixteen.

Of course it was fiction! I didn't see how I could have mistaken
it for a real journal. Some parts of it came out of India's life, but
she had changed them to support the theme of frustrated talent.
All the parts that did not fit and support that theme were left out.
But that's what writing fiction *is*. Why did it seem to me to be lying?

An artist lies in order to tell the truth, Picasso said.

''But what if the lies don't feel like truth?''

Then the artist has failed.

''But the first time I read it, it felt like truth, and now. . .''

Sometimes the reader has failed.

''But how can I tell whether. . .'' I stopped arguing with Picasso
and went outside to watch the sunset.

I stood on the edge of the cliff, now facing the sun, my eyes almost closed against the blinding gold shimmer spreading across
the cold waves. The sea smoothing out to the horizon reminded
me that the huge, pure, impersonal realities were still going on,
beyond my petty worries. That soothed me, but as usual the peaceful feeling deepened down into sadness. The ocean almost always
leaves me feeling sad, convinced that I'll never measure up to this,
and worse, that I keep forgetting to try. It makes me wish that I
could compose timeless, wordless music, instead of writing about
the small cruelties of short lives.

I started walking along the cliff edge, my left side catching some
warmth from the sun, my right side chilled. I could go only a few
yards before coming to deep gouges and gullies that fell off into
the ocean, so I would turn and walk back. I paced back and forth
on that strip of sandy rock, showing first my right, then my left
side to the cooling, fading light. And I judged India Wonder's book.

Yolanda had been kind to it. There were some good pages in the
beginning. But it was not a good book. It was sentimental and overwritten. It was all off balance, covering too long a period for its

length, with too many events and changes to fit convincingly into one person's life. Emma, who had seemed so wonderful, so heroic when I first read the book, now seemed too self-pitying and self-centered. How could I have identified with her so completely? My only excuse was that, well, I was only sixteen at the time.

I paced until the ocean was all gray and the glow at the horizon was cold and weak. I was cold too, and I ached all over, right up to my eyes, which ached most of all, maybe from all that reading, maybe because I, for some stupid reason, needed to cry. Tears came and were blown dry by the wind, before they even reached my cheeks. I hadn't cried at the funeral of India Wonder, so I was crying now. For me, she had died all over again. Or had she been dead a long time without my knowing it? Maybe I wasn't crying about a death at all. The woman who had died wasn't my India Wonder. My India Wonder had never existed.

28.

I spent Wednesday morning pacing the cliffs and the rest of the day driving slowly down the coast, stopping at Bolinas to eat and wait for the commuter traffic on the bridges to die down.

By the time I got back to Berkeley, it was dark, and the restaurant was so full of people that for a minute I thought I must have lost a day, and this must be Thursday. But the front door was locked, so I knew it was still Wednesday. I went through the alley and came in the back door, through the kitchen.

Five tables had been pulled together, piled high with papers and envelopes, zip code guide, staplers. Carla Neeland was in charge, giving orders from the far end of the tables where she sat above the others, up on my father's cashier stool. Around the tables sat women and girls stuffing envelopes. The girls had driven across the bay with Yolanda. They were still in high school, writers from Yolanda's workshop. They were excited and impressed at working with "real" writers on India's memorial, and they made me feel about a thousand years old.

Of course, this would be the night that all four of my brothers turned up, kids and all, so that the rest of the tables were full of family. They chewed on chunks of fruit, my father poured green tea for everyone, the kids played tag around the tables, and everybody talked at once.

My mother and Yolanda stood together in the middle of all this. "Guess what, Yolanda and I have a lot of friends in common." Mom, of course, knew most of the Quakers Yolanda had met in Canada.

"You didn't tell me John and Jennifer Wellson are your grandparents," said Yolanda. "They were the patron saints of the movement up there."

I nodded as Mom went to pick up three-year-old George, who had fallen and was starting to howl.

"Did you read my article?"

I nodded again.

"You think I shouldn't have said those things about India."

I didn't want to talk about it. "I'm surprised everyone came to do this...this shitwork. People like Jane have more important things to do."

Yolanda shook her head. "You don't understand. It's hard to express grief. This is one way. To work together...it's one way to show our love for India."

I didn't want to talk about that either. "Excuse me, I haven't seen my brothers for a couple of weeks." I went to sit with the family and learn the latest news. One set of nieces had just gotten over chicken pox, my brother Steve had a new job, Rob and his wife were back together again, Helene was pregnant, and Will's family might go to live in Hawaii. And the sniper was still on top of the Wells Fargo building.

"Your friend Jim is there," said my father. "He was interviewed on the news last night."

I just nodded. My mother was watching me the way she used to when I was coming down with a cold and she knew it before I did. I started to apologize for filling up the restaurant with people on my folks' day off, but I could see they were enjoying themselves.

Together we drifted over to the tables where the work on the mailing was going on. I was surprised to see that even Pamela Righbottom was there, stuffing envelopes and talking to Yolanda's girls about real seasons and the *New York Times* and how they must all get scholarships to good eastern colleges. I heard my mother ask softly, "Is that the way you talked when you came?"

My father winced. "I suspect I did."

"Without ever listening?"

My father rocked his head and grinned. "We don't mean to be rude. We just need time and. . ."

"Civilizing." My mother giggled and drew him back to the family. I stood behind Pamela for a minute. She felt my presence, stopped talking and turned, nodded at me. She seemed friendly enough, so I spoke, said I didn't expect her to want to be bothered doing this kind of work. She looked up at me, lifted those heavy eyebrows and said, "Carla and I have so little time left together, I just. . ." I swear there were tears in her eyes. I was too amazed to say any more.

I picked up one of the flyers. It announced the memorial tribute to India Wonder sponsored by six organizations including Yolanda's community writers' workshop. The program was listed more or less as Carla had planned it, with the addition of several very famous names called "sponsors." It wasn't clear from the program whether or not they were all going to speak.

"What do you think?" Yolanda was looking over my shoulder. She seemed to be following me around. I just nodded and moved around the tables to sit down in the only place that was left, beside Celeste Wildpower, who had tied up her orange hair under a green scarf that matched her eyelids. Right away she asked me when I was coming to see her to start training my spiritual powers.

Antonia Moran, sitting directly across the table, heard her, shook her head at me, then started puffing smokey accusations at Celeste about ". . .young people being pulled off into all these freaky cults instead of committing themselves to real solutions to the problems of this world."

Celeste raised her hands, fluttering them to wave away the smoke, like the sign of an evil spell. "I haven't noticed that your political organizations have led to any solutions." Antonia sputtered and puffed back at her, but Celeste waved away her smoke and her words. "You won't listen so you'll never understand the politics of spirituality." Antonia snorted, while Jane asked in a soft, wickedly innocent voice if that was the title of Celeste's next book. While Celeste bit her lip, Antonia laughed, inhaled on a cigarette and attacked again. I watched as they fought over my soul (although Antonia wouldn't have admitted I had one) as if either of them could decide for me what to do with it. Yolanda's girls just kept their eyes lowered or tuned in on the conversation at the other end of the table.

That was where Carla Neeland and Margot Stackpole sat talking about suing Doubledom. "Look," Carla was saying, "publishers are *always* breaking contracts; it's time someone did something about it."

Margot shook her head. "I don't have any money to..."

"Yolanda's *husband* might do it for a share of the settlement. If you *don't* get anything, you don't have to pay him."

"I thought you were against hiring male lawyers."

"There *are* exceptions."

Yolanda looked up from the zip code book. "You'd get *mucho* support from every writer who's ever complained about her publisher, which means just about every writer. But Doubledom let you keep the advance, didn't they? Dick says they'd call that sufficient compensation."

"Doesn't matter," Carla insisted. "Sue. Properly organized a suit could get you *far* more support for your book than it could *ever* get on its own."

Margot threw down the paper she was folding and burst into tears, shaking out her hair and throwing out her breasts as if her misery had to be projected to the second balcony. "You all think my book couldn't get attention any other way! India told you all that it was bad, she told everyone it was bad!"

Everyone stopped work, all except Jane. Everyone was watching Margot except Pamela, whose eyes were on Carla.

"I'm tired of being a joke, of people laughing at me behind my back. Now you want me to sue Doubledom just so you can use me..."

"Of *course* we want to use you," Carla said quietly, leaning over Margot from her high stool and coiling one arm around her shoulders. Something made me look at Pamela. She had frozen with an envelope in her hand. Her eyes blinked at Carla and Margot, and her face was pale. "But *you* get something out of it too. Publicity. Maybe even another *publisher*. Something that will *move* you to a fresh place. A new start."

Margot's tears disappeared as quickly as they had started. She and Carla lowered their voices and began planning strategy. I watched them leaning their heads together as their hands moved more slowly. Carla, so black and thin, sharp and intense, leaning sinuously over Margot, so pink and lush, like an overripe peach. I turned to sneak another look at Pamela, but she had disappeared, gone, left.

Someone was knocking on the front door. I could see through the glass that it was Sylvia March, hovering behind the glass like a lost ghost. I gestured, pointing around toward the alley entrance, but she just hung there until I got up and opened the door. "My baby-sitter was late! Then I got stuck at police barricades near Shattuck. You know that sniper is still up there!" She reeked of wine.

"Just in time to take my place," said Jane, getting up. "I have to go home now."

"It's only nine-thirty," breathed Celeste, as if the best hours were just starting.

Jane didn't answer, but Yolanda said it for her. "Jane was first to arrive, been here since seven. And she'll be first up and writing tomorrow." Jane gave everyone a silent wave and let my father usher her out through the alley.

For the next hour everyone talked about the sniper. One by one my brothers picked up their sleepy kids and left. Then Yolanda said she had promised not to get her girls home too late, so they all left, Antonia going along for the ride back to the City. Then Celeste decided it was time for her to go, so Carla scooped up all the flyers, envelopes, phone books, lists, and Margot. By eleven everyone was gone.

I went upstairs and pulled the TV out of the closet. Maybe I was too late for news of the sniper. All I got was an earthquake in Brazil, another murder in Oakland, a dog story, a new political scandal, a small oil spill, an airline accident and dozens of commercials.

When the phone rang, I was sure it was Jim. I planned to tell him that I had decided to quit writing and marry some nice man, maybe him.

But it wasn't Jim. It was the silence. "What do you want?" No answer, of course. "Yes, I'm back now, is it still me next?" Nothing but silence. "You sick bitch!" I yelled. "Save your calls for the others! Reduce your phone bill and hire a shrink! I'm off the case. I couldn't care less who killed India Wonder!"

29.

The sniper came down sometime during the night, and Jim showed up at the restaurant at ten a.m. ready to hypnotize me. "My people went through Wonder's house from top to bottom and didn't find anything except for the manuscripts in her room, and you had already been through those, right?"

"Right."

"What's the matter with you?"

"Nothing."

He looked at me for a minute. I just looked back at him. He was wearing that suit again, with a tie and all, a close shave around his sideburns. But his skin was yellowish pale and his eyes were red. I guess he hadn't slept much since the last time I saw him. "I guess you're disappointed because I promised to wrap up this case, but I had that sniper."

"Yeah. Okay. We go to your office?"

He shook his head. "That place is a madhouse. Some place where we can be quiet."

"Upstairs in my room?"

"If that's comfortable for you."

I took him up the stairs and into my room, closing the door behind us. He looked around, at my bed, at the bookshelves covering the walls, at my desk and chair, then at me. He looked uncertain. "Are you sure you're in the mood for this?" When I didn't answer, he said, "Choose a comfortable place where you like to sit."

I plopped down on the bed, then scooted back to sit up against a pillow. He turned the chair around to face me and sat down on it.

"Now, is there a question you want to ask...about what hypnosis is?"

I shook my head. "Just go ahead."

But he went on as if I had asked a question. "It is just a state of deep relaxation. You know how sometimes you can't remember something, and then when you stop trying and just think of something else, it pops into your head. In hypnosis we just induce that state of relaxation where you can remember what you want to remember."

I nodded quickly. He was like a salesman with a spiel he just has to go through, even if you're already buying.

"Two things are necessary to a good hypnosis: motivation and expectation." He looked at me as if waiting for an answer. "Motivation and expectation."

I nodded again. He didn't look convinced that I agreed.

"You have to want to remember and you have to believe that you can remember."

"Okay, okay."

"Okay." He sighed, really tired. "Now I'm going to ask you to put your hand out in front of your face. Palm away, looking at the back of your hand. Fingers together. Thumb separate. Look at your thumbnail, concentrate on it. Feel everything relaxing as you concentrate on your thumbnail. Feel your hand coming closer to your face, feel your fingers starting to spread, feel your eyelids getting heavy." He kept saying these same things over and over, but my hand wasn't moving closer and my eyelids didn't feel heavy and my fingers stayed glued together. His voice didn't sound like him, but not like someone else, in between, like him trying to sound like someone else.

I didn't want to sit there all day, so I tried to let my body go limp, tried to relax and not think about him as Jim but as a voice I didn't know. My fingers let go all at once and spread apart, but my hand was a long, long time coming close to my face. Finally Jim's voice said I could just let it drop into my lap. By that time my eyes had closed.

"Now I want you to think of something pleasant, easy, taking a walk, a pleasant walk, like along the marina. The air is fresh and the sky is blue. You're walking along and you look at the water and you look at those elegant, fancy restaurants that look out over..."

"No, I hate those places, hogging all that view of the water, serving that rotten, expensive food. When I was a kid the marina was open and free for everyone to..."

"Okay, okay." He tried to keep his voice soothing. I tried to go limp again. "You're walking up in Tilden Park on the road out from Inspiration Point. You like that walk." I let my head nod an inch. "That fine, broad road, all smooth asphalt so you don't have to watch where you walk. On your right is the side of the hill, on your left, you can look out on all of Berkeley. It's a clear day and you can see all across Berkeley to the bay, all across the bay to San

Francisco, beyond, beyond, blue sky, blue, all clear and beautiful, and everything is all right, and you feel just fine and so relaxed and so good and..." His voice kept getting in the way. If he just told me to think of that walk, I could do it, but his hypnotist voice kept nagging at me the way some people do when they go for a walk with me and can't keep quiet but have to tell me to look at the bird, look at the sky, and so on.

"Now there's a big balloon up in the sky, floating, a big red balloon, and a line from it is attached to your wrist. The big red balloon floats up there, lazy, light, floating far up there, and the line is tied to your wrist. It floats up and it gently tugs at your wrist, gently..."

Here we were again, back to trying to move that hand. He kept nagging at me about the big red balloon, and I kept trying to let go of my arm and let it float upward, but it sat there on the bed while he kept saying over and over that the balloon would go up, but I kept watching that balloon stuck, immobile, anchored to my two-ton wrist.

Very gradually the wrist began to lose weight, though not enough to float up without some help. I lifted it a little, just to encourage it, and it floated up another inch and I could hear Jim's breathing change as if he had just lifted my two-ton wrist, by himself, after straining for an hour.

"Now you're floating high above the city, the bay, the ocean, free, high in the balloon, gently, safely floating..."

"No, I'm not. You can't attach it to my wrist and expect me to suddenly jump into that balloon. You have to slide me up the wire or something, get me up there gradually. I'm still down here!"

Silence. "Okay." He sighed. "Let's try something else."

We tried deep pools and snowcapped peaks and cool green leaves. We tried sailboats and wings and a magic carpet and warm sands and the top of a redwood tree and the bottom of a deep valley by a shallow creek meandering silently over smooth blue pebbles. The creek dried up at the beginning of a stairway that went down, down, step by step, deeper and deeper, one level at a time, to deeper, darker depths into which I sank, sank, leaving my body behind.

"And at the bottom of these steps is a television set. You turn it on and you see India Wonder's house. You are a viewer, watching the party at India Wonder's house, on this screen. You can turn up the volume and you can adjust the picture to bring something in more clear. It is the night of the party. You turn on the television and you see..."

"I do not! I hate television. Why do you pick such banal images? Do you think I'm one of those people who sees life cramped down to the size of a TV screen?" I opened my eyes.

Jim was more pale than when he came in. He was sweating. And he was furious. He stood up and pushed the chair back to the desk. I had humiliated him, made him fail at the work that meant most to him. Probably if I had stolen his gun and turned it on him, he wouldn't have felt as degraded as I'd made him feel. I thought he would leave without a word, but he stopped at the door, though he didn't turn to look at me. "Have you had any more phone calls?"

"Last night. Silent."

"Stay around the restaurant next few days. Don't go out alone."

"All right."

"If anything...comes back to you, call me." He turned the knob and pulled the door open, keeping his back to me. "Sometimes after hypnosis you remember something." He didn't wait for me to answer, just went out, closing my door softly behind him.

I was glad that it was already time to go to work, glad that the restaurant filled right away and stayed filled, glad that I didn't have a minute to myself until closing time, when I started to go upstairs again, but Mom stopped me.

"Let's have a cup of tea." My dad was already getting a pot. My mom led me to a booth and sat me down, the way she does our blind customers, not pushing or guiding too much, but taking care no one stumbles. "Now, why don't you tell us about it before we have to close down the restaurant because the look on your face has scared all our customers away."

By the time Dad had brought the tea, I was letting my story and all my feelings pour out. "...because the point is that India Wonder didn't *have* any friends. All those people Yolanda says loved her, huh! They didn't even like her. Any one of them could have done it. They all had motives." I started ticking them off on my fingers. "Antonia Moran not only wanted her husband, but thinks India's book killed the Left. Pamela Righbottom wanted revenge because of her father. Sylvia March messed up her life under India's influence. Even Jane Lee was envious of her fame. Yolanda—wait till you see the article she tried to publish. She thinks India stopped her flow of grant money. Margot Stackpole thinks India stopped publication of that awful book of hers. Carla just was using her, playing up being India's lover so she'd get her poems published, love poems, hate letters! And Celeste Wildpower was losing India's endorsement of her witching away writers' blocks, which is a lot easier than working as a nurse!''

"No one loved her?" My mother frowned. Looking at her face was like seeing my own, older and wiser and infuriatingly calm. "Not even her husband? Her daughter?"

"Oh, he loved her in between screwing all her friends! And her daughter never forgave her for leaving when she was little. She probably hated India most of all!"

"Children of famous people often do," said my father. "Look at George Sand's daughter, for instance."

I shook my head. I didn't want to look at George Sand's daughter or at India's daughter or at anyone connected with India. "You know those people aren't good writers, not real writers at all. Antonia just wrote one book as a political act, no more important than walking one of a thousand picket lines. Jane edited it, probably rewrote most of it. Celeste never wrote a book at all; Jane ghosted it. Speaking of ghosts, Pamela is just a ghost of her father. The less said about Margot's book the better. Sylvia writes bad imitations of India, and Carla—well, anyone can read sex poems aloud with a jazz background and colored lights flashing and..."

"What about her play?" asked Mom. "You saw *Delilah* three times and raved about it."

I wished she wouldn't remind me. I wished I could say I hated it, because I didn't like Carla, and I couldn't stand the idea that anyone so bad could write something so good. "All right, all right, so there's Carla and Jane and Yolanda, only three of them who have really written anything!"

My father scratched his beard. "Three real writers out of seven. That's not a bad average. Four out of eight, counting you."

"Oh, me!" I guess I startled them. They both looked at me as if I'd just announced that I would never write another word. Then they waited, because they knew I had finally warmed up to what I had to say. "And India Wonder was the biggest phony of them all. I reread *Emma Pride's Journal*. It's full of sloppy writing and soppy thinking. And I called it the great human document of the twentieth century. Shows you how much of a real writer I am, if she was my inspiration."

I guess I expected them to protest, to tell me that I was a real writer and going to be a great writer. But my father was looking up and over my head, far away, nodding his head slowly up and down. "For me," he finally said, "it was Empton Carrell. I was sixteen when I read *Never Going Home*, and for me and my friends it was the voice of. . . ever read it?"

I shook my head. I'd never even heard of Empton Carrell.

"I found a copy at the library a couple of years ago, opened it up." He sighed. "Unreadable. I never should have tried it. Unreadable."

"Emilia Dale Portal."

We looked at my mother. She was smiling and looking over both our heads.

"Let it go now, now
Never tell how it held
With cold blood bonds, nor how
I fell when it loosed my soul,
Abandoned, left, lost.
Let it go now. Now.

"I memorized pages and pages like that. I still get a little shiver with that one. Haven't thought of it for years. Bet you never heard of her." I shook my head. "You still find one or two of her poems in anthologies. Not bad. Not great."

My dad was nodding. "Not bad. But not to grow old with, like Blake or Dickinson."

"Shaw and the Brontes."

"Willa Cather and Zora Hurston."

"Hardy and Hopkins."

"Wharton."

"Butler!"

I sat and let them toss the names back and forth like big, blue bubbles. I'd watched them do this before. And when I was little, they'd read parts to me, to show what they meant. Lucky for a writer to grow up that way, probably had more to do with my starting to write than any one book.

"But you know," said my mother finally, "none of the great writers ever affected me just the way Emilia Dale Portal did. When I was sixteen."

Then she and my dad sat looking at me as if they were waiting for something again. Waiting for me to grow up, I guess.

That night I dreamed I was watching India's party on a huge television screen. I saw Jane come out of India's room, carrying a thick envelope. Then the scene changed, to the living room, and India lay dead on the floor in Reuben's arms. He raised his head, the camera came in close, and his head filled the whole screen. He looked straight out at me and said, "You. You did it."

"No, no!" I woke up moaning, "No, no, no." It was six a.m. For an hour I lay in bed forgiving India Wonder for being the person she was instead of what I had made of her.

Then I called Jim and told him I'd remembered Jane in my dream. "So you're not such a bad hypnotist." I laughed, and after a pretty long time, he forgave me and laughed too. And when he told me that Celeste Wildpower had barred him from the seance, I promised to go and give him a full report.

Then I called Jane Lee and asked her what she had taken from India's room the night of the party.

"The manuscript of my new novel. India had read it and given me a jacket blurb."

I wanted to believe her. I didn't want it to be Jane.

30.

It was like the ending of India's life all over again. The fire was blazing in the fireplace. We all had taken nearly the same places as we had the night of the party, except that Reuben Wonder, instead of standing in the doorway of the kitchen, was sitting, pale and still, in the green armchair near the fireplace. Georgie sat on the arm of his chair, keeping her hand on his. She was looking even more angry than usual and, because I sat on a footstool next to her, I could hear her taking short, furious breaths and see her eyes flashing. Every time she looked at Reuben, he gave a tiny shake of his head as if asking for her patience just a little longer.

On the other side of me Antonia Moran was chain-smoking, giving Reuben an occasional worried look. Jane Lee and Yolanda Dolores sat side by side on the couch. Yolanda held a notebook where she wrote something down as she looked around the room. I didn't see how I could have thought of her as soft. Now her face looked broad and tough, her body thick and strong. But Jane still faded into the worn cushions of the couch. The more I stared at her, the less I saw. Maybe it had something to do with her eyes, the way they disappeared behind her round glasses. Yet I knew that in her way, she was as tough as Yolanda.

Margot Stackpole sat a little apart from them, on the end of the couch. Her T-shirt had been washed, had shrunk tighter than ever, and the words RESERVED FOR LOVE had run slightly, gotten smeared over and around her breasts. She was the only person who was smiling, her lips nervously twitching as if invisible strings jerked them back to show her teeth. Carla sprawled on the floor as she had during India's party, but this time her perfect black head rested between Margot's knees and one hand clasped Margot's ankle like a dark chain. Carla's crimson sweater and pants clung skin tight, and she wore a jeweled nose ring that made her face look fierce as she glanced around the room, not observant like Yolanda or nervous like Margot, just restless.

Antonia expelled a cloud of smoke like a safety valve hissing steam as Celeste walked in. "The labor movement was taken over by materialists, the black movement by thugs, the homosexual movement by freaks, and now the women's movement by witches." Celeste must have had her hair done for the occasion. It was flame-bright and frizzed out like an electrified halo. She wore a black cape that kept flashing an orange lining that matched her hair. She was gripping Sylvia March's arm, pulling her into the room. Sylvia was carrying her son and moaning something about her baby-sitter. Both she and the baby had been crying. She stumbled once, but Celeste held her up. This time she was really stoned. "I can't stay, I'm too exhausted, the baby has . . ."

"We all have to be here," said Celeste, looking around the room like a teacher taking the roll. "Where's Pamela?"

"Gone," said Carla. "She went back to New York."

"Didn't the police stop her?"

"She left a deposition. Had her lawyer call the police and say she had to start teaching fall semester. Would be available, fly out for official hearings or trial." Carla's voice was casual. She stroked Margot's knee. I almost couldn't believe the way she had screamed at Pamela for deserting her.

"But if Pamela . . ." Sylvia's blurred voice and helpless shrug said it for us all. If Pamela had gotten away with murder, home free, we were all wasting our time here.

"Let's get this over with," said Antonia. "What do we do, sit around a table? turn out the lights?" Celeste glared; Antonia puffed smoke back at her.

Celeste cleared her throat. "That won't be necessary." Her voice came out in a high-pitched whine like the voice of an old crone, a fairy-tale witch inside Celeste's young body. "Nor will there be tapping, spirit gongs or levitation. We make the call. Whether it will be answered is up to the decision of a higher power." All of us, even Antonia, froze and looked at her, waiting, almost believing, for about four seconds, until Sylvia's baby hiccoughed.

Celeste cleared her throat again and looked all around the room, meeting each pair of eyes, trying to get back the attention she had for those four seconds. "No gimmicks, only the willing hearts of those gathered." Most eyes veered away when she said that. "Connection helps. So I will ask you to join hands."

I reached out and took Georgie's hand in one of mine and Antonia's hand in the other. Yolanda hesitated a minute before putting her notebook down in her lap and joining hands with Antonia and Jane. Jane gave her other hand to Margot, who was clinging to Carla. Sylvia sat cross-legged on the floor between Carla and Celeste, who sat on the other arm of Reuben's chair and took his hand. Sylvia's baby toddled out to the center of the ring, sat down on the rug, and put his thumb into his mouth.

"Children are sometimes a great help," said Celeste. "They are more open." There was even more of an edge to her grating voice, like the nurse scolding her patients to take their medicine. "It is my usual policy to exclude those who cannot open themselves. But in this case there is more to be gained by including everyone, even the one who may not want to be here." That got everyone serious again, reminding us that someone here was probably a poisoner. But what if it was Celeste herself?

"I ask you to close your eyes and to repeat after me the following: Lona say belie. Dar mem toray." No one said anything. "Lona say belie. Dar mem toray." A few of us tried. Reuben's voice mumbled and rumbled under ours but dropped out the last two words.

"Everyone," nagged Celeste. "Lona say belie."

"Lona say belie."

Celeste's voice rose. "Dar mem toray."

"Dar mem toray."

"Jane, we need your help!" Celeste's voice had risen to a higher, peevish tone. I opened my eyes. She was glaring at Jane.

"What does it mean?" Jane's voice was a whisper.

Celeste shrugged.

"I want to know what it means, what it does." Jane's chin had dropped and she was looking down into her lap. "I don't like using words I don't understand."

Celeste nodded and looked pleased. She was being taken seriously. "Right, a very powerful incantation, a very ancient sound. But I don't know what it means."

Jane began to shake her head, but Reuben murmured, "Please, Jane." His eyes were still closed. Jane nodded and sighed, and we all closed our eyes again.

"Lona say belie. Dar mem toray. Lona say belie. Dar mem toray." We repeated the two phrases over and over. Each repetition was the same, yet different, gradually changing. Those who hadn't gotten it quite right in the beginning were starting to learn it, so no one was mumbling. Then the different voices began adjusting pitch so that we were together in tone and volume, like a single voice, with Reuben rumbling an octave lower. I started feeling a little sleepy, the way I had felt when Jim tried to hypnotize me, tingly and loose, hanging between Georgie's cold hand and Antonia's sweaty, hard grip. "Lona say belie. Dar mem toray."

"Toray, toray, toray. Memem toray." Sylvia's baby was chanting a little song weaving in and out and around our chanting. "Toray, Mommy, toray!"

I giggled and opened my eyes. Everyone's eyes were open, and most people were smiling, but Celeste looked furious and Sylvia looked scared. "I told you," her voice slurred. "I'll take him home." She started to get up but couldn't seem to get her feet under her.

"You can't go."

"Maybe if someone held him."

"He won't go to anyone else," Sylvia whined.

"Maybe he'll join the circle and hold hands."

While they were all making suggestions, the baby suddenly curled up, put his thumb in his mouth, and lay fast asleep in the middle of our circle.

"Good," said Celeste. "Oh, very good."

We were solemn again, but mainly because I think most of us wanted to give up. My arms ached from stretching out to hold hands. We had all let go of each other, and Antonia wasn't the only one who looked impatient.

144

"I think," Celeste whined, "we will try another approach. I ask you to maintain silence. Absolute. No speaking." She rummaged in a dark sack hanging from her shoulder, half-hidden in the folds of her black cape. Everyone watched her, looking as if keeping silent would be impossible. Carla stroked Margot's leg languidly, but kept darting her eyes around the room. Antonia breathed hard and fast. Both Jane and Sylvia sat with their hands folded like little girls ready to rebel against the teacher. Yolanda kept taking notes.

Finally Celeste stopped digging in her bag, reached out toward Yolanda, gesturing that she wanted some paper. Yolanda handed her the notebook and pen. Antonia breathed and opened her mouth, but Celeste silenced her with a look. Celeste was taking charge again pretty well.

She tore off sheets of paper and handed them around. "Now think of India. All silent, think of India, in whatever aspect you choose. A memory of something she said or wrote, an aspect of her physical being, a moment shared with her. While the pen is going around, think of India, and when the pen comes to you, write down a question you wish to ask of her. One question. It will come to you. Think of India, only of India, and when the pen comes to you, write down the first question that comes. Only that. Think of India. India."

I tried to visualize India, but I couldn't. I named parts of her face, her gray eyes, her long white hair, but I couldn't really see them in my mind. There were no moments shared with her, except at the party. And, right now, there were no quotations from *Emma Pride's Journal* that inspired me. When the pen was passed to me, I wrote, where is the manuscript of the new book? then passed the piece of paper to Celeste.

The pen went around several times. Yolanda and Antonia very quickly wrote something. Sylvia held the pen for a long time. Jane passed on the first round, then wrote a long, slow question. Georgie and Carla both hid their hands as they wrote and folded the paper many times before handing it directly to Celeste. Margot wouldn't write anything until after Celeste had. Reuben covered two sheets of paper, before we passed notebook and pen back to Yolanda.

Celeste shuffled through the pieces of paper, read them silently several times, closed her eyes, then opened them and read through them again. Then she threw all the papers into the fireplace, and watched while they blazed up for a moment and were gone. "All join hands again," she whispered. "Eyes closed." This time there was no chanting, just silence that deepened, very restful.

"India," Celeste whispered, her voice sounding very soothing, not squeaky as it was when she spoke up. "Your friends are here. How far have you gone? Are you utterly diffused into the all-being? Is anything left to us? If the transition is not complete, let us know, touch us, answer us. Answer."

I pulled myself out of a half-doze, sank into it again, fought it. I'd promised Jim a full report.

"Do you know all now? Answer our questions. Is there peace beyond life? Where is the manuscript of your new book? Why did you die? What were you afraid of? Will you live again? Have you found peace? Who killed you? Why did. . ."

A loud sob came from my left, an awful, grating sound that ended in a shudder. As I opened my eyes, Antonia pushed my hand away and turned to the chair where Reuben sat, his head bent forward, his shoulders heaving. Georgie was bent over him, clutching his hand, while Antonia grabbed at his other hand. "Go get water," Georgie snapped at her, but she wouldn't leave him, so I went to the kitchen to pour a glass of water while Antonia and Georgie took turns yelling at Celeste.

"Can't you see this is torturing Reuben?"

"Enough of this degrading farce!"

"No wonder India repudiated you—how she ever lost her wits and took you seriously is beyond me!"

When I came back with the water, people were on their feet putting on their coats. No one looked at Celeste. She stood alone in the middle of them, huddled in her cape, like a black mound with orange fuzz poking out of the top. Her hair was starting to droop. I handed the water to Antonia. Georgie grabbed the glass from her and held it to Reuben's lips. He took a sip or two, then pushed it away and looked around at all of us. His eyes were dry, and he was very pale, but very controlled. "Please don't go. Let's give Celeste one more chance. Just once more. Please."

Jane sat down first, leaving her coat on. The only sound was a wet sucking smacking as Sylvia's baby half woke, sucked his thumb a bit, then dropped off again. A soft sigh traveled around the room as everyone settled and looked at Celeste.

Celeste didn't seem to know quite what to do. Her mouth was pursed, her eyes and hair droopy, and her voice was thin and weak and whiny. "Too much resistance. I don't know how I can be expected to produce results with. . ." She broke off, looking lost, humiliated, ready to cry, like a teacher who has lost control of an unruly class. People started reaching out to join hands again, not waiting for her instructions. I felt my hands being grabbed and saw everyone closing eyes as if they wanted to hurry and get it over with so they could go home. So I closed my eyes too.

The next thing I knew, someone was shaking me, big hands clamped on my shoulders, shaking me so that I thought my head would snap off. And shouting. "Indy, is it you! India!"

"No," squeaked Celeste. "No, no." I opened my eyes, right into her face, about an inch from mine. Why didn't she make him stop shaking me, shouting at me? My head, oh, my head hurt, and Reuben kept trying to shake it off my shoulders. He was kneeling on the floor in front of me, shaking me and calling, "India, India!"

"No, it wasn't India," said Celeste. "Let her go."

He let go of me, and I thought I would fall over, but Celeste caught me, steadied me, and then I was all right. Antonia and Georgie had taken either side of Reuben, helping him up, then leading him out of the room and up the stairs. Sylvia's baby was howling. And everyone was staring at me, all except Yolanda, who was writing in her notebook. My head was about to explode. "What happened?" Talking made my head hurt even worse. If I could just take it off, bury it somewhere, and walk away!

Everyone started talking at once, but Celeste waved a hand and silenced them. Only the baby made a sound, whimpering. Celeste's voice croaked, "You remember nothing." She nodded at me. "You spoke. You remember nothing of what you said." I was afraid of what would happen to my head if I nodded it or shook it.

"She looks quite ill." Someone handed me Reuben's glass of water. I drank it down as if I had just come through a desert on foot. "More?" I forgot and shook my head. A wrecking ball swung inside my head, from ear to ear, smashing everything in between.

"Headache?" Celeste was nodding at me as if she knew all about it. She touched my wrist, taking my pulse while everyone watched in silence for the full minute. Then she pushed back my eyelid and looked into my eye, nodding again. "She's all right." She lowered her voice. "I told you, didn't I? You have it all, just under a thin veneer. You could be a Blavatsky, a Cayce, a . . ."

"What did I say?" The headache was dulling down to a steady pain.

"I took it down," said Yolanda. "Shall I read it?" Everyone looked to Celeste, who nodded at Yolanda with great dignity—authority. No one, not even Antonia, was laughing at Celeste anymore. "It sounded like, 'Tree—no—tree—pad—alone' or 'own.' Next words I couldn't get, then, 'pine alone—hideaway—bury—silence—pain—window—pad—pain.' Or pine. Or maybe it's pain again, but is it pain that hurts or window pane? I'm not sure. Then you seemed to be counting trees. 'One—two—three—three pines.' Repeated twice more. Same numbers. Something, something 'of one's own.' Then you started counting again. That's what I heard. Anyone hear different?"

"A room of one's own," said Jane quietly. "I heard, 'a room of one's own,' as in Virginia Woolf."

"*A Room of One's Own,*" Yolanda nodded. "India often talked about it, quoted from it in *Emma Pride's Journal.* Used to say everyone needed one...apart, even secret."

"Did she?" My voice sounded far away, echoing through my swollen, empty, sore head. "Did she have another room, secret?"

"Yes." Georgie stood in the doorway to the front hall. She looked around the room as if it were empty, as if we didn't even exist for her, and she spoke fast, rattling off words as if they had no meaning, no interest to her. "Some years ago. My mother got a room. Where she could get away from us, from her correspondence, from everything, a room. Of her own. Where she could work."

"Where?"

"It was her secret. Even our knowing would be an intrusion. So we never asked. Now, enough. I am tired and Reuben is very ill. Last one out please turn out the lights." She turned and was gone. I listened, but couldn't even hear her going up the steps.

Everyone moved, getting into coats, getting out. It seemed to me that they all avoided looking at me, except for Jane, who was watching my every move, her little round glasses glinting at me, her brain constructing a book with me in it, only I wouldn't be me anymore. I felt afraid, the way some people are afraid of a camera which might steal their souls.

I held out my hand to Yolanda, palm up. She hesitated, glanced quickly again at the notes she had written, then handed the paper over to me.

I let Celeste lead me out and put me into her car along with Sylvia and the baby. At least when the car started moving, the baby quieted down, but Celeste and Sylvia never stopped talking about me, talking as if I weren't there.

"Frankly, Celeste, I never quite believed before. But now I do. Jessie really did contact India, didn't she?"

Celeste waited a long time to answer, completing a left turn onto University Avenue. "I don't think so."

"Then what..."

"More likely telepathic. Jessie picked up something, no doubt of it, but more likely from a present, embodied mind. Yes, I think that's it."

"Oh." Sylvia sounded disappointed.

"Not that she couldn't—if she'll let me work with her." Then Celeste went on and on about my duty to develop my "powers." When we reached the restaurant, she took my pulse again. "You're fine, but I could come in with you and do a little suggestion on your headache so you can sleep."

I told her no. But she insisted on coming in anyway to talk to my parents. "I wouldn't want them to think I did anything that would harm you, harm anybody. You'll be fine tomorrow."

We walked down the alley to the back door, where she stopped me. "I want you to wear this." She reached up to her neck and pulled a thin chain out from the folds of her dress. As she pulled it over her head, it tangled in her hair, and a few orange strands stuck in it, glimmering in the faint light from over the door, as she held the chain out to me. There was a tiny, felt-wrapped lump hanging from the end of it. I shook my head, but she nodded hers harder as she slipped the chain over my head. "Not that you are in any danger. No, I don't really think...and yet...just don't take this off for a couple of days, not at any time, for any reason. Promise!"

I opened the door. Mom and Dad were still in the kitchen, cleaning up. I saw the look on their faces when they saw me, and I said, "I'm all right, all right, just tired." Then I went straight up to bed, so I never heard what Celeste told them.

Off and on during the night I half woke to see my mother or my father standing by the bed looking at me. They moved in and out of my room, and my sleep, all night, like friendly ghosts. Each time they left, I went deeper into a sleep with, thank God, no dreams.

31.

It was past noon when I woke up. My headache was gone, but I felt hungry, weak and shaky as I showered and put on my waitressing skirt. Before I went downstairs, I stuck Yolanda's notes into my pocket in case I might have time to study them.

The Sunday breakfast crowd had thinned to a few people. Mom and Dad were getting ready to close for cleanup before the early dinner customers started coming. They said Jim had called to say he was busy with his kids, but would call again. I sat down to a huge bowl of rice, eggs and fruit. By the time I finished it, Dad had locked the door, and he and Mom came to sit with me.

"I guess Celeste told you that I'm a medium or something."

"Or something," murmured my mother.

"Tell us what happened," my father said, combing his beard with his fingers, looking more curious than anxious, now that he could see I was all right.

"I don't know what happened. The seance seemed like a complete bust. Nothing was happening. Then all of a sudden, I...I don't know, I passed out or something, and when I came to, they told me I had...said things."

"What things?"

I reached into my pocket, pulled out the sheet of paper, and handed it to my dad. He read it and passed it to Mom. She read it and frowned. "That's all?"

"That's all."

"I thought mediums had controls," said my mother. "Entities called Marvin or Penelope, who said whole sentences and relayed questions to the..."

"The dear departed," said my father. "You're a hell of a medium."

"But Celeste says I have possibilities!" We laughed. It seemed like a long time since I'd laughed. "Anyway, she doesn't think I contacted India, just picked up something telepathically. And I was just barely getting started when Reuben Wonder shook me out of it."

"Why?"

"I don't know. I guess he got all excited when he thought India was speaking through me, or . . . anyway he started shaking me and yelling and I woke up with a terrible headache."

"How do you feel now?"

"Fine."

"Do you have any idea what this means?" Dad was studying the paper again. He loves a puzzle.

I nodded. "India had some secret workroom, 'a room of one's own.' Nobody seemed surprised—as if they all sort of knew about it. But no one was supposed to know where. Not even Reuben. A hideaway where no one could disturb her."

"With trees around it," said my father, pushing the sheet of paper forward on the table and leaning over it, the way he leans over the chessboard. "Pine trees. Or panes? Window panes looking out on pines."

"Or pains." I made a face to signify pain.

He shook his head. "Window panes looking out on pines. There are miles of hillside houses from Richmond to Hayward."

"You think that was what the counting meant, the number of miles? One, two, three. Three miles."

"From where?"

"From her house?" We shook our heads, and Mom got up and left the room the way she does when Dad and I get stuck between chess moves.

"I guess pad refers to the room, her secret pad."

I shrugged. It wasn't India's kind of slang. We started again, playing with the words, pine, pain, pane, one alone, pad, one-two-three-three, a room of one's own, pine, pain. Dad leaned back and looked over my head. "Tell me again. Everything. Every detail leading up to when you went into the trance."

I started with a description of everyone sitting around. I described each of Celeste's attempts to contact India, and told how each failed.

"You held hands? You closed your eyes?"

"Right." I waited for him to react, but he only shrugged for me to go on. He didn't speak again until I got to the part about Celeste having us write down questions for India.

"What questions?"

"I never saw them. She read them, then burned them, then started reciting some of them aloud, but that was when Reuben broke down and interrupted."

"Can you remember any of the questions?"

"She asked if India knew everything now, if she was at peace. She asked where was the manuscript of her new novel. That was my question. And, of course, she asked who killed her. Then Reuben broke down and everything stopped."

Dad lowered his eyes and narrowed them at the paper. His long nose didn't exactly twitch, but got that quivery look around the part that hooked slightly. "But the question about the new manuscript was your question, and the message you spoke was a partial vision of a secret workroom, which is, of course, where she would have been working on the new book."

I nodded. I was getting excited too, but it wasn't my nose that quivered. I always get jumpy in the stomach. "Which is how she could keep everyone from seeing it."

Dad nodded faster. "Which is why you didn't find it in her house." He bent over the paper again, and so did I.

"What if I tell Jim to check and see where she might have rented a room. Up in the hills, pine trees. Most of the houses up there have some little rental unit. Aren't they all registered somewhere?"

"The legal ones," said Dad with a sigh.

"There might be a simpler answer." Mom was standing over us, holding a couple of street maps. "There is a Pine Street in Richmond, one in El Cerrito, Pine Place, Pine Court and two other Pine-somethings in Oakland, Pine Alley in Berkeley. Also Pine-haven, Pinewood." She spread the map across the table. "The nearest one to India's house—you said she lived in Ocean View—is Pine Alley, right there, see how it snakes around the freeway?"

We bent over the map. Pine Alley was only a few blocks from India's house. "It makes sense she would find a place close to home."

"And the counting," said Mom. Dad and I looked at her and waited. She shrugged and smiled that little glowing smile of hers. "Couldn't it be just an address? One, two, three, three. 1233."

I shook my head. "Pine Alley's not that long."

"Maybe," said Dad, "your telepathic channels developed static—repeated three's."

"Or," I said, standing up, "it's 123 Pine Alley, apartment 3."
"Where are you going?"
"It'll only take me a minute to go down there and find out. If I'm wrong, we can try something else."
"Maybe you ought to wait until Jim calls."
"No time. Everyone else heard the message too, and they're figuring it out. When Jim calls, tell him where I've gone. Tell him to meet me there. No, I can't wait. I want to get there first. Maybe I'm too late already."

32.

123 Pine Alley was a long, low concrete building almost hidden between two tall brick warehouses. A narrow corridor ran along one side, dark and shaded and drafty. As I walked my bike down the corridor I passed dingy gray metal doors, each marked with a number splashed in rusty paint like dried blood. Doors number 1 and 2 had no names on them, but I could see that both sections were used for storage; boxes were piled up against the muddy, small-paned windows, those that weren't broken out and replaced with plywood. Door number 3 was also unmarked, and something dark covered the windows on the inside. I walked all the way down the corridor. Doors 4, 5 and 6 were labeled ARTANE PRODUCTS. Through patches of dirty window panes I saw more boxes, but nothing that told me what ARTANE PRODUCTS might be.

I walked back to door number 3. Now that my eyes were getting used to the shadowy corridor, I saw something I had missed before. Just above the gray metal hasp lock, in pencil, almost invisible on the gray door, was the name *Crawley*, India's maiden name. My heart gave a couple of good thumps and I forgot the cold draft as I recognized her slanted, scrawled printing.

I leaned my bike against the brick wall of the building next door, and set the chain lock. Then I turned back to look at the gray metal door that sealed India's secret room. A simple hasp lock, like the one I had just set on my bike, fastened it, kept me from—maybe—all the answers I had been looking for. I even tried my own bike-lock key, while I still had it in my hand, but that would have been too good to be true. It didn't open the lock.

The thing to do was to telephone Jim's office, then stand by the door until a cop came to take my place, then wait until Jim and a locksmith could open it. I decided to do that, but at the same time I was looking around to see if India might have hidden a key near by.

There was no place around or above the door where anything could be hidden, no ledges or nooks, nothing but bare, gray concrete walls, no framing even around the windows. Behind me was the solid brick wall of the building next door, going up two storeys beyond this one. The path under my feet was broken concrete, gravel, ground-up bits of broken glass. There was an oval pad of concrete just in front of the door. I got down on my knees to look more closely, but I was afraid to rummage around with bare fingers in all that broken glass.

Then I saw it, just under the tip of one corner of the concrete pad, a thin hollow where the pad tipped above the uneven gravel— a faint glint of metal. I took a pencil out of my pocket and poked it in, then slid it through that narrow place. It came out easily, a key.

Now was the time to telephone, I was thinking, as I tried the key in the hasp lock. As it clicked open, I told myself that my parents had probably called Jim and that he or someone from the police would be here at any minute. I couldn't resist just one tiny, private peek before they came.

The door squeaked and rattled open on total, black darkness. The dim light from the corridor hardly affected it at all. I stepped onto something soft, a rug. I sensed rather than saw a small room, with a wall only a few feet in front of me, and with something bulky over toward my right. I ran my hands along the wall on either side of the doorway until I found a light switch. I flipped it, but nothing happened. Then I tried walking slowly forward, with my hands reaching up toward the ceiling, waving back and forth to catch a hanging string and pull it or a naked globe to switch on. Nothing.

In only four steps to the right, I reached the bulky object. A table? A desk. I made my hands creep slowly over its surface. Paper, pens, a cup full of more pens, and finally! a lamp with a little button switch on the base. I pushed it and got some light.

Not much. It was one of those narrow, rod-shaped lamps designed to focus light only on the surface of the desk, on an area two or three feet square where you're writing. Something had been done to this lamp to confine the light even more, an extra shade placed over it. I touched it and found that it was just a piece of sheet metal shaped and bent over the top of the lamp. Nothing held it in place, so I lifted it off and got a bit more light, not much more, but enough for a dim impression of the rest of the room.

It was a little longer than I thought at first, with a narrow, empty space running off from the left side of the door, where the two windows were. I stood on the right side of the door, where there was barely room for the small desk and wooden chair. Dark rugs covered not only the floor under my feet, but the walls too. I touched the wall above the desk to make sure. Patches of carpeting were nailed up, different colors and textures and odd shapes and scraps, overlapping each other. I felt all along the shadowy walls and found them completely padded with nailed-up rug patches, sometimes in three or more thicknesses. There was no way of telling how many layers of carpeting covered the windows in the far left corner of the narrow room, far from the desk, as if the writing space had been placed as far as possible from any opening to the world. A padded room. Padded window panes. Pad, pane. As a medium, I guess, I tended to be awfully literal.

I was surprised that the air was not more close or cold or dusty. Then I noticed what looked like the shape of a pipe and a grate up in the high ceiling. There must be a ventilating and heating system to protect the stored material in the rest of the building. It kept a constant temperature and enough air circulating for one unmoving, unspeaking human being to breathe.

I tried to push the door closed, just to see what the room was like to work in, but it got stuck half-closed on some loose carpeting. Still, it was black dark beyond the desk. I replaced the metal shade on the desk lamp and sat down on the stiff chair, picked a long, thin black pen out of the cup and held it over the one blank sheet of paper that lay on top of the desk. This was how India sat, this was where she worked, not in her room at home full of letters, not in a hillside room overlooking pine trees, but here in this narrow padded cell squeezed between warehouses in industrial Berkeley.

The sheet of paper gleamed white under the square of lamp light, but everything else was black, shadowed, hidden. I couldn't even see my elbows. Not only was I surrounded by darkness, but by absolute quiet. I'd never known such quiet. Not in Berkeley, not even in the wilderness on camping trips. Between those two high buildings and between rooms stacked with boxes, this space was, as the saying goes, quiet as the grave. India Wonder had found the ultimate room of one's own, free of distraction, hidden from light and sound, hidden even from the conscious knowing of other minds. Hidden from everything but the white sheet of paper, waiting.

I sat looking at that sheet of paper, letting it expand and contract as my eyes let it in and out of focus, letting it take me in, letting that tingly, heavy sensation spread through my body the way it had when Jim tried to hypnotize me. I was beginning to feel as I had felt at India's coffin and at the seance. But this time I knew what I was doing. This time I balanced, fully conscious on the edge of some other way of knowing. I wasn't going to let myself just fall into anything this time. Whatever was opening up to be explored, I was going to climb down into it carefully this time, with a strong line hooked onto the edge, connecting me so I could ease down or back up again.

As I touched the pen to the paper, I could feel, all around me, rising up out of the darkness, the vibrations of the life lived in this space, deep and high, strong movements collecting into something like dark clouds thickening, closing in around me. Cautiously, slowly, I let myself breathe them in, deep, deeper, let my eyes close, let myself swim down, down to where I knew I was going, to where India was, to where I would become India, what she was here, what she knew here.

The pen began to move across the page. Slowly at first, stopping and starting. Then faster. Faster and faster, as my eyes filled with tears that leaked out from under closed lids, as my brow beaded sweat, as my neck and shoulders tightened into pain, as my feet grew colder, colder, as if I stood in my own grave as the pen flew across the page.

Enough. Be careful, I thought, as the faint feelers of pain rippled across my head. I had almost reached the bottom of the page, could feel it under my hand. Enough, time to slowly, carefully come back, through the clouds of vibrating currents.

But then there was some break, some interruption, some change in the vibrations in the dark behind my head. The chill in my feet shot upward, shaking my body into a shudder and making my head snap upward and begin to turn. But only when it was already too late.

Hands had closed around my throat. Before my own arms were even half-raised to fight, to clutch backward at whoever was choking me, I was spinning downward, diving out of control, down through layers of deeper dark, to the bottom of the grave where I would lie with India forever.

When I had fallen almost to the bottom, almost to the end, my eyelids flickered once. I tried to come back out of the dive, struggled to rise, to blink my eyes open again, to focus. Just once more I blinked my eyes open and saw the goddess of death standing over me, leaning down to take me. I tried to fight, but my own fear shocked away what was left of my strength, as my eyelids fell, as I sank, as I died.

33.

Her tentacles were wrapping around me. I tried once more to fight her off.

"Easy, Jessie. It's all right. It's me, Jim."

A disguise to fool me, to trick me into opening my eyes. If I opened my eyes and looked at her again, I might turn to stone. Could I risk it? I opened to a squint. Jim bent over me. "It's all right, Jessie. I got an ambulance. You're all right, but we're taking you to the hospital, just to make sure."

"Another blanket, I think," said a cool, bored voice. They were wrapping me and strapping me on a stretcher like a mummy. I couldn't even get my hand out for Jim to hold it. That made me feel so sad that tears welled up and trickled down toward my ears, and I smiled, thinking that funny old song was right, I've got tears in my ears from lying on my back in my bed while I cry over you. Had I sung it out loud? No, I couldn't have. My throat was closed up.

"I'm going to follow the ambulance in my car. I'll be right there when you get to the hospital. Okay?"

I nodded and closed my eyes, but then started crying again, for no reason.

"Going to give you a shot," said the cool voice. "Very light sedative, just to relax you. Take a little nap, wake up feeling fine. Okay?"

I kept my eyes closed while I nodded, felt the needle prick my arm. Then I was rocked, turned, rolled out into the light, the sharp, cool air. By the time they lifted me into the ambulance, I felt the shot taking effect, a delicious, woozy, drunk feeling starting from my fingers and toes, rippling through my body.

When I woke up, I was in a hospital bed, and Jim was sitting beside me, holding my hand. Mom held my other hand, and Dad stood behind her, leaning against the wall, pale, tugging at his beard as if he would pull it out.

"Who's minding the restaurant?" I was surprised that I could speak. It didn't hurt at all.

"Joe," said Mom.

I made a face to show what I thought of that idea, and got just a shadow of a smile from Dad. I started to tell them to go home, but a doctor came in and started poking and peering at me, asking questions that I had a hard time answering. What happened? Simple question, but I just couldn't seem to find a simple answer.

"You think someone tried to strangle you?" The doctor shook his head. "Just this bruise on the neck. You'd have an ugly neck there if...you can talk all right, doesn't hurt?" I shook my head. "Maybe cut off your air enough to knock you out. I don't find a thing wrong, but let's keep you overnight anyway. I think Inspector Merino wants to leave you here with an officer to watch." Jim nodded at my parents. He didn't look at me at all. "You can go home in the morning."

After the doctor left, I talked with Mom and Dad for a minute, just to show them I was all right and they could go. I was afraid Dad would be sicker than I in a little while. "You might as well," said Jim. "I'm just going to ask her a few questions, then I think she'll get some rest if we all just leave her alone." Mom nodded and gave my hand a squeeze before she let it go.

"If anyone calls, Jessie is still unconscious."

"Right," said Mom. Dad nodded.

"Write down who calls and what they say."

Mom and Dad nodded, kissed me, and left.

Jim dropped my hand, pulled up a chair, and took out a notebook. "Start from the beginning." I told him everything, starting from Mom finding Pine Alley on the map and ending with the goddess of death.

"When I called, your father said you were over there, so I drove down. I found the door wide open and you on the floor. The desk light was turned on its side, like someone wanted to light up the room more. To search. All four drawers of the desk were pulled out, cleaned out. Nothing left but a stack of blank paper.

"So, whoever it was came for the manuscript, not just for...me." I hoped that was true. It was better than thinking about someone following me everywhere.

"Who knew about Pine Alley?"

I sighed. "Everyone." Then I told him all about the seance. "I guess any of the others could have figured it out the same way my mom did."

"And got there just after you did." He looked disgusted. He leaned back in the chair, not looking at me. "I've sent out some people to question everyone again, but I don't think there's much chance of getting that manuscript now. Too easy to dump it, destroy it, burn it, stash it."

"Somehow I can't believe any of those people would destroy a manuscript by India. Fifteen years work? No matter, even if it insulted them or ridiculed them or . . ."

"Incriminated them?"

"Well. . ." I thought about that.

"But you may be right. There's always the chance that the killer wants, partly, to keep the manuscript, to have it found." He sighed and shrugged at such a slim hope.

"It's my fault." I had to say what I knew he was thinking. "I knew I should call for a cop, then stand outside and wait till he came. I knew it while I was going into that place. If I'd done that, we'd have the manuscript, maybe even the killer, and I wouldn't have made all this trouble." I was thinking more of my folks now. They were worrying and suffering a lot more than I was. Jim didn't answer me, as if all this wasn't worth answering.

Then I remembered my automatic writing, and my hopes bounced up again. "What about that sheet of paper I was writing on? Was that stolen too?"

Jim shook his head. He pulled the sheet out of his pocket and handed it to me.

I had written in large, backhanded script mixed with printing, a little like India's handwriting, but mixed with my own handwriting, smaller and slanted the other way. The words were scrawled and spread far apart, so I hadn't written as much as I thought.

All those who have worked daily as literary laborers will agree with me that three hours a day will produce as much as a man ought to write. But then he should so have trained himself that he shall be able to work continuously during those three hours—so have tutored his mind that it shall not be necessary for him to sit nibbling his pen and gazing at the wall before him. It is my custom to write with my watch before me, and to require from myself two hundred and fifty words every quarter of an hour. I have found that the two hundred and fifty words have been forthcoming as regularly as my watch went. This division of time allowed me to produce over ten pages a day of

"*That's* what I wrote?" I was not only disappointed, I was embarrassed. What would Celeste think of my "powers" if she saw this? "That's all?"

Jim nodded. "Is that something India Wonder wrote...or said?"

"No, no! Trollope."

"Who?"

"Anthony Trollope. He was...never mind. He's just about as far from India Wonder as you could get. That's from his autobiography."

"And you memorized it?"

"No. Yes. I mean, I guess I did. I didn't know it though. Damn."

"What in hell is this?" Jim had reached into a pile of stuff on the bedside table: my wallet, keys, change, ring, whatever they found on me.

"Oh, that's a chain Celeste put around my neck after the seance, to protect me, she said, some kind of...charm?"

"What's in this little sack on the end?"

"I don't know."

"You've been wearing this thing, and don't know what's in it?" He started ripping at the tiny felt sack. What if I had let Celeste put something on me that would make me sick, faint? I *had* been feeling strange lately. Jim pulled something small and pearl-like from the sack.

"What is it?"

He turned it over, poked it with his fingernail, raised it to his nose, then shrugged and looked at me. "Garlic." He put the chain back with my keys, then touched my hand, but only to pat it as he stood up to go. "Try to sleep. Call me in the morning, and I'll come drive you home. You'll be safe here. There's an officer, Phyllis, right outside your door. She'll be there all night. See you tomorrow."

I tilted my chin up to kiss him goodbye. He hesitated for a second, then landed a light kiss on my forehead.

34.

I went home Monday morning, crawled into bed, and fell asleep again. I lost count of how many times I half woke when the phone rang and my mother said, "She's still in the hospital. No, still unconscious, no visitors. May I ask who is calling?"

By Tuesday I could stay awake, but I still felt exhausted. I promised not to answer the phone if Mom would go down to the restaurant to catch up on all the things she must have let go. I tried to read, but every two sentences I lost track of what I was reading. I got up, took a shower, washed my hair, and ate something from the tray my mother had left. Then I went back to bed to rest up from the effort.

I must have dozed off again, because when I opened my eyes, Jim was sitting on the edge of my bed. I smiled and put out my hand. He squeezed it and said, "How you doing?"

"Fine, just...lazy." He nodded. "What about those private eyes in the movies who get hit over the head and ten minutes later are chasing the murderer again?"

Jim smiled. "That's only in the movies."

"What have you found out?"

"Not much. Made the rounds. All the suspects are very concerned about you. Of course. None of them knew about Pine Alley. Of course. But thought they knew who did. Each of them named a different person." Jim sighed. "Have you remembered anything else, anything that had slipped your mind?"

"Slipped is right. My mind is so slippery, everything has slid right out of it. I'm a blank." I moved over in the bed and motioned for Jim to sit back with me, put his feet up. He leaned back with a sigh, and I couldn't see his face anymore, but it felt good to have him lying next to me.

"That...goddess of death who leaned over you, what did she look like?" I shivered, and Jim put his arm around me. "Didn't mean to upset you. Easy. Still chilled?" I didn't answer, but I was shaking less. "I was thinking...that goddess of death might have been a real person bending over you, someone you saw but didn't see, didn't recognize because you were only half conscious."

"And scared."

"Yes." Then Jim gave a funny, embarrassed little laugh. "You don't want to give me another chance to...to help you remember."

"Hypnosis?" So many strange things had been happening to my mind lately that I wondered if it needed to be left alone for a while.

"Not unless you want to. It wouldn't work anyway unless you..."

"Motivation and expectation? You think it wasn't a hallucination or a spirit? You think it was a real person, bending over to finish me off, but interrupted because she heard you coming?"

"Maybe."

"Okay, let's try."

Jim took his arm away and let me rest back on the pillow. "Don't expect too much. You know how it was last time."

"Last time I didn't know about a lot of things I can do. Don't worry, I won't resist you this time."

He went even slower this time, and said very little. Single word suggestions were enough to start me off: water, sky, trees. Abstract words were even better: peaceful, wide, free, deep.

"You're so deep, you're almost fast asleep. Not quite. But you're so deeply relaxed that it won't worry you to go back to Pine Alley, to India's secret room. Into the darkness. See the desk. The spot of light on the top of the desk. You're not afraid. You won't feel anything that happened to you there. You'll just watch it. Nothing will hurt you, and you won't feel afraid."

We went through it all, from the moment I sat down at the desk. Sometimes I described what I was doing, and sometimes he asked me questions. I told what was happening until I began to feel a shiver coming, and Jim would remind me that I didn't have to feel it again, just watch it. "The hands close on my neck, press. I reach back to. . . nothing. Blackness. Black."

"All right. You're all right. Are the hands still on your neck?"

"No."

"Where are you?"

"Lying on the floor. On my back. The rug smells moldy. My leg, twisted, cramped up under me. It aches. Now something is coming over me. Coming down over me."

"You're not afraid. You're just watching."

"I'm lying there. I try to move. I can't. Face up, helpless. She's coming down over me. I'm helpless."

"And now you open your eyes?"

"I open my eyes."

"Who is it?"

"Yolanda."

"What does Yolanda do?"

"She. . . comes down. Her face comes down closer, closer. I'm afraid."

"You were afraid then. You're not now. Go on. What happens next?"

"Blackness again. Black. Then I open my eyes again. The face is yours. It's Jim bending over me. It's you."

"Fine. Okay, you did just fine. So relaxed, a deep hypnotic state that's very restful. You're going to come back up now. And you'll feel wonderful. All the fear is gone, and you'll feel rested. You'll feel really good. I'll count to three, and then you'll open your eyes, wide awake and feeling good. One. Two. Three."

I opened my eyes.

"How do you feel?"

"Awful! I mean, I feel fine, but if it was Yolanda, I feel terrible. I think I liked her better than any of them, better than Jane even. It couldn't be Yolanda. Her weapon is her writing."

"It hasn't always been," said Jim. "I uncovered a juvenile record. Usually these things are destroyed, but hers was serious enough to. . ."

"I know, but that was twenty-five years ago!" I was glad he didn't scold me for holding out on him. I felt miserable. He put his arm around me again, and I buried my face in his chest, so warm and broad and firm. Both his arms came around me and I kissed his chest, then his neck, then his lips.

I put my arms around him and kissed him again, longer this time. At first he just let me. Then his mouth started to kiss me back and we slid downward together on the bed. His hands never moved, but if they were passive, his other parts were not; an instant erection was pressing against my thigh. I thought for a minute about how making love meant commitment to Jim, and about how commitment would complicate my life, but I only thought for a minute. Then I started to wiggle out of my robe.

"No." He sighed and let his arms drop away from me, shaking his head. "Jessie. No, I better not . . ."

"Don't you want to?"

"You can tell I do. But it wouldn't be right, it . . ."

"Oh, we'll work all that out." I started to lick his ear and he gave a little quiver but kept his arms still, and finally I got the message. I leaned away and looked at his clenched jaw. "Something's changed. Sure. You've gone back to your wife."

"You said I would. You were right. I guess I was lying—to you, to myself. So I don't want to lie again now." He looked at me with a mixture of embarrassment and desire and, I was glad to see, a touch of regret as I rewrapped my robe around me. "I'm moving back in this weekend, so technically, I guess, I'm still free. And I know it wouldn't be like . . . like taking advantage of you because it would suit you better if I didn't . . . feel anything special for you, if I had my wife to go back to so I wouldn't be hanging around and getting in the way of your work. But I . . ." He took a deep breath. ". . . I wouldn't feel right, in myself, about it." He shrugged and smiled. He was all red. He was ashamed of acting decent.

I nodded and kept watching him as he got up from the bed and straightened out his clothes. His pants still bulged a little.

"I made a fool of myself, and I insulted you."

I shook my head. "Neither."

"I . . . well, I guess I'll go see Yolanda."

"Are you going to arrest her?"

"I don't know. I'll have to hear what she says. You stay in. Don't answer the phone. Keep under cover a little while longer."

"Still unconscious in the hospital."

He nodded. "Just to be on the safe side."

"Okay. And look. I'm really glad you...I hope it works out with your wife."

"Thanks, Jessie."

As soon as he shut my bedroom door behind him, I fell back against the pillows. I lay there, giving in completely, waiting for the tears to flow.

But they didn't. Instead I felt my whole body flooded with relief—total, warm, joyful relief. I laughed. Then all of a sudden I felt full of energy, and I had a terrific idea for a story. I got up and sat down at my desk, uncovering my typewriter for the first time since India died. Hello, old friend. "Hmmm," it answered warmly, as I switched it on.

I don't know how much later I looked up to see Mom and Dad standing in the open doorway, smiling.

"Look, she's a writer again."

"Not going to marry a cop?"

"Or become a medium?"

"Of course, I'm a medium!" I answered. "What do you think a writer is?"

"Hmmmm," said my typewriter.

That night Jim phoned to tell me he had seen Yolanda but had not arrested her. "Just asked questions. Got the same answers as before. She never heard of Pine Alley, never went there. But she was scared, she knew I had something."

"You didn't tell her I'd seen her?"

"I decided not to. She's too smart, her husband's a lawyer. I thought it would be better not to lay out all our cards, keep her thinking you're still unconscious, still in danger."

"What for?"

"Well, I've talked this over with my partner and my boss. They think my plan is a little bit dramatic, but they don't have any real objection, so if you're willing..."

His plan made sense. On Friday, the day of the memorial service for India, all the speakers were to meet at the church a couple of hours before the program. "You stay covered until then.

After they all arrive, I'll bring you in to confront Yolanda in front of the others. Then we'll see what happens. I hope you won't get too bored staying in for a couple more days."

"I'm too busy to get bored. I'm writing a story about..." but I never talk about what I'm working on.

35.

It was already dark when we drove onto the bridge to go over to San Francisco. "We should get to the Unitarian Church about seven," said Jim. "All the others should be there by then, rehearsing the program. We'll walk in on them and confront Yolanda."

"What shall I say?"

"Whatever comes into your head. That she tried to..."

"I don't know what she tried...all I know is that I opened my eyes and saw her."

"Then say that."

"And then?"

He strugged. "Then we'll see." He seemed different, withdrawn, hard to talk to. So I didn't try.

He found a parking place right across the street from the big old stone church. I'd been in the big church a few times, but I must have gone to the smaller, new wing dozens of times. That was the place used for readings and lectures, and that was where Jim and I were going now. We were even going to the same room, a square space with gray walls rising to a central, stained-glass skylight.

I led the way down the hall. "I guess I've heard all of them read in this room at one time or another, all but Jane, she never reads. Carla did a multi-media thing here once: jazz, poets, dancers, film all going at once. It's nicer in daylight when the sun comes through the skylight." I was talking too much, nervous, almost wanting the people in that room to hear my voice, hear me coming, so that my entrance wouldn't be so shocking. But the whole point was to shock them, to catch Yolanda off guard, and if they heard me coming, I would defeat Jim's purpose, our purpose. Jim didn't shush me, just kept looking at his feet moving along the gray floor, stopping at the glass doors to the room, then looking at me, giving me a quick nod, businesslike.

I could see all of them through the double glass doors, but no one was looking toward us. Carla, all in black, shadowed Reuben, Margot and Antonia, who sat together holding sheets of paper they studied while Carla talked. Sylvia and Georgie stood off to one side, passing bits of paper back and forth between them, shaking their heads, then nodding as they read them. Jane sat in one corner on a folding chair, reading a book. Yolanda stood in another corner, silently watching the others. Celeste sat on the floor directly under the central skylight crosslegged, with her eyes closed. A soft, silky beige gown flowed around her, and her red hair flowed just as smoothly around her face and shoulders, no frizz at all. She looked soothed and soothing. She opened her eyes and looked straight at me as if she had been expecting me. She touched her throat and nodded, to tell me she knew the charm she gave me had kept me safe. Then she closed her eyes again and stayed that way.

Jim swung the door wide open, then stood back and put his hand firmly on the small of my back, ready to push me if I hesitated. I walked into the room.

"Jessie!"

"Oh, look, Jessie's here, she made it!"

"How *are* you?"

"Jessie, thank God you're all right." Yolanda moved faster than anyone else, coming straight across the room to put her arms around me. "You're all right," she repeated. I drew back and looked into her eyes. I must be wrong, I thought. I must have been mistaken. No, the memory was clear. The goddess of death who bent over me was Yolanda. I opened my mouth to say it, but nothing came out. Was I supposed to say it now? Say whatever came into my head? But nothing did.

I was surrounded, touched, my hands held and stroked. Jane kissed me on the cheek, silently. Even Georgie put out her hand and almost touched my shoulder. Only Reuben stayed in his chair, pale, staring at me through the gaps between the others. Margot hugged me. I hardly recognized her. No T-shirt. She wore a dark blue dress and her hair was pulled back into a thick braid. No makeup. Like India. She had dressed up like India to read from India's book, and she looked exactly right...she even looked thinner. I had a premonition. Margot had found her role at last, she would read India Wonder in one-woman shows from now on, and she would be a great success.

We moved closer to Reuben and pulled up folding chairs to make a circle. Margot and Antonia sat next to him again, Georgie behind. Celeste was still on the floor, her eyes still closed, but everything about her totally alert to what was going to happen. Yolanda sat down, but then got up again, moving around restlessly. Jim faded back.

"Tell us what happened to you," said Jane.

I took a deep breath, swallowed, and said, "Yolanda, you tell us." I was glad I was sitting. I felt as scared as if I were the guilty one. Everyone turned to look at Yolanda, who stopped moving, stood still, and looked at me. "After you knocked me out, I opened my eyes and saw you bending over me."

"I didn't knock you out."

"I saw you." We were both speaking so quietly, almost whispering, but you could hear every word as if we were yelling. "I opened my eyes, remember? I saw you bending over me."

Yolanda sighed and leaned against a chair, shaking her head slowly. "You were down on the floor when I came. I saw you were alive so I ran out to get help, then I saw the police car coming and I knew you would be all right. So I didn't stay."

"Why didn't you tell me that when I questioned you?" Jim had moved in closer. He stood between me and the others. I could relax now. I leaned back in my chair. My heart was pounding.

Yolanda shrugged, then shook her head. "*Estúpida.* A throwback to when I was a kid, and to see a cop...I was going to a phone, honest, Jessie, to get help, but when I saw that police car drive up...it was like right back to the days..."

"The days when you piled up a record: assault with a deadly weapon, grand theft, resisting arrest..." Jim went on and on in a heavy voice as if Yolanda had committed these crimes just yesterday. He sounded funny, like an actor in a bad movie. Not like Jim at all.

"A juvenile record." Yolanda shrugged. "Years ago." She didn't look worried or guilty, she even looked relieved. "I know you can't understand the panic...even I don't...I saw that cop car and next thing I knew I was on the bridge."

"Why didn't you tell me that when I questioned you?"

"I didn't know Jessie had seen me. What did it matter that I was there? A reflex, an old habit, don't tell the cops anything unless you have to...but I..."

"Suppose you tell me now, everything."

"I put together in my mind what Jessie said at the seance. A room of one's own. Pine. You must have figured it out the same way, Jessie."

"Why didn't you call and suggest that to me?"

"It sounded. . . a far-out possibility. I decided to drive over, take a look. When I got there, I found the door opened, the desk ransacked, Jessie on the floor. I bent over her to see if she was. . ." Yolanda stopped and looked at me. "God, when I thought you might be. . ." She was very pale, her cheeks no longer apple-red, but her lips were still dark, a sort of bluish-red.

"And you wanted a look at Wonder's new book," said Jim "Before anyone else got to it."

Yolanda nodded. "I was curious. . ."

"To find out what she said about you."

"And the others."

"What did you do with it?"

"I told you, it wasn't there! The desk had been emptied." The color was coming back into her cheeks. If she was always scared of cops, she must have hated them too. She looked at Jim as if she hated him.

Jim was looking right back at her, with an even meaner look, quieter, the look of someone with power to back up his hate. "I'm going to read you your rights, Ms. Dolores, Mrs. McVittey, whatever you call yourself."

"Oh, Jim, I don't think. . ."

"Keep out of this, Jessie. Thank you for your cooperation." I had touched his shoulder, but he didn't turn, didn't move, dismissed me without even shrugging my hand off. "You have the right to remain silent. . ."

I jumped up from my chair, but I didn't know what to say. I believed Yolanda. This was all wrong, a mistake. The others were all frozen in their chairs. Celeste was watching from the floor, her eyes wide open. Only Jane moved, getting up to stand beside Yolanda. I heard her say, "I'll call Dick. What else?" I couldn't believe what was happening until I saw Jim push back his coat and unhook something from his belt. A set of handcuffs. They jangled as he pulled them free and started to walk toward Yolanda.

"No. No." It was Reuben Wonder's quiet voice. He sounded exhausted, repeating, "No, no, no," like the soft running down of an unwound clock. "Enough. No. It was me."

I saw Jim's back and shoulders relax. He turned to Reuben Wonder and nodded his head, unsurprised. This was what he wanted. This was what he had really planned. Jim knew all the time. Why hadn't he told me? So I'd make a convincing accusation, I guess. "I didn't think you would let it go this far, Mr. Wonder."

Reuben shook his head. "I didn't mean to. Everything started to move...too fast. I will go with you and explain everything. All I ask is...I would like to stay for the memorial service." He gave a shrug, almost a smile. "I'm not running away anywhere. I couldn't if I tried. It would be safe to let me stay for that...and then... what you want."

Jim nodded. He looked like Jim again, and he looked very sad.

Georgie had stood up behind Reuben, holding onto his chair the way she had right after India's death. She looked frozen, too dazed to do anything but hold onto the chair. Yet she didn't look surprised. She looked ready to faint but she wasn't shocked. She knew. She had always known.

Antonia was the one who looked really stunned, sitting there so close to him. Her cigarette dropped from her mouth into her lap, where it smoldered until Margot reached across Reuben to sweep it to the floor. Then both Margot and Antonia, at the same time, drew back from Reuben, just a few inches of recoil, staring at him as if they had never seen him before. Tears were spouting from Antonia's eyes, and her mouth twisted. She may have hated India and wanted Reuben, that mouth said, but not this way, and not this Reuben, so completely different from the man whose devotion to India put him beyond her reach.

36.

"Jessie."

I moved to stand beside Jim, where I could face Reuben. I kept one hand on the back of a chair. Like Georgie, I was wobbly in the legs.

"Jessie, I never had any idea to hurt you. I just pressed a little nerve on the side of your neck. A trick I learned in the commandos. It just puts you out for a few minutes. I laid you on the floor, gently, not to let you fall and hurt even a finger. You'd be out a few minutes, that's all. I couldn't figure out why you were in the hospital so long. I worried, I thought, maybe I forgot how to do it, pressed too hard or something. I'm sorry." He looked at Jim. "Yolanda is telling the truth. I was leaving when her car pulled up." Then he wasn't looking at anyone. "I always knew where India's secret room was."

"You'd been there before?" I asked. "You'd read the manuscript?"

Reuben looked down at his folded hands. I couldn't see his face. "In this book there is a dirty old man, leering at young women, a fool, humiliating India. In this book I'm worse than in the first one."

"Where is it now?" asked Jim.

"I destroyed it. Took it home and burned it."

Jim ignored our gasps. "Is that why you killed her?" His voice was quiet, almost casual. "Because of what her book said about you?"

Reuben was quiet for a long time, head down, looking at his hands. When he raised his head, he looked at Jim and at no one else. "I'm dying, you know, a few months at the most. I devoted my life to India, so she could write, and that was how she paid me back. I thought, maybe. . . if I could be free of her, marry a younger woman." Margot was squirming in her chair, moving off to the edge of it, as far as she could get from Reuben. "With India gone, and the book gone. . . maybe that was what was making me sick. Her and that book. Get rid of them, marry a young woman who would bring me happiness, not ridicule, would bring me back to life. Crazy. I know it was crazy, but. . . "

"Is that what your defense will be?" Carla hissed at him. "Temporary insanity?"

Reuben didn't even look at her. "My dear Carla, I will never come to trial. I don't have that much time."

"Where did you get the cyanide?" asked Jim.

Reuben sighed. "I have always had it. For years. I am surprised you didn't catch that, Jessie. You were so thorough. Ah, but you are too young. You wouldn't know the pill was cyanide. The suicide pill. Remember *Emma Pride's Journal*?"

I remembered. "The suicide pill her husband kept, from when he was a commando and was supposed to bite the capsule if he was captured." Reuben nodded. "You kept it all those years!"

"When we came home from Washington, I was not quite ready to let it go, but I was afraid Georgie...the child might find it. So I put it into our safe deposit box. Then we forgot it. Only a few months ago, when we went to check something in one of India's contracts...there it was, in the corner, under all those papers." He hesitated. "I took it home. I thought...I thought I would take it myself, when the pain should be too much. I kept it in my pocket. Then...then I started to feel better. A remission. I thought I would live...I thought that once free of India, I would live." He stopped, hesitating again. Georgie opened her mouth to speak, and that seemed to make him rush on to finish. "When everyone at the party started talking about her book, and India announced it was coming out, I...I just went crazy. I put the capsule in her drink. She..."

"No, no, no, no." Georgie protested over his voice until she drowned him out.

"Yes," he said quietly.

"No! I won't let you!"

"You will. Be still, Georgie. This is none of your business. This is between your mother and me, the last thing between your mother and me." He looked at Jim. "Handcuffs are not necessary, I hope. I was only waiting to confess after the program. I would like to stay for that."

"No," said Georgie. "Give it up, Reuben. It's enough now, enough sacrifices." I understood exactly what she meant. And I felt as if I had known all along.

"Georgie's right," I said. I let go of the chair, stepped around Jim, and knelt down in front of Reuben Wonder so that he would have to meet my eyes, even if he kept his head down. "You're lying, Mr. Wonder. India had been holding that drink for quite a while when the subject of her new book came up. You didn't have an opportunity to slip anything into it."

"I put it in before?"

I shook my head. "I believe you when you say you always knew about the room in Pine Alley. In fact, you padded it and furnished it for India, didn't you?"

He nodded.

"Then why didn't you go destroy the manuscript right after India's death?"

"Because..." he stopped. He knew I had him.

"Because there wasn't any manuscript, was there, Mr. Wonder?"

The tears had filled his eyes and started to spill over. "You made those phone calls too. So we would think there was a murderer. To protect India's image. But you wouldn't have let Yolanda or anyone else actually be arrested. You'd stop everything if it came to that." He had covered his eyes with his hands. "You went to India's secret room just to mess it up, make it look as if the manuscript had been stolen." Then I had to say the worst part. "And you didn't find the pill and take it from the safe deposit box. India did."

Georgie was patting his shoulder and nodding at me. Antonia Moran's tears were smearing her makeup all over her face. She and Margot had moved closer to Reuben again. Yolanda and Jane sank into chairs behind Sylvia and Carla; all of them wore the same look, not of shock, but of recognition, like when the thing you're searching for is found in plain sight. I had never seen Carla silent for so long. She looked irrelevant, a mere, thin shadow. Celeste, on the floor next to me, watched Reuben closely, like a nurse, a priestess, whichever Reuben needed. Jim was backing up slowly, moving back almost to the door, as Reuben took his hands away from his face and raised his wet face to look around him.

"None of you understood, none of you knew what these past twenty years have been. None of you cared." He sighed. "At first, when *Emma Pride's Journal* was published, oh, those were good days. A best seller! Pictures, interviews, honors. India, the center of attention! I enjoyed it. I told her, enjoy it. When it all dies down, I thought, we'll get back to normal.

"But we never got back to normal. Letters from all over, she had to answer everyone. The book kept selling, selling. The more her reputation grew, the more people wanted from her." His eyes moved around the room. "India, help me get published. India, come to my writers' class. India, help the blacks, the Lesbians, the chicanas. India, I can't write. Help me save my marriage, break my marriage, raise my children, leave my children, save my soul. Always the call for help, and always she had to answer.

"Books should be published anonymously! To protect her from all of you. And yet she enjoyed the attention, at first, until she drowned in it. She couldn't write. You don't have to write, I told her. Yes, yes, she must. Because she had to? Or because everyone expected it?"

Jane murmured, "She could have stopped at one book. We would have loved it, and her."

Reuben shook his head. "She didn't believe that. She believed that all the love she got because of the first book depended on everyone waiting for the next. Like you, Jane, you can't imagine how she envied you, because you could work. You, Sylvia, with your dozens of journals. Even Margot's trash, production. India got admiration, fame—is that love? That's why she had to do so much for people, so they would love her. You don't know how India wanted love. And if they would love her only for what she could do for them, then she had to stay famous, admired, powerful enough to do it. How? Another book. She must write!

"She tried everything, even witchcraft." He looked down at Celeste, not with contempt, but as though he wished she were a better witch. "And the time passed, and she grew more and more afraid that anything she did write would not measure up to her fame. You were right about that, Yolanda. Cruel, but right." He had not turned to look at Yolanda who sat behind him, her tears falling like his. "The only mistake you made, the irony, was saying she must publish her new book. Even you thought there was a book." Reuben sighed and bowed his head again. "How could there ever be a new book? She was cut off from real life. No one was real, not with her. They fawned on her like Sylvia, or tried to own her, like you, Carla. Sometimes they even insulted her, just to prove they were not impressed by her fame. You, Antonia, you don't know how many times you hurt her. Nothing in her life was real anymore. How could she write out of...this?" He had raised his head to look around again, then bowed it.

Georgie patted his shoulder. "I'm not sure," she said, "which of us started the rumor about the new book. It was so many years ago. My mother demanded we keep up the fantasy, as if it would make the book happen. Besides, there was the money. Three large advances. I don't see how she could have paid it back."

"And then..." Reuben was looking around at all of us again. "The last few years...everything started to slip. The way it happens when you get old. I got sick. India's hypertension started to affect her memory a little, her thinking. She got scared, maybe it was too late now to ever do the book." He looked at Antonia. "You know the fear when age begins to blunt the mind, even a little." Antonia stared at him, her old, razor-sharp mind taking in everything. Her tears had stopped, and she was sharing his pain, deadpan, like a tough old soldier who has seen death a thousand times.

"That was when she went back to the Church," said Georgie. "Probably she started thinking about suicide, though she waited a while before she said anything to us. She must have hoped that priest would talk her out of it, threaten her with eternal hell-fire or something. But she probably never told him. She must have realized it was too late for her ever to believe in hell again."

"Her hell was here," mumbled Reuben. "Things were turning, people turning against her. It started with Carla, you and those letters! I told her that was your own rage and ambition, just you, but she took it deeper, said it showed people starting to turn against her." Carla sat still, her face open and quiet, but her eyes blinking like someone who was trying to take a slap in the face without flinching. Then she got up so quickly that she upset her chair. It fell with a crash as she pushed open the door behind Jim and rushed out into the hall.

"And then came Yolanda's article."

"What article?" asked Margot, but Reuben ignored her, and everyone else just watched Reuben and waited.

"Do you all think she was stupid!" Reuben's voice was stronger. "Do you think she didn't feel the resentment, the envy? You, Sylvia, after years of running after her, helping push her into the corner she was stuck in, even you were turning bitter toward her. She saw everyone turning on her, unless she could do something. She shut herself in that room for hours, hours! Then she saw I was dying, soon there would be just the stink of cancer for a few weeks, then even I would desert her. Alone to face all of you!"

"She talked to you about suicide?" I asked, looking up at Georgie.

Reuben rested his head on his hands while Georgie nodded and spoke. "It was when she changed her will that I realized she was thinking about not outliving Reuben, making the transfer of everything simple, if he was too sick. I talked to her, I tried everything, I told her she should see Reuben through to the end. She cried and said she couldn't save him this time, what was the point? But she said she would hang on, she would try."

Antonia lit a cigarette and puffed on it with determination. Then she mumbled, "She needn't have staged such a death. . .at a party, for God's sake."

Reuben shook his head. "You never understood her, no, she didn't stage anything, wouldn't do. . .wouldn't mean that."

"I don't think she planned it," agreed Georgie. "My mother was self-centered, but not...she had taken the cyanide capsule from the safe deposit box and wouldn't tell us where it was. Then she said she threw it away. She must have been carrying it around with her.

"When she decided to give the party, she said it was to tell everyone the truth. To say there was no new book, to say she wasn't writing anymore, except letters that would help others. I thought it was a good idea. I thought she was coming to terms with...but something must have happened at the party to make her decide that she couldn't go on. I think...." Georgie turned to me and tried to give me a smile, the kind of smile you make when you want to soften something terrible you're about to say. "I think it had something to do with you, Jessie."

"With me!"

Reuben put his hand out to touch my cheek. "Nothing you did, Jessie. Only what you are." He withdrew his hand. "Young and talented and starting out, looking up to her like...how you looked at her that night! Awe, worship, as if she was a goddess. She was your god. You are too young to know what a terrible burden such worship can be. You, after thousands of others. And her fear of seeing your young worship turn to...."

I opened my mouth to tell him he was wrong, that it was impossible that my love for India could have turned to anything else. But I knew he was right. Even in the process of looking for her killer, learning just a part of the real India, I'd begun to despise her because she didn't completely match the India I had made up in my mind, to suit my own needs.

"Just a minute." Jim spoke slowly, trying to understand. "You're saying that India Wonder killed herself just because...she couldn't write another book?"

Antonia, Celeste and Georgie ignored him, too occupied with Reuben to notice. But the rest of us turned to look at him. I waited for Yolanda to say something. Then I was sure Jane would say it, but she only shrugged. She was right, he wouldn't understand if she did try to explain.

"And you, Mr. Wonder," Jim went on, "lied, even were ready to confess to murder, to cover that up for her?"

Reuben shrugged the identical shrug my father does sometimes. "After all these years, I should suddenly change?" He almost

smiled. The nobility of that irony in grief—could I ever write that
down, show it? "I would hope you might do the same, Inspector.
Do you have to say in your report that she killed herself?"
Jim nodded. "I have to. But I can say she did it because of...
failing health, hers and yours. That's close enough."
Reuben nodded. "Thank you."
Carla pulled open the door and rushed in, brushing roughly past
Jim. "The church is packed. All the dignitaries showed up on time
for once, even the governor. I seated him and a dozen of the most
famous writers on the platform. You all will find vacant chairs in
between them." There was a silent, frozen moment when I thought
maybe I couldn't, none of us could move. Then Carla looked at us
and, instead of giving some harsh order to make us go, she smiled,
almost gently, and said, "Last one in has to sit next to Norman
Mailer." Reuben smiled back at her, and we all started to move.
"Sylvia, Georgie." Carla pulled them aside. "I have to talk to you
on the way in. I have an idea."

37.

I sat in the front row next to Reuben, saving a seat for Georgie
on the other side of him. I could name all but one of the twenty
famous people sitting on the platform, and most of the thirty or
forty more celebrities filling the front row with us. I let my eyes
skim past them to the gold lettering stretched across the long,
creamy wall, my mother's favorite saying: WHAT DOES THE
LORD REQUIRE OF THEE BUT TO DO JUSTICE, TO LOVE
MERCY, AND TO WALK HUMBLY WITH THY GOD. The
big old church rustled with the movements of the hundreds of people
crowded into it. That hushed rustle and the smell of the mounds of
flowers made me drowsy. Gradually everyone quieted down,
waiting, expectant, but minutes passed and nothing happened.
The seat we saved for Georgie stayed empty. Carla and Sylvia were
missing from the platform.
Then I saw a small door open in the side wall where the three of
them exchanged whispers and nods before they finally came out.
Carla and Sylvia took their places on the platform, and Georgie
came to sit with us. She took Reuben's hand and smiled at him, but
before we could ask her about the delay, the program had begun.

Celeste Wildpower stood first and moved out to the edge of the platform. She didn't move her arms or chant, just stood like a creamy beige stalk rooted there. The quiet that she had kept for so long in the other room had grown to reach out over us. Her voice was like high, thin music from far away, as she said she would offer a burial prayer created by an Eskimo woman shaman. "To our sister, our sister, farewell. Safe journey. To the sky that bends over us, to the clouds that rain upon us, to the sun that warms us, to the air that comes in and out of us. Where our sister dwells." She repeated this three times, then sat down.

Carla, all in black, was still only a shadow, except for her eyes, which caught the light a certain way, and shone. wet? "The first speaker will be India's oldest friend, Antonia Moran."

Antonia began with, "Nothing has ever inspired me more than walking beside India Wonder under a picket sign almost forty years ago." She told stories about Old Left days. Some of them made us laugh a little, just enough to ease the tension, to make me feel warm and close to the other people there. She was an excellent speaker, and she proved it by, as soon as she sensed the warmth, stopping.

Then Carla introduced Yolanda. Without comment, Yolanda listed dozens of groups India had helped. The list went on and on. At the end, Yolanda looked once around the church and said, "Everyone here must have a similar list." Then she sat down.

"Many of you," said Carla, "cherish a letter from India written in answer to one from you. For India always answered. Sylvia March will now read from one such letter."

Sylvia started off shaky and hardly audible, reading the first letter she had received from India. It was like the letter I had received, but it was definitely to Sylvia, personal, individual. Her voice got stronger and firmer as she read, even though she had begun to cry. When she finished, she put the letter down and said, "India's daughter, Aurore Williams, has asked me to announce that India's new book will be published as scheduled next fall. The title is *Letters to my Daughter.*" A rustle started, but Sylvia wasn't through yet. "Then Ms. Williams and I will collaborate in preparing India Wonder's complete letters, a task of many years, to fill many volumes. We ask you to assist by sending us letters you received from her." When Sylvia sat down there was a ripple of uncertain applause—was it all right to clap in church?—then everyone decided it was, and clapped hard.

Then Carla was up again. She looked very stern, almost angry, and there wasn't any doubt about those glistening eyes. "I have written many poems to and about India Wonder. I was asked to read one of them today." She stopped, swallowed, then looked even more stern. "I could not choose one that would give us the essence of our friend, our sister, India Wonder, as well as her own words. So we conclude this program with a selection from India's own book." I could hardly believe it. Carla—to step down, to refuse to exploit this opportunity—she made me feel almost as naive and believing and hopeful as I had felt at India Wonder's party.

Margot came forward, then stepped back a little from the microphone and the lights, letting her blue-draped body blend into the shadows. Her voice came soft but clear from those shadows, like a familiar tune played on a viola.

> Today was a good day.
> I awoke with a headache. The children quarreled. My husband demanded comfort. And that typing job must be finished if we are to pay the bills this month.
> Good reasons not to write. Yet, I did drag myself to my desk, sat down with my usual dread, spent my usual hour of despair until faintly, like far-off music, came the words, a sentence, two, a paragraph. Two whole pages!
> Tomorrow I may read those two pages and know I must discard them. So be it. Even discarded, they are priceless, for in reaching toward them, I penetrated my own disguise. I reached beyond myself and found my self.
> Today was a good day.